THE HOUSE OF RUST

THE
HOUSE
OF
RUST

A NOVEL

Khadija Abdalla Bajaber

Graywolf Press

This publication is made possible, in part, by the voters of Minnesota through a Minnesota State Arts Board Operating Support grant, thanks to a legislative appropriation from the arts and cultural heritage fund. Significant support has also been provided by Target Foundation, the McKnight Foundation, the Lannan Foundation, the Amazon Literary Partnership, and other generous contributions from foundations, corporations, and individuals. To these organizations and individuals we offer our heartfelt thanks.

This is a work of fiction. Names, characters, businesses, places, events, locales, and incidents are either the products of the author's imagination or used in a fictitious manner. Any resemblance to actual persons, living or dead, or actual events is purely coincidental.

Published by Graywolf Press
250 Third Avenue North, Suite 600
Minneapolis, Minnesota 55401

www.graywolfpress.org

Published in the United States of America

ISBN 978-1-64445-068-0

2 4 6 8 9 7 5 3 1
First Graywolf Printing, 2021

Library of Congress Control Number: 2020951327

Cover design and art: Kimberly Glyder

For Mombasa,
I thought you were trying to kill me.
It has been a privilege.

CHAPTER ONE

When Aisha was younger her father used to take her out to sea.

Her mother had been beset with pains and, Aisha suspected, rather sick with the sight of her, so her father, bereft of sons, would heave Aisha up onto his shoulders and leap onto the boat.

Pay attention, he said, guiding her hands into the stomach of a red-edged changu. Feathered filaments torn, raggedly inflating within blood-speckled gills. Ali laughing a bright summer laugh, crooking his finger in the tuck, hooking from the inside. His little finger gleaming and wriggling like a worm.

He had looked into her face and what he saw there stopped his smile, his mirth fading. She would remember this ever after, sensing that she had failed not just at a task, but at possessing some important instinct. That she had both disappointed her father and yet done no more than expected the first time. It was not unforgivable. There were lessons here.

Ali snatched the struggling fish up by the tail and motioned to the sea with it bristling in his fist. The command need not be spoken this time but she heard it all the same. *Pay attention, Aisha.*

He flung the mutilated thing over the side, and just as the cold cord of its guts began to cloud the water pink, a black fin cleaved the wave, quick as a scythe, and vanished. A light white froth, milky as boiling rice, bubbled up in a fizz before it too dissolved.

Pay attention, Aisha. *Everyone must have their share.*

Aisha guts the fish her father brings, scales glittering under the saw of the old blade. The dull side scrapes, the sharp slant angled toward her body. They fly off the fish, these scales, like sparks off a whetstone. They stick to the dark skin of her arms, glitter hotly on her neck and cheek.

She makes the cleanest line, carving tail to jaw, pulling out guts with quick tugs and rinsing out the hollow in murky water. By the end of it the fish are clean and Aisha is not.

The cat in the alley curls its tail around the leg of a chair but scrambles away when it is approached. Aisha pauses, and puts out the chipped plate in the shadow of the flat. Days and days, she would watch as a child, waiting for the cat to approach—but it never comes when it is watched. Aisha had learned how to leave. In the morning the plate is clean, a lumpy swarth of ants scattered around the rim, collecting.

In the morning she sees that the offering has been accepted.

At market, Hassan fumbles when he gives her the egg tray. Everyone talks of his entrepreneurial spirit as if he is destined for wealth, but he moves as humbly as a beggar and rarely meets Aisha's eye when she does business with him. *The boy likes you*, Hababa observed, knowledge grave as though it were from the mouth of a witch who read portents.

Aisha wished Hababa had not said it. The knowledge of it annoyed her.

But that is why Omar, Amina's son, has his uses. Too young to go in anyone's place alone, he accompanies her, six and grumbling, glowering at other men. He folds his arms and pronounces each character of the alphabet in Arabic and then in English, like a little minister berating the congregation.

Ibrahim, the Zanzibari merchant, laughs at him and neatly splits an orange with his knife. Omar sucks at the rind as she returns him home to his family where she puts away the groceries while Omar sits kinglike on the kerosene-powered refrigerator.

If his mother is not around, Omar is insolent, ducking his head to sneer as Aisha tries to shift the lid he sits on. "One day *I'll* be the only one who goes to the soko."

Possibly, but Aisha does not tell him that. He was a terrible haggler and would be one for the rest of his life. Still very small, thinking of sweet oranges to come to him on all days.

He means that one day she will not be asked to do this for his mother, that they will not need her or need him watched—it is likely in three years she will be completely unnecessary to them, but she does not reveal that she knows.

She savors the trips to the market, even if it dirties her shoes, even if it is only a mud-crusted path walled on all sides by the old buildings that make it a labyrinth—stones hunching toward each other like suspicious, gossiping crones. Even if the basket is heavy. Even if she sweats. Even if the other girls look at her like they can smell it: salty and rank, the ugly stink of fish.

On the twisting path she can imagine she is walking toward something rather than in between things.

After all such errands are done, Aisha hunts back to Hababa's. Hababa spits out mabuyu seeds into the scarred palm of her hand, and the squat *ping!* goes off in Aisha's head, a cartoon-bullet noise. In her other hand, discolored with burns, she stirs at a heavy sufuria with a flat mwiko, salt and crackling sunflower roasting.

When she can be coaxed—with some strategic sweetness on Aisha's part—Hababa expends great energy in regaling Aisha with tales, some real and some imagined.

Hababa sees slights hidden in perfectly crafted manners, the thousand and one ways in which blessings turn into curses, winding like a snaking braid bound tight enough to make the bride look eternally surprised. Hababa speaks of upcountry folly being punished by beautiful women with hoofs peeking beneath their buibuis, of crows throwing murderous parties and guzzling blood like palm wine, of blessed virginal heroines and their prize of a prince. Hababa turns day into night, makes gardens full of charming snakes, makes heroes and villains

3

switch places in the space of two words. Hababa tells stories about punishable selfishness and valiant tolerating duty, about her own latent wickedness, lurking in the ribs of her, waiting to spring. Hababa warns her about strangers, about wanting more than she is given. Hababa warns her about a number of things.

"Everyone has wickedness in them, but women be most wicked of all," Hababa warns in her low, vibrating hum. "God gave each of us an inner selfishness, like a wild dog that wants with uncontrollable greediness. We are often thinking wicked and cruel and inconsiderate thoughts, it is what we must fight to prove ourselves true. You must be especially sure to remind yourself to be grateful, Shida. You must be sure to never behave in a way that lets wickedness colour your intentions."

Shida. Sometimes Hababa forgot and called Aisha by her dead mother's name. Sometimes the story drifts and Hababa's eyes become filmy, gelatinous, as though she has slipped, without alarm, into the undertow of another time. In such moments the blue sclera of cataracts give her the eyes of a cat, as if Hababa had moons hiding behind her stare, appearing for a ghostly breath between vanishing acts.

Aisha never corrected her, never uprooted time for such a reason. A time ago she used to flinch at her mother's name but it was spoken so rarely, eyes averted, in a whispered, head-shaking croon—people whispered Shida's name with careful pity. But for Aisha, in her mother's name hung rainstorms and rust, a dirty, zingy metal taste. Ungalvanized, galvanizing, *sharp.*

"Be kind to your neighbours; if you cannot love them then be kind to them. You will be found by a good and righteous man. Every heart is ugly, we must make our manner and welcome sweet. Discourtesy, rudeness are the makings of an ugly soul."

Hababa would go on speaking, vacant, as if repetition had dissociated and distanced her from the present world, gazing at the door, expression hollow and lost in strange climes, unknowable to Aisha. The sunflower would singe, smoke—and she would come back to herself with a hiss. Anger would wake her.

The sea does not sleep, and there are things in the water that would eat you alive.

A foreigner couldn't outlive it, wouldn't live long enough to fear it. We ourselves we know—we watch the razing green tide the same. The white froth of the wave, we take the same delight in it, *relish* the cool wind gliding over the bluest back. The sea is beautiful.

Sometimes it drags things away, tugs you down so gently, so slowly—you do not realize you are drowning until your third breath takes in more water, the back of your tongue struck with salt, and six feet of deep.

Locals of all faiths and faithless know to utter a prayer. God's name at least once. God's name crowds the hearts of coast folk, carried easily in the roof of the mouth—there is no such thing as taking God's name in vain, for it is always spoken, even in afterthought, ever present. If words have a shadow, then it is He who gives it shadow and shape.

It is spoken, too, before swimming. The locals give the water due respect and they are for the most part left unmolested, should the water feel that day that there are no lessons to be taught and no manners to be imparted.

The locals know, there are things in the water that would eat you alive.

CHAPTER TWO

Omar liked their little apartment, even though they were fussy about the noise. His mother had painted the door a pale blue herself. The scabby brown-red landing it faced between flights of stairs going up and down to other apartments clearly got a lot of traffic. Inconsiderate neighbours with their dirty shoes! He beat at the floor with a stiff broom, dried red onion skin flying about with all the dust and hair upstairs swine swept downward to land on *their* floor. If he was bigger he would pick a fight, but that would not be for some time yet.

Grumbling, he did his never-ending work. It was the only thing Mama was particular about—he heard from his own peers given ludicrous tasks, like washing clothes and such. Omar was wary enough about complaining. A good son was always mindful of his parents' wishes.

Omar was once sent to his mother's workplace, that machine gun—fire room. The vibrating needle punch work of seven seamstresses embroiled in the ceaseless wars of fashion had rung up his head. Mama had smiled when she'd seen him, accepted the parcel, and he had to flee back home.

Once he was within home's walls, Omar understood how the silence of the apartment must have been all the more dear to Amina. Even when his mother came home, her work never ended, needle and thread in hand, completing embroidery on some dress or other. Everything had to be done quietly, for Mze Saleh was in the next room sleeping the uneasy, suspicious sleep of a night watchman. Only a doorway veiled in thin beads separated the sitting area from grandfather's room.

Grandfather, grandmother, and mother, working all hours of the day, treading in and out, like they had only come inside to briefly affirm the hour. Omar, still a child, must be deposited in the care of a trusted neighbour or left in the streets to play with children or be minded by dull Aisha. When he was at home by himself, his ears rung just as hard with silence as they had in the sewing factory.

Mze Saleh guarded property at night, Hababa Rukiya worked kneading the flesh of brides, and Amina sewed in a shop.

Omar swept the landing and scowled, and played, and was bored, and was *useless*.

A woman is like a rib, crooked—to straighten her would be to break her. But when Mze Saleh said it, Omar couldn't help but mark the quiet pride he took in his wife's skill. Mama Rukiya's hands could manage smooth and lay easy any bride, the twisted became straight silk, not a strong-arming but with a firm will and delicate erosion.

This wasn't a skill she would pass on to her grandson, for such work is womanwork.

They spoke of his grandmother like she was a holy witch. Her strength kneaded weakness out of ailing limbs and vigour into the supple flesh of the newborn. She had the craftiness to make the moon rise up in the skin of the bride.

With awe Omar watched her brew. Mama Rukiya soaked mbarika leaves in water heated just short of boiling, and grated and minced fresh spongy manjano bleeding its sun-yellow juice, and ground sandalwood back and forth into fine paste.

There was not a blemish she could not smooth, not a knotted sinew that escaped her skill undefeated. As she had grown older, though her vigour had not waned and her craftsmanship had only improved, she no longer travelled so often to her clients' homes—they came to her. It was not a house of men, just a boy who was not yet a man and an old askari who had finished his dangerous years as a man. Once he became a man, Omar would not be allowed in the house for the hours the brides would come. He would have to set his own pallet each night in the sitting room instead of sharing it with his mother. He would be man enough to be taken note of, treated properly. Until that day, young brides, whether they were crying or laughing or waiting soldierly in the sitting area before Mama Rukiya admitted them, always interrupted themselves by pinching his cheek and bringing him sweets.

One day he would be a man, not want sweet things so shamelessly.

For now, his mother held him in his sleep and stroked his curls, so like hers. If he had a father, he would not be able to sleep between him and Mama, and be so tenderly mothered. So perhaps for now, it was nice.

The day Omar stole the chicken was the worst day of his life.

Omar only took notice of it when he was playing with the other boys. One of them had kicked the ball hard enough against a wall that the lady inside the ground floor flat came out to scold them. But not hard enough, it seemed, to spoil the calm of the glossy red hen who sat on the limestone flowerpot they'd been aiming for.

There were plenty of chickens in the stalls always, chickens tied together by their feet and dangling on the hips of racing bicyclists, chickens frothing the shoulders of vendors like mite-glittering furs, chickens even on the roofs of crafty neighbours who'd come to an accord with the landlords to put up city coops. Chickens on their way to the plate. And one unflappable chicken, rising as they were being scolded, to go about its business, making its pedestrian way through the streets, as though it was strolling home from market.

Omar followed. The other boys boldly escaped the scolding, hunted along with him. They followed it as it took corners, smaller paths. One said he would pluck it alive for its feathers, another said he would stew it with whole onions, another wanted to know if the suffering of a chicken was the same as the suffering of a cat, once caught.

9

Omar said nothing, for its feathers were beautiful and its flesh was sure to be sweet, but its suffering was not interesting.

No matter how slowly the chicken went its self-important way, they could not catch up. Slowly his peers fell away. *Beautiful feathers, for a duster?* All that walking must make the flesh tough, if it hasn't got more feathers than flesh! *Stoning a cat or kicking a dog, that's better than kicking an uncatchable chicken too stupid to feel fear, Omar!* It would be like torturing a tree.

Omar kept on, even as he grew more and more alone, and the roads went so deep into Old Town that the vendors had fallen away. No one was selling anything here.

Then it was only Omar and the chicken, and soon the chicken went through the open gate of a walled little plot. Beyond the wall loomed the roof of a house, and above the wall peeked the head of a pillar, domed like a minaret. It was all built of shag coral, more deeply soaked in time than any old house he'd ever before seen in Old Town.

Not a minaret. His stomach swooped strangely. A pillar tomb.

A crumbly house with a wall that barely held. As the door beyond the gate opened, Omar hid. He could hear neither water, nor ship, nor crow. Only the rusted hinge, the drop of handle on the inside as the bar groaned.

There was a hand. Only a glimpse was needed to see how finely it was formed. Its movement was graceful, the sleeve tucked elegantly, and the way it beckoned the chicken within and then shifted away so it could enter, like a guest, was as graceful as any host.

Omar had never seen a chicken so courteously invited within a home.

The door closed. Omar waited.

He waited and then he neared. It was an ugly door, wood all rotted up, the handle a piece of old ironwork, scabby coloured as the floor on the stairway at the apartment. The kind of handle no one would want to touch, certainly not with a bare hand. Its gruesome appearance was a warning.

The pillar tomb loomed behind him. The yard he'd walked through was all gritty weeds and broken glass. If he were to disappear, his family would notice it earliest, at dinner. He was stubborn, like his grandfather—who despite the apartment going electric still insisted they continue using the same old kerosene fridge they'd had for longer than Omar had been alive.

Mze Saleh might have looked like a thin wispy old man merrily pedalling his bicycle to his workplace, but his work required him to be brave, but cautious and alert. His employers slept through the night while he guarded their lives and property.

The boys would want to know where the chicken had gone. If he told them, they'd laugh at him. *You went up to the door and fled without looking inside?*

Omar could be brave and stubborn like his grandfather.

Just because a thing be a drifter, Mze Saleh would say later when his grandson returned home in tears, *doesn't mean it belongs to no one.*

One of two things he might find within, a host and a guest, or an unaccompanied chicken. An interesting story in this boring old town, or a dinner chicken to close the evening with his family. Ah, black pepper chicken, in garlicky broth so rich its fat floats glossy and swims up against the lip of the bowl.

Taking hold of the rotten handle, Omar opened the door.

～

In the grand green roof of Mombasa's heart, the crows slept.

Be they busying the day in Lamu, Malindi, Kwale—night flew the crows back to Mombasa like businessmen returning to their families. After a hard-working day of menacing house cats, stealing from the distracted staff of untended kitchens and gardens, killing songbirds, defecating on the common people and their property, and dancing gloatingly in garbage, they rejoined their brethren.

The one called White Breast sat on the beams of the great marketplace, bony shoulders packed between his brothers. He slept with one eye squeezed shut, while the other peeked out at the shadowy innards of what the humans nowadays called *Marikiti.*

Crows' names did not come from their mothers, but from their peers. Certainly none had the arrogance to name themselves. White Breast would have no name were it not for his defect, as he had no other qualities that made his name beloved or fond, and when he tucked his beak close to his chest and brought his wings in a forward huddle, why, no one could see the ghastly pigeon-like feathering that distinguished him from his peers. He sat among hundreds of his brothers, whose own sleep usually lent peace to his, but this night—he had listened to worrying happenings.

Lord Crow would have known what to do, what to say, but he had disappeared many years ago. It fell to the Old Burned One to decide what was an emergency.

Earlier that afternoon, terrible news had travelled among the crows with the speed of a rumour. It was uncrowlike to whisper and should have earned rebuke, but the Old Burned One had ignored it, if at all heard, and it seemed that Gololi could get away with anything. Her feathers black as the unrepentant heart of a murderer, her beak as deadly as a surgeon's rusted scalpel, her eyes beady and bulging as big black beetles, her wings perfumed with the rot of the fish market guts she bathed in. Crow as crow. Why, nearly perfectly crow, had she in her possession actual brains.

Gololi had flown over Old Town and seen a human boy enter the House of Smoke and Shadows, the forbidden territories.

"Brother," the crows demanded, "tell us what happened next!"

The earth had not turned to dust, the buildings had not been set aflame, and the trees did not rip out their roots to march the streets.

"He left," Gololi had said slowly, chilling the crow-blood of her brethren, "unharmed."

White Breast knew he should not engage. If the Old Burned One heard them whispering it would be troublesome. It did no good to further inflate Gololi's huge head by paying her more attention, and yet. "What does this mean, Brother?"

"It means, of course, that Old Snake did not eat him."

Even alluding to Almassi terrified them, fearing that the monster would be summoned. What pleasure Gololi took in this! An idiot proud of her own daring. "If you do not know, do not pretend then, Brother," White Breast said coldly. "Inventing what you have not witnessed is an untruth, and that is uncrow."

"This crow says no lie, Brother. What Almassi does not eat, he teaches hard lessons to."

One of these hard lessons had earned the Burned One his name.

"He belongs to Almassi now." Gololi's sigh was self-important. "He left and came *here*, to market! So miserable the merchant asked him what was wrong. He bought two kilos of kashata, returned to Almassi. And then he went home and cried to his family, like a brat."

Almassi liked sweet things more than crows liked bloodshed, and liked bloodshed more than crows liked anything, and liked crows least of all things.

There should have been a big meeting, an honest convening to decide what to do next, how to react, as crows.

Gololi was far too pleased with herself. That she had flown so close to Almassi's estate was a credit to her bravery, but what could be more uncrow than stupidity, which she possessed in even greater abundance than ugliness?

White Breast fell dreadfully quiet. That night, when he should have been asleep, he had peeked at his kin, heart pumping as though he were stealing the sight of them.

Gololi's grand news had quietened him. How could he tell them what he had seen when he flew out far and alone, soaring above a sea it was foolishness to go so far in? Where had he become tired, there'd be nothing to perch onto. A crow does not fly far to eat the air alone, he flies to migrate. He certainly should not risk flying the sea unpartnered to dazzle his own heart, for such fancies were traitorous, uncrow.

How could he tell them he was not the only fool out there?

That he had seen the long inky one, the monstrous serpent who groomed the sea bed, wailing in the water?

The long inky one who was never far from his fisherman companion. It was one thing to be sickened by such a creature's domestication, but this weeping was new, alarming. White Breast flew ahead, searching until his wings tired. Luckily he found a floating, sea-chewed piece of wood for pause.

Then he knew why the inky one had wept, and knew then, with horrible clarity, what had befallen the fisherman.

Gololi had brought news of the odious Prince of Snakes.

What did White Breast have that might ease or delight his brethren?

Only a plank beneath his talons, only the wood of a boat, smashed apart like a child's toy.

A dead fisherman, and no sleep.

CHAPTER THREE

One day Aisha's father did not return.

Last seen as a sun-glare blot on the horizon, the sails of his vessel flashing like mirrors, plunging into the unknown, daring a distance unfathomable to those other ordinary people who had sought roots, steady earth, who carried with them the firm, clear knowledge of what could and could not be. All those happy people whose fathers did not vanish with all the ceremony of a bottle cap rolling over the edge of a table, dropping from sight.

He had a lot less to risk than most, didn't he? A poor man of simpler means leaving neither sons, nor wealth, nor grand property. Only a skinny, strange-eyed daughter and a gossiping mother with swollen ankles.

He usually disappeared with little or no warning. Once or twice he'd sail away in the afternoon, only to return the next. If evening had come and she did not see him, Aisha usually went to her grandmother's to help with dinner and wait to be collected. And if he did not collect, as he had done now, then she slept over. Staring up at the unending farness of the ceiling, Aisha dreamed she was pinned to the bottom of a deep, dry well, waiting for a moon to show itself.

Daytime. A fleshy lizard crawled above her head. A door slammed. She had overslept and couldn't see how. It was hard to comprehend the morning itself when one of the shark hunters was in the majlas, scowling shyly at the floor. He had not taken a seat. Hababa's silence was like the sea ruminating the thunder; they had been speaking together and Aisha's entry gave the shark hunter an excuse to leave.

Aisha saw no plates or saucers for tea, only the smell of breakfast burning in the kitchen. He had not come as a guest. Aisha left to attend to the fire hazard, so Hababa could finish chewing her teeth, and when she came back disapproval had deepened sour lines in Hababa's face. She told Aisha her father had not returned, that no one knew where he was. Hababa was more angry than scared, the centre of her mouth twisted in a scowl not even the tea she sipped could shift.

Aisha's hands did not shake. Her grandmother must have had the same eerie inkling Aisha had, of the dark sea truth. If there'd been mystery she might have wept in terror and in fear, but whatever had befallen her father seemed to both women something inevitable, *earned.*

Hababa spoke darkly through the steam of her cup. "Five days, he must return by then or he's lost. He'll be dead and free of us."

Aisha's hands did not shake, but her head had begun to buzz. Such words are too hard not to have a heart behind them. An allowance of five days. If his absence extended beyond this Hababa would ask the imam about the funeral rights for those lost at sea. A funeral in five days, body or no body.

Hababa went to lie down. Her head was hurting her, she mumbled. Aisha did the tasks of the house quickly, prepared the things she would cook for lunch, and left quietly.

Whatever slivers of the Tudor's shore not bearded in mangroves were cramped with rickety mtumbwi. On the rust-eaten hull of a half-sunk speedboat, a man wove his net, pick tugging at the handmade holes. He eyed Aisha with habitual suspicion as she picked along the slippery, algae-mossed shore.

The sea smelled foul, as if it were turning out whatever dead things were rotting in its bed. Farther in the centre of the creek was the unlucky sailboat, scaly with flaking paint, its sails looming skeletal, the bones of a body no one dared bury.

Aisha didn't want to look at it longer than she had to, prowling before she chose a group of scrappy men near where the mangroves began. Perched on the thick roots, one of them held a spear whose point trembled keenly, poised over some restless target in the water.

Aisha crouched.

The spear flew, water bursting. The men laughed around their brother's disappointed mutter. Then all as one they seemed to take notice of her.

"Who is this fishling?" Mze Zubeir huffed. "If you look for someone among these men do you not possess a brother to send for such inquiries?"

"No," Aisha said, standing. "I'm looking for my father. Have you seen him?"

A shadow passed over the men's faces, but discomfited courtesy won out. They maneuvered about her, gesturing that she sit. The man sent his spear into the soft sand; it stabbed deep and quivered there as he rushed off.

Zubeir crossed his legs, balanced on the root with the aloof ease of a feline. "You are Ali's whelp."

He spoke not unkindly. The shark hunters of Mombasa were made dangerous by dangerous work. Straightforwardness neared rudeness, but if anyone knew of a sea farther than most fishermen dared go, it would be they.

"I understood your company was the last to see my father's boat."

He nodded. His treatment of her was refreshing for now he answered reasonably, without reminding her she was a child and a girl, with a girl's destiny. "You know the strangest place to catch shark? It'll astonish you."

"No, sir."

"Near the train tracks that bridge the creek."

Macupa Causeway? Aisha was dubious. Past the creek was a tangled mangrove wilderness—sharks swimming past the reef, past the port, risking the proximity of human settlements just to sniff at a measly railway . . .

Zubeir didn't seem to care what she believed; fishermen told tall tales often, but this one had purpose and intention. "Don't put even a toe in that water, I tell you. Little girl like you could wade upright there with your eyes above the surface. Not many go, so not many know. It is a secret I'm sharing with you."

"Interesting, Mze Zubeir." Aisha frowned. "Now, my father—"

"It's the metal in the tracks. Whenever a train slides over, it charges the rail. The shark's snout is sensitive to the tiniest electricity, attracting it like a school of fish," he hummed. "Now your father, may God keep him, has much the same instinct, but not the teeth that would make it less foolish. In his koko of a brain is a reckless silliness that keeps him danger-bound."

Aisha's fists curled over her knees.

"You look like him," Zubeir said, off-handedly. "There are some places even we do not hunt. Water too deep for a boat of twenty men, too far. Your father has gone alone. You couldn't pay us for a search party. My men would rather eat their own hearts than risk those waters."

She crunched down on any heated retort when the man with the spear returned. Sun glared off the metal pot. Aisha kept her silence in quiet mutiny as the tea was poured into two chipped cups. He offered the first and the nicest to the guest. Aisha took it carefully, not ready for the ugliness of anger to turn into the ugliness of rudeness, and murmured her thanks to the sand.

"When you saw him last," Aisha began, raising her eyes from where she'd been watching the mint bob in the sweet, dark tea, "which direction was he headed?"

"Face the direction of the Ka'ba and make prostration."

A wave of rage rippled through her veins, sparking violently in her fingertips. "I have a right to know."

"You have no right to anything, not a boat, not a favourable wind, and certainly not directions to your death," Zubeir said. "You want your grandmother cursing me?"

"If you don't have the courage to look for him, if you are so weak of heart—"

"Aisha," Zubeir warned gently. When she looked back to him she saw the tiredness around his eyes. "Yes, I remember that he used to bring you, a *child*. How could he make you dream of the water only to expel you from a future in it? Shouldn't have put that sea-longing in you. Go home," he said, conciliatory and *useless* to her. He urged softly, "Take care of your Hababa, pray for your father, pray for the rest of our like if you can. Pray for yourself. But leave the sea alone."

Aisha's eyes itched; the hot cup burned her palms. Prayers and prayers. As though that meant there could be nothing in between. When no one was doing anything, when no one would.

She dragged the pot toward her, lifted the lid, and poured her untouched tea into it. Zubeir sighed. "Girl—"

"Thank you," she said sharply—for the tea, for the time, for the *reminder*—and left.

She returned the way she came, but after the stairs leading back to the firmly anchored world, she began to wander. The thought of returning to Hababa's house made her insides roil. To return to that place complicated by stubbornness and grief . . .

Her father's foolishness was known. A careless dreamer . . . the butt of a joke, a man who now existed only as a fool in a cautionary tale. Brave and reckless, he had his successes, but he failed just as excessively. Some days they thought he was dead, taken by too strong a tide. His peers praised, envied, and were disdainful of him at turns. They said her father was the greatest fisherman, that men could throw in their nets and bring only sand, rock, the bones of things eaten by the dirt, but Ali was a master of the waves, coming in every evening, boat full. But Aisha also knew that if he died, if his mother wanted to bury him, they would say it was just. What else did a fool expect, to venture out so far?

Master of the waves? Had they seen the dark shape beneath his boat, they'd have killed him out of fear.

She had adapted to his temporary absences, but she was not ready for anything more permanent, to bury him. Without a body he had no death, no name.

And she understood the wisdom of Hababa's demands, understood the place where loving a person was only easier once you had buried them, when the disappointment and the futility of it could no longer be borne.

When she came to, it was a hollow waking. Her feet had carried her back to the house she had lived in with her father, where her mother had gotten sick and slipped away, escaped.

The cat was there just like the first time she'd ever seen it. Stretched a brazen yellow over the step like a long, dried banana leaf. Aisha waited patiently for it to scramble and bolt.

It sat up, resting on its haunches. Orange tail whipping lazily before curling around its paws, it regarded Aisha, blinking slowly, waiting, too.

"I have waited so very long for you," said the cat. "Have you forgotten me? Where is my share?"

CHAPTER FOUR

Aisha stood still, so quiet she hardly dared breathe. For a moment madness rushed her, gaining pitch in her skull. The wild panic that she had lost her mind gripped her—but it passed, dissolving like the foam on a wave as it arrived on the shore.

She licked her lips, tasting salt. Words crackled in her parched throat like burnt up paper but she spoke: "Peace unto you."

"And unto you," the cat returned equably.

Aisha nodded calmly. "I seek refuge with God from the accursed devil," she said under her breath. "I seek refuge with God from the accursed devil. I seek refuge with God from the accursed devil."

The cat did not scatter. "I am no jinni," he said, though he sounded as though he approved of these formalities. "A jinni is quicker to take offence. But where have you been? You have neglected to feed me. Where is my share?"

Not knowing what else to do but lean on the crutch of courtesy, Aisha addressed his tiny feet. "My father's missing, I've had to stay with my grandmother. I beg your forgiveness."

The cat gave a long, slow blink before settling better on his haunches. "But you returned here, for what purpose?"

"Lost in dreaming, I forgot that I do not live here anymore, or at least will no longer."

When the cat said nothing, Aisha stepped alongside him, opening the door. It would be rude to step over him. "Come in?"

Skinny but well groomed, the cat inclined his head with the sonorous grace of a prince accepting trivialities. Aisha, dusty and sunburnt in the dry afternoon, felt awkward.

The cat followed her into the small room that served as the majlas. She left him there and lit the kitchen's small cooker to brew tea. She had no mint and nothing to sweeten the tea except for a tin of candies they used during sugar shortages. She piled a saucer with small, crackling minnows that she had preserved.

When she returned, she expected the cat to be gone, as if dreamed. How astonishing that the skinny yellow cat who had refused to be touched all these years now allowed her to host him.

Sat properly on the carpet between the throw pillows, the cat had been waiting patiently for her return with the tray. She apologized, the habit of a host as she'd seen it performed. "Forgive me, for I've no milk for you," she said, setting the plate before the cat. "May I pour you the dark tea?"

"You may."

Aisha did so into one of the decorated cups they kept for guests, inwardly relieved that she had not risked offending the cat by bringing a cup for herself and only unsightly cutlery for him. She gave him what any guest was due, dropping the sweet in tea to dissolve.

She set the pretty cup by his paw after she had poured her serving. Raising her cup to her lips without drinking, she observed the cat through sweet whorls of steam.

The majlas had served on multiple occasions. Aisha had been born here. Her mother had spent her forty days recuperating on a mattress beneath the only window. She never properly left afterward, only grew more ill, receiving well-wishers there. Each morning Mama would leave her bedroom to come lie down in the majlas, wasting beneath the light, yellow to amber, getting up only to return to her room. Some days she got up and attempted a woman's work. Cooking and cleaning, noisy and aggressive, angry to make up for her stillness. Aisha would try not to get in her way and fail. Fits of dizziness, fainting, fevers, and chills would take her mother, and then she would lie down and turn toward the wall to hide her wrathful tears.

When she'd died the guests had come here to pray for her, for the family. Aisha hadn't cried: it had felt too much like begging for pity.

The cat ate neatly and nicely, small mouthfuls with small sharp teeth.

Aisha cleared her throat politely. "I apologize for neglecting you. It was careless of me to forget—"

"It was."

The clench of her jaw hidden behind her cup, she reminded herself that she must approach this encounter diplomatically. "Forgive my nosiness, but what is your name?"

"You may call me Hamza."

A name, not necessarily his own, or his only one. "I am Aisha. Forgive me, but you have never spoken to me before. Have you always known the language of man?"

"Anything can be learned if one takes keen interest."

The cat lowered his head, pink tongue lapping at the tea. When the cat spoke he never moved his mouth. His voice seemed to come from his throat in much the same way a purr might, but this voice was clear, full of a calm levelness that was measured and precise, wise and never wasteful with its speech.

"Long you have gone."

"My father is lost at sea."

"I had heard."

"If you know anything," Aisha said, "I would be grateful if you shared it."

"Ah," the cat said, "and if you learn it what will you do?"

"If he is dead we will continue with life."

"Was life at a standstill? Will you stop loitering in your hours?"

"I don't want to sit here for word games," said Aisha. "I have never been good at vitendawili. I need to know. I could stay with Hababa forever, and continue life with no answers. I would have already buried him, but my heart would eat at itself until it died. I am uncertain life without my father could sustain me. No one would blame me for staying and pretending. Leaving would never have seemed like an option for me, not for a girl. And yet," she struggled, considering her rough, ugly hands. "There used to be a spear beneath my father's bed, but he sold it. I've no boat and no hint of direction in which I might set sail, it has been years since I've *been* on a boat, and I don't know if I remember enough to have an inkling of how to steer one. Even if I acquired any of these things, a boat, direction, seamanship . . . I am guaranteed to drift or die in the endeavour."

"Three things you have said you do not have. All three I can procure," the cat said. "Go home, make your afternoon prayer, your dusk prayers, your evening and night prayers, and think. You cannot return to this house without your resolve. I will wait for your answer, and the next time you come, it is to meet me on this step and decide whether you love your father or the memory of him. For I tell you, Aisha Ali, if you have no intention to find him then you must promise never to come here again."

"You really will help me?"

"There are things in the water that could eat you alive," Hamza said, and Aisha saw it, the lift of its lip from small, pale fang, its approximation of a sharp, sharp grin. "Though I'm sure you already know this and quite well."

When Aisha returned to her grandmother's house, Hababa did not ask her where she had gone. Chopping greens, turned away, chillies and black pepper aplenty sizzling in the pan, so that Hababa could say that was what made her nose run and her eyes wet. She was a tall woman, grandmother, hunched up on that tiny wooden stool to pretend she had never once wept in her life.

Hababa convened with neighbours, stubbornly keeping to the pattern of her usual life. *Five days I give him.* Hababa's palm had accompanied this declaration, slicing through air as if in negotiation, a haggler who would not move from her price but underline it twice. *I will bury that boy in five days.*

Whipping her palm through a sufuria full of batter, the oil bubbling gently, Aisha shaped the batter as it fell through her fingers into the hot oil. A tail of bubbles followed the wet shape and then it would bob up, round and golden, kaimati. When she was done, she tossed and flipped them through molten sugar made shiny with the tartness of lemon.

Hababa congratulated her on the shape. "You will make a happy household, God willing."

The thought of eating any of it once this was said turned Aisha's mouth to ash.

A troupe of three wedding singers alighted upon the front step, hollering Hababa's name. Bright birds with deeply lined faces, they sat before Hababa in a close circle as though to put their wings over one another and tuck their beaks into their neighbours' necks. They spoke effusively, begging news and crooning sympathies. Aisha slipped between their jostling elbows with dark kahawa in its thin cups. It was as if her father were already dead and Hababa was divvying morsels of him to them.

They slurped and rubbed their lips, sugar-sticky fingers spinning through the air molding the words as they left their mouths. *Surely you must extend the date, you have survived worse, Swafiya—the heat alone! Whatever wave your boy is perched on must be boiling!*

One of the singers caught sight of Aisha, suddenly taking interest. "You poor thing," she whined, pupils glowing and narrowing like the yellow point in a parrot's alert eye. "Your Hababa will take good care of you, as you must take good care of her!"

They all nodded solemnly, their gestures stirring the room, sounds of agreement and unsolicited advice spilling and rolling against Aisha's ears like waves.

Aisha smiled, a stiffness to her mouth, eyes averted, wan, returning to the kitchen during another woeful chorus when another spoke, cutting through the colorful fog. "There's power in a name," they said seriously. "Shida? The old ways are not quite just, to be a child of a woman whom you have called 'hardship' and 'trouble' . . . what lousy inheritance is that?"

"She was born during a great drought."

"Then she should have been given a name that spoke to you of rain."

Blood rushed in Aisha's ears, the root of her chest burned. She could not explain the reaction—this affirmation making her throat close, to hear someone speak of the rights of her dead mother.

The wedding singers seemed to be in possession of information on all the world's happenings. Every house that hosted them for a time would receive tidings known only to spymasters that enjoyed their work a little too thoroughly. They possessed all news, from this and that divorce, this and that scandal, and the disappearance of this and that foreign dignitary.

A European diplomat had come for vacation with his family. Within a week he wandered, whistling, out of Madaraka. He'd eaten royally at a Mombasa club before going to the airport and flying back to his home country.

"His family must have been very surprised to be left behind."

"More surprised to find out that when the plane landed, he was not among the arriving passengers?"

Yet these other mysteries did not lighten Aisha's heart, though Hababa made an effort at being consoled. The more time passed, the more her grandmother's resolve and grief deepened.

In the past the wedding singers' visits meant humiliating Aisha by begging her to dance to songs they promised to play at her own wedding. They would tease her until her face burned and she would have to flee, the stress of refusing them anything agonizing. The kitchen became a sanctuary. Hababa and the wedding singers would sing songs that made their hearts thrill and their eyes fog, their thin, wiry voices twisting the heart out. They would untie the wood blocks from their lesos and clap-clap-*clap* a frenzy that called for rain and love like a war-lord howls for blood. Whenever they had kahawa, Subira, the oldest wedding singer, cataracts eclipsing her sight, would begin the solemn ritual of reading the grounds. Looking for portents and trying to descry the future, but even holy-hearted Hababa would titter only lightly before leaning in to listen to the near-blind discern the shape of the future.

That day no one read the grounds. It was one thing looking for portents and another to dare misfortune.

CHAPTER FIVE

On the tables of kings, candle wax had dripped down the cat's skull and whiskers. An obedient, trained creature, but at heart: a philosopher and spy. Of all his brothers, he was the stillest. The king laughed, releasing the mice to test them, but the cat did not play. He stayed, an exquisite statue, listening to the courtiers and accepting graciously praise for his obedience. The flame burned high, the cat outstayed the night in a court of grand excess, molten wax melting along his spine, scorching his ears. The wick ate its way down, the cat was perfect and mute. He was listening, he was watching. Until the wick spluttered between his ears, and the light went out on his fur.

It was not only the cruelty of those who thought themselves too shrewd that the cat remembered. Long ago he was sheltered from rain, and scorching desert heat. He had slept in a humble man's sleeves, nestled in his cloak, in his pocket, in his hood. Brothers and sisters ever around, ever their bodies squashed against him. The man had shared his little food with them and kissed them, and loved them all, numerous and unnamed. Those happy days, pure in his heart. Their man was a scholar, writing what he saw and heard, pressing invaluable words into leather and leaves. Cat kin danced on his hands, spilling their bodies over his writing implements, but he laughed at their interference and was never angry. When the man died they buried him far from home. A cat could not weep, but it could cry. The moon was there. A moon that was once divided, halved and then put together in the same night. The cat had not forgotten. The moon remained, just as he remained. For as long as possible, he would watch it, too.

Today, the cat waited on a wall in Old Town. He had remembered cruel kings and humble scribes, he had overseen the journeys of both the wicked and the kind. The cat was a facilitator of interesting conclusions, deserved ones.

Today, he was Hamza, and he lay in wait for a girl to know her own name.

~

In some faiths, family were buried next to one another—as though they could grasp hands in death. Between his duties leading the young shark hunters and keeping them busy, Zubeir used his free time to remember God. God and death. And love. The inseparable things.

Makaburini made any pedestrian hasten their step, eager to be away from it, sometimes cowed into a quick, quiet prayer. Zubeir's dead were scattered from one end of the plot to the other. He took his time. He made his duas where he could not ask permission.

His butcher father at one corner by the wall, twelve grave mounds from his mother whose grandfather was once an old lord of Pwani. Zubeir had inherited his father's solemn face and his mother's wry and brilliant expression; even as a young boy he had been handsome and dark.

Years had passed, people were born and they died, and he had only ever loved one woman. His sly handsomeness was indeed being wasted!

He paced from his mother's grave to his father's, and back again. There were crows in the trees, surveying his march, but Zubeir did not interfere with the politics of birds. Before the impressionable young shark hunters who looked up to him, Zubeir maintained his easy calm and assurance, for these were no pretences. But when he was troubled, he went to the dead, to pray, to eat his thoughts toward their conclusions. He could never lie in front of his parents; they knew his every trick, for it was their example that had taught it to him.

That Aisha's eeriness was a strain little different from her mother. Shida, the wedding singer, who had had such life in her that it crushed her bones. Her spirit had been too strong for the vessel, snapping the outer shell like boiling water forced through thin glass pipes. When Shida broke, she cut all her keepers. The people hadn't spoken kindly of her until she'd died, as they'd been too afraid of her. Shida had hated pity even more than she hated praise. Dead, people said they knew her. None had ever understood her. Viciously clever, a woman like that could whip herself up an army if she wanted, simply by singing the right song.

She always knew how to sing the right song.

Living without a mother was no easy feat, but that woman had been a burning tree. She should have been a war-lord, not a mother. Zubeir's mother had been all things good. Nothing could pass through her hand without having been improved by it. Whenever he walked through the market and the familiar scent of henna came over him, his heart swelled with love for his mother who had spent her life at the knees of brides, painting beauty into their hands like blessings and spellwork. Neither his father nor Zubeir himself could have suffered life without her. Girls like Aisha and Shida, he could not see the delicateness of the bride in them. Shida had borne it in anger, and Aisha was a child. It was no easy feat, to grow up without a mother, and yet that half-feral heart that Shida had possessed had, through her absence, also been inherited by the daughter. Aisha's eeriness was not in the snarl, but in her eyes.

Aisha moved like an animal. Had the flat, direct stare of an animal. She never blinked unless she reminded herself; he saw her sometimes pause to look down, timed, before she looked up again. A vacant, dull-looking girl, she'd have been excused and gotten away with it, been called meek, if not for how flat her gaze was. It was like staring into the unknowable sea. To be unknowable was selfish in these parts, showed a lack of trust and a lack of neighbourliness. *And we are all neighbours here.*

31

She was no great beauty, nor exceptionally religious, nor as intelligent as the sort of women who end up running businesses or becoming great matriarchs. She was an isolated careful fiction of a girl. Doing what she was told, yet keeping the rest of her to herself.

Her father had similar inclinations, he felt a failure and lacked confidence—but he was always a sweet boy, earnest and trying his best. Obedient except for when he stepped out of his father's shadow to learn how to be a fisherman. He did not join the shark hunters, which was perhaps for the best.

I might have guided him, Zubeir had thought sometimes. Now it haunted him like a regret he had earned: he had felt wary of interfering, for it was not his place. He had kept his distance, watching from afar, marvelling at the weakness and courage of such beings.

Ali, Aisha, Shida—all keeping their hearts to themselves and never speaking a word of them. Selfish things.

Neither could he be unearthed. When the girl came to ask him to save her father, he had refused. All three members of that family had a sort of recklessness in them—girls like that took pains never to look defiant, but the sun had been a brand on her brow, a circlet of fury. He saw her desperate, but not yet blind.

Zubeir joined a funeral procession quietly, hoping prayer would take his mind off of things. When the old man returned to the pier, snapping at the boys to look sharp and get ready to practise their diving, Moudi frowned, too wise to be fooled. "Is she going to bring us trouble, Mze Zubeir?"

Zubeir squashed his most devout student's cap down onto his great big hair. "She would have to find it first."

Zubeir had grown up glimpsing hidden things and seeking them out with caution. Glimmers of shadow in doorways, a certain haze in the corner of a room—how many crows gathered, he counted their number, they were not uniform, their faces all different. He might as well have given them names, but knew to speak them would be to invite correction and conversation, and other things beyond his control. Well, Zubeir and the unseen things, they noticed one another.

He noticed the cat. He noticed the things in the water. Knew about Ali's secret friend because what else would have made more sense? Unlucky brat like that does well to have a beast on his side.

Ali's beast, and Aisha's companion.

Show me what trouble you will bring, fishling.

CHAPTER SIX

Aisha prepared a dinner of broiled cassava leaves and spiced chicken while Hababa observed. They ate, they prayed, and then they lay down to bed.

She had tried to hope, before. Taken to the roof of Hababa's bungalow, she hardly saw anything, the sea was shielded from her. Orphans, widows, women were expected to scan horizons till their eyes hurt, so that if her father came she would be there to greet him, a good daughter, a good wife, a good mother, a good host.

The day she heard Baba was missing, her body was slow, and she realized now she was still stunned. His being missing had awoken in her the extraordinary, a monster of childhood, the serpent that lurked beneath her father's boat, tearing apart the fish it was thrown. Then the cat had given her his name.

Her fingertips tingled; beneath her skin there was a stinging sensation. A nearly painful, humming heat, like fishing thread fizzing through her fingers, plowed away by the bolting merlin. The tingling spread to her elbows, a numb ringing in her arms as though she had jarred the bone down onto a table too hard.

Before Hababa turned off the light, Aisha had held out her palms in front of her; her veins squirmed and burned but her fingers, her hands, her wrists were still and steady. Then all at once she could only see their shadowy outline, a vapour coloured in with charcoal.

"Rose water."

Aisha, a still branch, turned on her side so that the mattress could make a noise and that noise would be a question.

"That was what he gave me as a wedding gift." Hababa was speaking in the dark, which carried her voice around the room like a soft silk to be treated delicately. She made a hard, angry noise in her throat, to tear it. "The scorn of it. He was very much in love with me, you know. Since we were children. He'd say, I will ask your father and he will not deny me. He laughed when it made me angry, and I got angrier when he laughed!"

Aisha pursed her lips before remembering that no one could see her, she need not perform with her face. She paused, uncertain. "Jedhi Swaleh—"

Hababa snorted, turning heavily toward the wall. "Was dead before you were born, thank God, I thank him every day. Other women weep to be widowed, I wept too. I wept for months, years, till today I weep, tears of grief and then relief. It is not such a bad thing to be widowed, Aisha, when you have a son who is meant to take care of you."

"Hababa . . ." Five days don't grow even a clot of blood. The boat had gone far, but my father is not without a companion. There is something in the water. Something that *knows*. "That is unkind."

"It is true."

"Did you love him as he loved you?"

"Sweet girl, love does not build houses or raise the dead." Hababa spoke in a quiet huff; when she sighed it was the shallow sound of regret long borne. "Your grandfather, I leave him to the dead, that I will take as his act of love. Your father, I give up to the water, in time maybe that will be his act of love."

Aisha's grandfather had been much older than his wife. Aisha swallowed, throat thick with a grief she was coming to realize would be her inheritance. "You said 'when we were children.' Who is the boy that loved you?"

And Hababa, who found joy and nourishment in the sharing of secrets and the sweetness to be found in a scandal, who collected the lives of others in words and hearsay and wrapped herself in the alive-ness of a thousand different actors performing the daily dramas that gave her world fuel to revolve, put salt in her food and language in the movement of unspeaking things—the mbuyu, the wind, the hiss of the water—she drew her blanket over her head like a beggar huddling into his cowl and muttered. "A boy. A boy. Sleep, dear one, before the sun comes up."

And she huddled and made herself small as if to tuck that one sa-cred thing back into her, the kind of secret Aisha understood could not be parted from with sweetness, cajoling, or flattery.

Hababa's secret was like the shoki-shoki, sweet and barbed, thorn-covered truth travelling from heart to throat to mouth in a slow journey. It would not show its face overnight.

The night unravelled, slow and sticky, a monsoon's heat with mos-quitoes swarming through the hours as the light rose. They deserted, returning in drowsy anger to the cool, dark roots of mangroves.

Aisha, well-bitten, rose. The skin beneath her eyes felt bruised; her spine ached as though it had been twisted into some unearthly contortion and held in place for too long.

Aisha rose to look into the sun's great eyes. She was not as near to the sea here but she still had her sea sense. She could see with her sea eyes how the water would be a blood run. By the time the sun was borne out of it the waves would be warm and bladed in gold, a hun-dred daggers shuffling over one another in slurry honey. She held tight to the breath she'd collected in her salt-lungs, squeezing it hard, and all at once, exhaled.

When she opened the door it was to the dawn flaring up, red like a sari, and pinkening on the smooth egg Hassan held between thumb and forefinger. He was bent at the waist, raising it up to her like a prince presenting a diamond.

She blinked rapidly, stomach flipping sick.

At her silence he rose in a fluster, rambling. "I heard about your father," he told her feet. "I'm very sorry—"

His five days are not up. But even that enraged inner voice felt disassociated from her, like it wasn't her thought or feeling at all. Her body after all was inordinately still and steady.

Hassan passed the egg palm to palm, and something uncharitable occurred to her: that she would never consider him handsome, with his eager kindness, the gap between his teeth. And it was only the flood of shame following that let her fall onto the crutch of courtesy, which allowed her to speak to him, chastened by her unkind thought. "I was going to buy some for Hababa today. I'll still need to go to the soko, but how much do you want for them?"

Her businesslike manner must have appeared too abrupt, for his shyness deepened; he cupped the egg between both hands as if he might crush it in his embarrassment. "I know that you're going through a difficult time . . . with your father—" When he chanced a look, she didn't understand how he could splutter so quickly and avert his stare, as if there was something in her stillness that prompted further hesitation and fear. "This is a gift, you needn't pay," he ran on. "Please accept these from now on."

"Charity."

He cringed. "Neighbourliness."

"Thank you," she said, so as to not be found ungracious, though her lips barely moved. She did not want the eggs, or his kindness. She did not know what she might be expected to buy, for in time, a kindness must be acknowledged and returned. Kindness can have teeth. A kindness, like all things, is a transaction, a pending promise, a debt. "Thank you very much."

He blurted out his thanks for her thanks. Warming with pleasure, he pressed five eggs into her palms. A sixth tumbled between their hands and broke, splattering eggshells against her ankles.

Aisha flinched, the ruptured yolk spilling over the steps in a slow, bright ooze. Hassan's profuse apologies were noises she could not properly register. He pressed at his kofia nervously and sprinted away like a thief, leaving Aisha on the steps with her hands full of eggs she did not need on a morning that came in a slow fade of red, pink, yellow, and gold. Mute.

When she assembled breakfast her hands moved like pulleys, the motions of a machine. She imagined she was assembling a box, a gun, a chair. Crack of egg, spit of oil, the meatiest part of her palm blazed from a burn she could only feel after she sat before her grandmother to watch Hababa sop up the ooze of yolk with the chapati.

Aisha swept the floor, mind an empty room where visitors came and left, a terminal made temporary with tasks and chores and housework. She salted sunflower, scrubbed her clothes, and prepared the meals that determined the passage of time.

Soon a guest even stranger than the cat arrived. Drops of water still clung to Aisha's brow and lips as she'd rushed between chores and completed her Wuḍū, so that there was nary a space between the last and her prayers to care about wiping her face. Hastily, she moved to the door, bracing herself for the usual drill of helping Hababa host. Swafiya was still performing her sunna salahs and it would be some time before she finished. Aisha resolved to put out the eating things and vanish. She had a lot to toss around in her mind, not knowing the particulars of her appointment with the cat.

Aisha opened the door with one hand, swiping at her lip with the other.

Aisha's grand-aunt, Hababa Hadia, stood on the step. If Hababa Swafiya was as tall as Hababa Hadia's pride, then Hababa Hadia was as short as Hababa Swafiya's temper; the point of her walking stick scraped down her weight into the stone of the first step. She had odd green eyes in a papery face, her wrinkles seemed to have been placed with symmetrical elegance and she had not a single blemish.

Aisha had only ever seen her once or twice before. She remembered her at her mother's funeral—small and witchlike. Though back then she had not needed to hold on to the arm of a small slip of a girl like the one at her side now.

She hadn't looked like she'd wanted to be at Mama's funeral either, and seemed to suffer Aisha's presence even less.

Aisha ducked her head quickly, at a loss for words, and extended her hand to offer her greetings. The green-veined, cream-coloured hand delayed in moving from the young girl's arm to Aisha's—offered with a cool suspiciousness and a kind of disdainful lethargy. Aisha kissed the cold skin, and it flinched beneath her lips, recoiling. The old woman took her hand back without wiping it on the girl's shoulder. *I should congratulate you on your restraint,* Aisha thought in amazement, *if I didn't think you were already impressed with your own tolerance.*

"I hope you're well, Hababa Hadia," Aisha smiled. "Please do come in."

The girl's face was as pale and mute as moonlight, eyes low as one beneath the hand that keeps them meek. They stepped over the threshold and Aisha guided them to the small seating area before going back to hunt for her grandmother. "I'll be right with you, Hababa Hadia!" she called out, so Hababa Swafiya would have some sense of who her guest was so she might prepare her fortitude.

When Aisha found her grandmother still praying, she tensed with nervous impatience. Took a moment to tighten the muscles of her face and keep in place her small, impartial smile. She went past the guests again to make the coffee, torn between two opposing wishes: for the guests to leave before Hababa entered and hurt her own feelings, and for Hababa to appear so Aisha wouldn't have to sit with them.

Neither of those wishes came true. Aisha served the guests, then sat there odd and formal, as if sitting for a portrait.

Her grandmother kept a small grainy photo in her cupboard, the only picture they had of Aisha's Jedh. His head had been turbaned in clean white cloth and he posed with a stately indifference, still dressed in the style of his village in Hadramawt. His face had been long and lean, no fat in his face or even under his eyes, giving him a sleepless look. He had been a cousin to Hababa Hadia, and in her grand-aunt's features Aisha saw the paleness and a vague suggestion of him in her—certainly she had the pride of one of those arrogant people who claim their blood has not been 'muddled' by Mombasa itself. Oh no, they were *real* Arabs.

Her grandfather had a quiet dignity. In Hababa Hadia there was a sharpness of arrogance and pride. Perhaps she had hated the idea of Jedh marrying a local woman who couldn't boast of purely Hadrami lineage, perhaps she hated that he would bring himself low to marry a woman whose sister had disgraced them all by running off to do whatever she wanted, perhaps Hadia thought Jedh should have married her instead.

Aisha had inherited that sleepless look from her grandfather, Ali had told her once, bringing out the photo.

He loved his father, who had died before he could protest Ali becoming a fisherman instead of tradesman.

There was an ornately carved bed that rose high off the floor, a gift from when Hababa and Jedh Swaleh were married. Aisha never saw her grandmother sleep in it, and whenever Aisha came to spend the night she and Hababa slept on mattresses. Hababa preferred sleeping on the floor; it was better for her back. And the bed was too high, she said, for an old woman like her to bother with dragging herself onto it. And yet, not once did she consider giving it away.

Hababa had never shown her the photo, but Aisha had seen her sit with the cupboard open, folded clothes sitting around her ignored, the door of it shielding her from view, and known that her grandmother had taken it out to gaze upon his face. She would sit there a long time.

No matter how much Aisha ate, even if one tried to fatten her, she'd always have hollows beneath her eyes like grooves carved out a mountainside. The girl's mouth was tiny and pink, Aisha's mouth was so broadly expressive that she struggled to make it pretend what it was supposed to pretend. Aisha's blood had Jedh and Mombasa in it too. The Mombasa that flowed from Hababa, went to Ali, Shida, to Aisha. Mombasa blood, the Uswahili that Hababa claimed wasn't *really* Swahili because wasn't her father an Arab? Her father's father was an Arab, all the fathers before, Arabs. But who, Aisha had often wondered, was Shida's father? And what of all the not-Arab mothers in that long line of so-called Arab fathers whose names no one clutched to remember, because it was better to be who your father was, to be Arab? The Swahili was in Aisha's blood, in her mouth, on her face. Not something that could be denied, or waved away—and Hababa Hadia must laugh at them, for she thought she was better than them.

Because she didn't have to pretend. No one could tell Hababa Hadia who she was, no. She got to tell everyone else.

But despite all that, Hababa Hadia could not laugh at Aisha properly. Jedh was in Aisha's face too. Her eyes were dark, near black, but the shape of them was indisputably her grandfather's, the hollows beneath them were the shadows of Hadramawt. If Ali had seen Jedh in Aisha, then how could Hababa Hadia see it without rancour?

Hababa Hadia cleared her throat. "Do you not go to school?" The girl was listening, because she moved a plate toward her grandmother with focused nonchalance, attentively not making eye contact. "Or have you remained to help with your grandmother?"

Aisha was not sure about going to school. She had no desire to study or not study, but was going through the motions of it. She was lucky to have the option. Disciplined, she did not look at the girl— few Hadrami girls got sent to school, few Hadrami boys as well—but the world was opening up in the miserly way a living giant clam did, and no one wanted sand in their eye hunting for the pearl.

She did not know, by Hababa Hadia's tone, whether she thought that girls should be in school or that they shouldn't. She was wary of the trap. Aisha offered her best peacefully brainless smile. Both an offer of submission and a complete withholding of meaning. She turned to the girl and raised her brows, amiable. "It's embarrassing but I haven't got a head for studying!"

The girl, surprised at being addressed, smiled shyly. "You only have to find something you're interested in," she said kindly. She met Aisha's eye briefly and was startled, remembering herself and her grandmother. "I like biology," she said more quietly, feeling her grandmother's impassive gaze on her.

"I should hope so," Hababa Hadia said. "She is going to be a doctor."

This bragging humiliated a girl Aisha had been talking to like an agemate. She was as short as her grandmother, but older too. Skinnier than Aisha was. She wore the big black, tie-under-chin buibui that her grandmother did. But her eyebrows were hidden by them.

She must have uncovered her face only on the step of Hababa's house.

A bride to be.

And a doctor to be, as well? How did that work?

"What class are you in?" Aisha asked. And quickly, so the girl would have a choice of which to answer: "Do you dissect animals?"

It was an odd, gruesome question—to ask it so abruptly suggested an intolerable amount of interest. The girl was too well bred to frown, and she smiled a little in confusion before nodding. "Cow hearts," she said. "We have a lot of specimens in the lab."

It was a question she may have been asked before, but perhaps not in front of her grandmother. Hababa seemed both interested and disapproving. Her brow had inched up with imperiousness.

"Is that something you're interested in, too?"

Aisha remembered to look away. She had an odd way of staring too long and too directly, and had to control her pauses. "I don't think I'm very interested in anything in particular."

"Not the sea like your father? Or even in improving yourself?" Hababa Hadia asked in a kind of drawl that felt less like kind instruction and more like a punishing observation.

"One can only aspire to be as good as your generation, Hababa Hadia. But we will always fall woefully short. It is impossible."

It was a line of praise, rehearsed, used many times. The child of fire is the ember, and the child of the ember is ash. If you be the fruit, then we be the rotting flesh, dripping maggots. The older women always said it, but they hated to hear it repeated to them with such a pious, courtier's tongue.

They'd said her bastard mother had the mouth of a warmonger, that she had never had the respect to tie her tongue, that she'd verbally brawled with older relatives who dared even look at her wrong. Shida's own mother had been a wild woman, and it was hard to believe she was Hababa's sister—but if she was wild, then Hababa had to be a steady, law-abiding rock to make up for it. If Shida was rash and combative, Aisha had to be sweet without being sly, even if that meant looking dull or stupid sometimes. Aisha could never hate her grandmother for worrying about her and being strict.

Hababa Swafiya arrived, composed and smiling, but without the ease she met with other people. Hababa Hadia could not rise to greet her, on account of her bad hip—so Aisha had to watch her grandmother, who had always been rather tall, bend halfway to the earth to kiss the cheeks of this relation who blamed them for their own expulsion from the greater family.

Aisha made sure to inch closer to her grandmother, so they would know that Swafiya had people too.

"It's unfortunate that your son has gone missing," Hababa Hadia said. "It must be hard to be without a husband, now without a son. Financially, things will be difficult."

"My son is not dead." When grandmother said that, Aisha did not dare clench her brow to betray them both.

Hababa Hadia was too crafty to show open scorn in her expression. She only had a chilling way of keeping her expression insultingly cool as though she was above engaging in argument when others were perfectly capable of undermining themselves for her. "I provide well enough for my family, and they can rely on me. I've been working since I can remember."

"Yes, that is true. Do you still make the . . . little platters?" Hababa stiffened, her smile sharp and hurt, demurring. "It's only that we are to have a wedding soon."

The girl's jaw clenched, and her eyes shuttered closed as though she had been forced to see an insect cruelly crushed, and powerless could neither act nor turn away. Aisha appreciated that she was embarrassed for, even ashamed of, her grandmother. Usually she disliked such creatures, who wanted to be like their female elders so they could step on others as they had been stepped on, perhaps harder.

"I may be interested in ordering from you. It is quite a large order, though, I don't know if you can manage it. You must be preoccupied with planning for your future and your granddaughter's future. I don't envy you that. God give you strength."

Hababa had to clench her back teeth and say *ameen*. Hababa Hadia had tricked her by offering a prayer like that. So that Hababa Swafiya would be forced to thank her before she could even think of berating her.

"Your father," the girl interrupted frantically, "is a sailor!"

"He's a fisherman," Hababa Hadia corrected. "He ferries prawn on foot."

"Oh," she said, crestfallen that she had not helped at all. "Some women do not leave their houses, do they? No doubt such men are rather necessary."

"My father doesn't ferry prawn on foot." This time Aisha could not stop anger from giving the words some heat. "He doesn't fish for prawn, either, you don't need to go deep sea for that. There's no shame in either, but there is a distinction. As there is a distinction between a general practitioner and a surgeon. He's not a mangrove, shore fisher. He goes far."

"Does he have a sailboat?"

"Sailboats are for rich club members," Hababa Hadia scoffed. "Of course not."

The girl quietened, overexerted, her courage drained away. Hababa Hadia had not liked that she had spoken. "It's only that I've read about it. In the newspaper."

Hababa Hadia's eyes sharpened, brightening at the sight of a new opening before anyone else could grasp it. Then they cooled, and looked rather sly and cunning instead of petty. "Is the unlucky sailboat still there?"

Aisha did not frown, "I wouldn't know."

"Wouldn't you? Isn't that where you run about? All over the creek? The beaches and the piers?"

"My granddaughter is young and a little wild, she was raised like a boy—" Aisha couldn't *bear* to hear the sickening rest, the kind of excuses Hababa made when she should have been going to war. She drowned it out, as anger rushed the blood to her face.

"It's there, no one will buy it. The owner won't sink it because that would mean driving it into the sea. He's frightened it'll kill him before then."

"There's no such thing as luck . . ." Aisha muttered.

"Whether it's luck or possession, you stay away from the things that have made a pattern of harming you. They're no good for you.

45

God give you patience in these trying times," Hababa Hadia said, rising. The girl could have been an elegant person but something about Hababa Hadia always made everyone scramble.

Hababa's offer to stay for lunch was waved away like it was a foul odor.

At the door the old cousins shared a cool embrace while the girl rushed about to find her grandmother's shoes, and then helped her slip them on. Hababa Hadia tolerated the service owed to her.

Hababa Hadia gripped the door-frame in one hand and her walking stick in the other, stepping out gingerly. With her grandmother's back turned, the girl gripped Hababa Swafiya's arm and thanked her for her hospitality. The entryway was too narrow for the girl to go past Aisha's grandmother and embrace Aisha without Hababa Hadia noticing, for which Aisha felt awkward relief, so instead the girl smiled a little sheepishly in farewell.

Hababa had a sharp and witty tongue, and her temper could lash out, but her forgiveness was just as quick too. Usually. It angered Aisha that Hababa would take such an insult from this woman, angered her most of all that she, her granddaughter, had to be silent about it. She was not a peer so she could say nothing. Rising to Hababa's defence would only shame her.

Aisha put away the things. None of them had eaten any of it or sipped the coffee. Hababa kissed her teeth. "A platter! She wants me to make her something so she can turn it away. Since when did Hadia look out for me? She's a vulture who only comes here for the dead. All this stuff about a wedding! She thinks she does me charity in my time of need with the promise of work she will not give me? God protect me from my enemies!" Hababa was so heated up she had to go and perform ablution, though she returned even more upset than before. "The enemy really does come here with God in his mouth!"

CHAPTER SEVEN

Aisha performed her chores like an elaborate dance, perfected from rehearsal and repetition. She swept the street and bought oranges and the sun rose and made sweat stream between her shoulder blades and made the walls damp and swollen, and then it sank quickly, plummeting into the water. Aisha sat on the roof, perched on hot stone; orange went from her temples, to her knees, to her ankles, draining away as if from the vial of her body.

And still, Ali did not appear.

Behind her eyes, the seam between wave and sky deepened red, a bloody cut. The call to prayer was a lament as the night-time made a slow meal of the rest of the day. Mouthful by mouthful, economical, the dark came.

Ali was not borne on its back.

And in her blood then was the slow squirm of minnows, darting beneath her skin. The tingling in her now followed from fingers to palms to elbows to shoulders, and the root of her skull ached as though there were teeth gnawing into it. The feeling did not pass as they supped on shark stew and puffy mahambri, not when she cleaned the sinia and scrubbed the bowls, not when they lay down to sleep and Hababa said, "Soon this will pass. Every day people are dying and being born, only men can leave those who depend on them behind and still be called brave. A woman is not praised when she suffers, she is praised for suffering in silence. I have not been silent and I have been reviled for speaking so loudly of my wounds. Forgive this old woman for shaming you."

Aisha, who had not wept even at her own mother's funeral, felt tears swarm the back of her throat. Her fingers uncurled toward the dark lump of Hababa's back and with careful daring, she touched the frayed edge of her sleeping robe and whispered, "You don't shame me, Hababa. Don't say such things."

"The only thing that gladdens this heart is to think that you will marry soon. The women were impressed with your cooking."

Aisha's throat tightened; her body felt hot and cold and sick all at once. Her mouth tasted of sand. "Tell me about the wedding gift."

"It was nothing."

"Does a gift insult?"

"When it is aimed correctly," Hababa said, "it can cut like a knife."

The dogs had stopped baying after Isha time, the howls that had echoed the muadhini had trailed into silence. Mombasa was ready to fall asleep, pots and pans were returned where they hung, the bellies of boats rubbed the shore along drowsy currents, and the mattress beside her shifted, occupied.

"Do you love my father?"

Hababa tuned slowly to peer at Aisha in the darkness. "I brought him into the world, he is this flesh."

"Do you think that he is dead?"

"Death is his only excuse for not returning that I will accept," Hababa said. "I am tired of blinding my eyes on horizons, waiting."

"What has he done that is so awful, Hababa?"

"Tell me, Aisha, do we not live comfortably? Like our ancestors, we will never live in palaces, but there is always food on the table, is there not? And when it is your time I will be able to afford a few gold bangles for your wedding."

Hababa awaited challenge in Aisha's silence and, receiving none, she sighed.

"What else does your father seek? He is sick, powerless in the face of his own ambition—he has a mother, a daughter, a home. He finds no solace in the company of men or women, nor in prayer, politics, or money. He desires only to exceed and abandon. All who love him, he leaves. He will always be in want and not look back once."

"Hababa," she started, but it sounded weak to her own ears. "Baba goes for us. He wouldn't put himself in danger if it wasn't to provide for us."

"Ha!" Hababa scoffed bitterly. "Let him hunt shark or break his boat against cliff sides with Zubeir, let him die *with* men. There is danger enough there, and money too. But he goes alone! Only men can abandon and be called courageous."

"My father loves you."

"Your father loves no one but the sea."

"And my mother?" Aisha broke in. "Did you love my mother?"

"I raised her. She was an orphan. No one was left to name her."

"Only you."

"Yes," Hababa whispered. "Only me."

Aisha felt tears burn up behind her eyes. "Was she always so sickly?"

"Her mother was, too. It was in the blood. I was strict . . . but she was a good girl."

"A worthy wife," Aisha surmised, flat and deadened.

"At the time I thought Ali would make a worthy husband," Hababa murmured as if in excuse. "It was natural, they grew up together. Who else would have married her?"

Hababa rarely ever talked about the circumstances of Shida's birth, or even her own irresponsible sister. *You were named for her, you know?* Ali had told her once. Aisha had never dared ask about this faceless wild woman whose example had forced Hababa to be so strict and law abiding—or about Jedhi Swaleh. They were Hababa's beloved dead, and asking her grandmother about them would have been like pecking at her, it would have been cruel.

Instead, Aisha took a deep breath, held it, and then she said, "Tell me about the man you loved who was not my grandfather."

Here Hababa stiffened, angry and hurt like a cat who'd had its tail stomped on. "A young girl like you should not ask any of what you have asked of me tonight. You have become wilful, Aisha."

"Did he give you rose water as a bridal gift? You were not widowed overly late, why did he not marry you then?"

"*Aisha—*"

"Hababa, please don't bury my father. I know he is trouble alive, I know that you have sacrificed much, but you must not bury him. If he has no body to bury he might as well not even have a name. Hababa, he will return, you'll see."

But her grandmother had turned away and soon Hababa's breath had evened low, in and out, like the calm tide. Aisha crept out of her pallet, went through the dark of the house quiet as a shadow, and left.

The streets were dark, unlit. The moon had gathered the stars like her children and refused to come out. Aisha slipped out of Sparki where men in their kiosks watched her with sleepy interest, past the mosque whose step was clear, except for the beggar who looked at her once and then turned over and went to sleep.

But for a car or two on the main road it was unusually peaceful. Aisha snuck across like a thief and was not caught. Theirs was a quiet city, but this restful turning-in, as though a curfew had come down, was eerie.

The streets grew only more deserted as she went. Impossibly empty. No vehicle, no man, woman, or creature disturbed her on the way to Makadara—if some otherworldy hand had cleared her path, was it to lead her to truth or to doom?

At the mouth of the maze, she felt lonelier than the dead. It was a dangerous place at night for a girl, but now she wished that the shadows hid someone, anyone, so she would know she was alive. She couldn't wake the neighbours, so she toed off her slippers, edging across. She wound around grimy puddles, hunting along the shadowed walls and toward the meeting place.

Her blood stood still as the night-time and sweat gathered beneath her arms. When she caught sight of the sky she did not know where the sea ended and where the sky began, black like tar, seamless and dark, without horizons. Mombasa was perched in an open mouth, teetering on sandy teeth.

The cat was on the overhang above her door. Aisha opened her mouth and he leapt across, scattering over the neighbouring roof in a yellow-orange bolt.

Astounded, Aisha watched him run away before her heart slammed into her throat. She took off, slippers tucked in her belted sash, heels hard on the jagged ground, breath cutting, soaring. She refused to think on him. She ran after the cat as he skittered and leapt, wall to wall, alley hang to crumbling roof tile, flying fast.

She hadn't dreamed it up. The cat was real, had tolerated her tea and poor hostessing, had spoken to her. Had looked at and spoken to her. To *Aisha*.

He was leading her somewhere—*leading*, for there was some purpose in this. Her lungs burned, the slap of her soles across stone abominably loud, yet no soul roused awake to call her back.

Then the shadow of Fort Jesus swallowed her in interminable night. Bolting through a lightless world, plunged in the belly of the deepest sea, pushing down on her shoulders, each racing step dragged slower, sucked at by resisting forces—hearing only her breath shorten out as though her air was lost with her sight.

Aisha burst finally around the corner and slipped, tearing her knees on the gritty gravel and stone that neared the port's edge. Her palms burned on silvery ground, limned in the gaze of a security light. She wanted to close her eyes, to hear the rest of the world, but the cat disappeared around the next corner. Aisha shot unsteadily to her feet, breathing hard—

"And who is this fishling," came the murmur, "running on such skinny legs at so late an hour?"

Aisha tasted blood in her throat. She twisted and looked up. Perched on the lip of the wall that lined the old red fort was a man so drenched in dark she could not mark his face until he had raised his smoking pipe to his scarred mouth.

Zubeir puffed, ponderous white smoke chugging steadily out of the end of his pipe.

Aisha stuffed her sweating palms against her dress. She wanted to bolt, blood racing at the thought that this delay would lose her the only opportunity at finding the cat and her father—terrified that Zubeir might drag her back to her grandmother and cause her disgrace. She licked her lips. "I need to go, Mze Zubeir! I really must go!"

"Let me not keep you!" Zubeir drawled. "I must visit your grandmother sometime—"

"You mustn't," Aisha blurted. "I've only forgotten something from when I was here earlier."

"Oh?" Zubeir inquired and shifted in his seat. "Let me help you look for it. I'll only be a moment . . ."

"I wouldn't want to be a bother!"

"No bother. Was it very dear to you, that you would brave such an hour?"

Aisha's face burned, she hadn't the time to be laughed at, or to explain. She did not dare think that Zubeir would believe her, or that the cat would appreciate her sharing. It hadn't spoken to anyone else. It had spoken to her. To Aisha. And the longer she spent dallying on indecision and wasting time with obstacles, the less real the cat became. The longer she stayed away, the greater the possibility of it becoming nothing but a dream.

"Did you know why I told you the secret of our sharks?"

"No," Aisha cried, distressed. "I don't!"

Smoke whittled up into the black, his throat rippling as he took breath back.

"Mombasa is full of such quiet and still times after sun sets. Let me be like the nighttime and give others its tenderness—like the freedom of darkness that night brings, the wordless respite in what it is willing to hide, and what escapes, what trespasses it shields . . ." He gazed upon the vanished horizon. "Tonight, I am like that night-time. Go on, Aisha. I will keep this secret. I have not seen you. On you go."

His strangeness alarmed her. The supernaturally empty streets alarmed her, yet his being an exception to whatever spell the cat had surely worked tugged her most of all. She readied to run but halted, staggered, and tugged. Zubeir would really let her go? Cursing herself, she twisted back toward him.

"Why?" she blurted. "Why did you tell me your secret?"

"Because." Zubeir's teeth were white, like a slash of moonstone. "You are your father's daughter. Tonight my secret will die with you. But if you survive, you will be worthy of it. Run along, little fishling, before this night-time shows you sharp teeth."

Aisha did not wait to hear the warning a second time. She twisted and *ran*.

On the sleeping beach the cat's escape left not even the palest dusting of paw prints in sand, fine and gritty as pulverized glass. He waited for her on the edge of the shore, head raised, gazing upon the space a moon might occupy. Aisha slowed as she arrived by him, gasping and gutted by her own mad run.

Waves lapped slowly backward and forward, swelling and receding, like the breath of a far larger animal—the soft exhale and inhale of black-blue lungs. The water skirted right to the very edge of the cat's paws but did not touch them.

Aisha watched what the cat watched. Relieved, she kept her silence. Her throat was still too raw.

"Peace," the cat said, and Aisha's face, already filled with blood, flushed altogether, humiliated by her forgetting the courtesy as she returned the greeting in a rushed, shrill ramble.

The cat's head lowered as he dropped on the sand an item he had been carrying in his mouth.

Aisha crouched, her fingers shaking on the worn edge, her gutting knife. Cradled carefully in her not-nice palms, her cut-up, calloused, dirty . . . Aisha stowed it away hastily, avoiding the cat's gentle inquiry as to her gratefulness and began tugging on her faded slippers. "It will do nicely. Thank you."

"May God grant you goodness."

"And you, too, may God reward you with goodness."

Courtesies exchanged, Aisha took unexpected comfort in them. Sometimes they had drained her, in the daytime, with people she saw every day but looked at her—their all too aware grimaces, as if they could not be happy nor expect her to be happy, and could not be in her presence without remembering that her mother was dead and that her father might as well have been. With the cat the courtesies held the familiarity of pattern.

She looked out to the flat black sea, to its slowly spreading and receding lip. Like a slumbering baby gnawing on a bone, worrying its teeth.

For a long time she waited by the cat, didn't dare prod or push. She was here. She had a weapon, or as close to one as the cat saw fit. She would not rush what had already been promised to her. The cat was full of courtesy, strange wisdom. Nothing was more foul and discourteous to him than one who gave one's word with no intention to keep it.

Then the cat began to *meow*, soft and then louder, a rise and fall of pitch. It was a harsh, disused yowl, like the scrape and whine of a rusty door. This sawing call through an unnervingly still night-time. She had never heard the cat meow before; he had always been silent, always escaped. In one day he had not only spoken to her, but also sang, and promised his company.

And slowly a shape rose, sung up from the rotten bed. A white prow, rousing drowsy upward, the flat sea rippling away as it slowly pierced air, night-time, dark.

The cat sang it out of sleep, out of a deep grave. The prow was too complete a piece, too smooth, too white. Ghostlike, it woke. And its sides were not smooth, packed wooden beams, but a long, spaced-out cage of ribs drifting toward them.

Where oars would be were long webbed wings. Translucent grey like the fins of a mythical beast, the boat trailed the water soundlessly. Approaching the shore unmanned.

Moonless night but the shape was ghosted in moonlight. Sea ebbed through the sides of this pale phantom in black slurry, in one part and out the other. No rigging nor sails, no explainable science in its integrity, in its construction.

The cat ceased singing but there in the water, not touching the shore, floated a ship made out of bones.

CHAPTER EIGHT

The boat was a skeleton of some sort of . . . fish. None Aisha had ever gutted, eaten, or held. Slender, long-ribbed like an eel, and the trailing fins of a flying fish; that thin, firefly-wing skin that does not tear so much as break into brittle shards. A half-skull jutted lower jaw, lengthy grey fangs curving up and in. Prehistoric.

She had cleaned enough underwater creatures to know their bones were flexible, translucent, easy to snap. Small and crunchy, got you in the throat if you weren't careful. But these bones had denseness to them, white as moonglow—mammalian, an ancient whale? The halved jaw with its gruesomely long teeth . . .

Something other, unseen by man. Only the wings . . . did such a fish fly? It was too large in frame to carry up like a bird. In life did its wings have colour? Ornamental, like the parrotfish or the spindly lion fish. Or poison? Too large to fly, but what remained of its jaws told her that it may have been a terror alive.

The cat paddled ahead with unbusy ease, a born swimmer. Its head was kept up easily above the water and its snout butted the side of the corpse boat. Padding a paw against the huge gap between the ribs, the cat batted for purchase and then climbed the slippery sides.

Tail flicked sharply once to dry and then curled around his feet, Hamza waited.

How disgustingly agile. She was not half so self-possessed. There was a building pressure in her chest, the gaseous expansion of hysteria.

It had come across and through her every now and then, a stillness interrupted by new waves of absurdism.

"I secured us passage, was this not what was promised?"

Cats had spoken, sung, shark hunters had let her go, and the corpses of leviathans rose out of the water every now and then.

"Is there something the matter? We are losing time."

"No," Aisha said. "Of course not."

"Then you must come on board."

Aisha watched the water's slow black breathing. Moonless night and a sky that did not split it. In the day it moved and frothed, jagged with colour, waves of glass bursting with light, but tonight the darkness hid its depth and what might have moved within those depths.

Stepping into it was like stepping into the bottom of the entire world. Her foot splashed through the water, still lukewarm, retaining the day's heat. The wedding singers were right: if Ali was truly lost at sea he would be boiled.

Wading forward, Aisha felt water sloshing up her ankles, swallowing up her waist. Her torn knee stung through with salt. Warm muck ebbed into her shoes, sucking at her feet.

No breeze passed but a chill erupted at the nape of her neck, moving through her body in a wave. It had been years since she'd been in the sea, even to swim. The itch of salt and sand was already on her, renewed, present, as if to remind her of how long she'd been away.

Her sleeves dragged heavily. She walked and the water came up to her hips, to her waist, to her ribs. Blood began to pound in her ears, the slow warm lick laving around her collarbones, rising to her throat, and when it hit her chin she gasped. At her mouth the water was warm as a body, and the sand grew murkier, slippery, sucking at her ankles. Aisha went onto her toes, the blood in her veins swimming in frenzied commotion, as if it could find no safe corner. Before she could choke on the water coming up to her nose, Aisha lunged with hands out.

Her hands slapped around the slippery ribs and she clung on, petrified of a depth dragging her away. The boat didn't even shake. She scrabbled and splattered and kicked at the water coiling around her ankles. The tops of the ribs were sharp, scraping hard against her belly when she climbed over them and landed in the boat with a faint clatter.

Water moved between the boat's ribs, licked her throat, and she stood quickly and saw there were wooden boards slatted between. Seats. The cat watched with patient expressionlessness in his queer, direct stare. His fur, only slightly wet, gleamed.

Aisha breathed hard, her chest rising and falling rapidly, her breath shallow, fast. Spooked by water, by *swimming*. She hadn't swum in many years but the sea at night was a different animal. A living thing, a mouth. She rubbed her arms, shivering. She left her ankles in the water ebbing into the boat and tried not to wince every time the water moved about them. Water clung to her eyelashes; she blinked the drops away and waited until her teeth stopped chattering.

"You must want the third thing." The cat lifted his chin. "Grab the oars and set forward."

The oars were the fins' slimy-looking nubs, like bones without sockets. They were so cool and dry they sucked the moisture right out of her palms. Her knuckles tightened, and with some difficulty she began to row. The boat moved like a blade through water, parting the surface as smoothly as a seamstress's scissors.

Aisha rowed and the oars made no noise. The water's muted whisper did not protest the boat's draw across the water, and what it touched was also without noise. She rowed, quick or slow, but either way, the boat moved at the same pace. It did not shake nor quiver nor rock side to side like a boat should have moving on the breadth of water, but was still, as a cave is still when the water runs through it.

She tried once or twice to speak to the cat in the eerie silence, but he was not receptive to conversation. He only blinked at her, slow and long, and said nothing.

The land blackened as it receded. A queer fear crawled over her, but she rowed.

She thought of Hababa, a line of mountains in a mosquito-laden night-time. Had she woken by now?

Would Aisha be back by morning? The water nipped around her ankles, her drying skin itching from the salt. When she licked her lips she tasted the sea and reminded herself not to do it again. No, the land was disappearing. It wasn't likely she'd return by morning, or return at all.

Once she asked the cat, "Are we there yet?"

The cat turned his head, his whiskers still, and said, "Keep rowing, we will know when you have arrived."

The second time she asked how it is that he knew of Ali's where-abouts.

"How is it that *you* don't say how *you* do?" the cat answered easily, satisfied when Aisha shut her mouth, reluctant to speak about what she'd seen in the water all those years ago. "I promised you directions, not explanations. Don't tire, you must row."

Aisha rowed, and for a while she kept her silence. She rowed, her limbs straining, her strength flagging, up, down, revolving, pushing. There was neither sail nor wind to blow it. Nor light to see the water except for the pale, moonlike illumination the bones themselves glowed with. Was it something in the marrow or in its very death itself that lent the skeleton that pale porcelain glow?

The cat did not answer or even make a show that he had heard. He only looked at where the moon might be, eyes fastened, as if all of his body, his limbs, his fibre and blood, knew the locus of it. Where it was even if it did not show itself. The cat had learned the moon by heart and they had answered one another for a time longer than most had been alive.

Perhaps this too is a sort of love.

So Aisha rowed and the cat watched the night's door.

"Here," the cat said, and Aisha dropped the oars as if burned. Sea squirmed along her ankles as the boat stopped at once, abruptly, like a wheelbarrow whose wheel has been stopped by a stone.

Aisha wiped her palms on her knees, the old teeth in the nape of her neck, an unwelcome chill. The water was still and dark, flat as a sheet of glass, but she could not see through it. She breathed raggedly in the wait, whispering, "What now?"

The cat only stared back with unflappable composure. "Did you not accompany your father before?"

"It was a long time ago."

"For everything that changes a million others endure," the cat returned. "Wasn't there something in the water with you then?"

Aisha rubbed the fraught edge of her leso between her thumb and forefinger, remembering old movement, an unspooled shadow, body black like an oil spill, and the water boiling white for a brief second.

She wet her lips, tasted salt. "Yes."

"And how was it called? By name? Greeting?"

"By share," Aisha said quietly. "By the giving of goods, of fish."

"A transaction then."

Aisha looked up sharply at the cat, but he did not care for any offence or harm, or fear the words struck in her. He only saw her, knew her, and anticipated her exactly. "We must attempt it, Aisha," the cat said. "What can you offer the water?"

"I don't have anything!"

"You haven't looked properly."

Aisha flattened her mouth. *Everyone must have their share.* But this was not a share . . . Her father and this beast had divided spoils between themselves. This was a transaction, and as with Hassan and the eggs, she didn't know what she was buying. But unlike with Hassan, the worst thing that could happen was only to be eaten alive, quickly and immediately.

Her fingers traced the sash where she'd tucked her gutting knife. It was the smallest of comforts to realize that it was there. Surely she couldn't offer up the knife after it had just been gifted to her. She ran the edges of her nails through the well-remembered grooves in the hilt, shocked to realize that of all the things she had owned—few and far between—this knife was the most familiar thing to her. It had worn the small bones in her palm to the hew and shape of it, its weight and extension, felt as fitted to her hand as bone into socket.

It was the most known thing to her in the entire world.

Her hand sprang away. There was no time to feel sorry for herself, and this was the last place for that pitiful luxury and dangerous self-absorption, but no, she would not part with this knife.

She flattened her mouth, determinedly looked around the boat, looked beneath her seat, hunted along the ribs, felt the prow.

The cat did not assist or comment, as she searched in futility. Had she pockets she would turn them out, only . . . her shoes. She toed them off, snatching them up before they could sink through the ribs of the boat.

Sink. Through to the depths. They hung on the hooks of her fingers by their straps. An Eid Al Fitr hand-me-down bought from a well-off merchant's daughter that scuffed, only a little the worse for wear but still well made, still the most useful of beautiful things she'd ever owned. She'd loved them for how they'd made Hababa preen and smile, happy to fulfil the grandmotherly duty of gifting. Her thumb scoured the stretched-out strap. The irregular beading where the sequins and embroidery had loosened. Hababa had worked hard to get them, done her very best to make Aisha look smart for Eid.

Aisha bundled them up, stretching her arm over. She took a deep, fortifying breath. It trembled in her, delayed in its tumble to her lungs, and then she let go.

They sank with a glug—not a splash but a sudden gulp as from a deep swallowing drink of water. The moment they met water their shape was gone, vanishing when they breached. No longer sea but an ink, dense and dark and deep, devouring the offering in one mouthful. Their plummet invisible to her, not even a tremor on the surface. She imagined none of it reaching the bottom, imagined it sinking forever. Her hand to her lap.

Slowly, it began: the smooth glass of the water cracked, crunching and fracturing like a black ice cube. Then, foaming, it boiled, spluttered.

Milky fizz of rice, bubbles rushing in mutinous mobs, bursting as they assembled. From it rose a dark, black orb.

Two round holes opened in the sleek dark skull of a creature, eyes larger than plates, blaring the sickly lantern light of a deep dweller choppy yellow on the water. Ink ran down its slippery eel skin.

Aisha's knuckles paled on her slippery knees, her heart lunged, once, twice, and skipped the third for one long plummet. This was that companion that had swum beneath her father's boat, that long spool of ink, that eater of thirds.

"There is a strange smell," said a reedy voice, though no mouth moved. "That smells like the sea and not, that is familiar—though I have never been given its name. Who is this and does it know me? And why does it disturb me with slippers and worn sole?"

Aisha's mouth ran dry. The chill that raced along her back and raised the hairs on her arms had less to do with the stillness, the lack of breeze, and everything to do with the voice. Water ebbed around that head, rippling out sedately from its eyes.

It *knew* her.

Not her name—no, that was never given out, names had power, even hers, and they could be used. One must keep one's name precious and sacred from beings who might know how to move one.

She answered, trying to stop the way her voice shook. "Friend, I come to ask after your companion, who has hunted with you for many years. Ali, the fisherman."

"Do not speak that name to me." The voice, shrill, was a plea of rage, scratching at the insides of her ears. "Oh, you will not speak that name to me!"

The creature's bitterness alarmed her. "Oh friend, you must help me! Or is it that you have eaten him?"

"Eaten him?"

"He has not returned home in days. If you have not eaten him then you must know what has happened to him."

"Might be that I should have eaten him. If this heart was not so soft it should have repaid betrayal with eating—thrice your father has betrayed me, and yet I have loved him, a fool of a friend! This heart so soft, like butter, you could cut it with a knife."

She did not know how readily she might trust this creature, but the accusation of Ali being thoughtless with a friend was not hard to believe—it was likely a truth, one that hurt her. "So you have quarreled," Aisha said. "I am sorry to hear it."

"And who are you, fishling, to look for him so? How do you know of me?"

"I have seen you move beneath his boat. Please, how did he come to know you and betray you?"

The head inched toward them, slow and curious. "I have known the fisherman for more than twenty years. Many, many years ago on a day so hot that the sun boiled like a yolk I swam, saddened and alone—you see, a thousand years ago I had been struck from the undersea, an outcast, forced to roam alone . . ."

"What had you done?"

"A minor trespass. Should I expect more interruptions?"

Aisha inclined her head, apologetic. "Forgive this one."

"Yes, well," the creature groused. As it circled the boat Aisha tried not to make it too obvious how keenly she tracked its movements. It would be offended if it noticed her suspicion. "Preoccupied with my own woes, I failed to pay attention. A sudden water shift, a brutal wave, tossed me about head over foot or tooth or hoof or claw, tangled in mine own body—which in the undersea was so long it could circle your continent thrice, but in this ocean, after having been so severed, can only barely wrap its tail around your red fort—this body could not even bring down a mere Portuguese warship. I am half a thing! Oh, even the leviathans would laugh at my crippling—I should hope to hear some creature's laughter other than fish who never laugh, they have nothing clever to say at all and are so poor of wit. I have been starved."

The creature paused to reflect, to pity itself.

"Tangled right into a fisherman's net, I was finished. I lay there in knots, scrubbing the gritty bottom of the sea, and I prayed to God, but how could this heavy heart believe that salvation would come? Anytime someone could pull me up and I'd be expected to put up a fight, even as tired as I was. Not many of us wish to die even as we say that we do, not so much as we wish only to stop *being*. Dying is painful; not existing is promising in its nothingness, and impossible, as you well know.

"Soon enough the net went taut, and I was being dragged up. Up, up, up! To this sickly place that is so dry and *up*—how intolerable that only birds can navigate it as we navigate the water, but they cannot even float or rest as we do, they must find a perch. The body becomes so heavy. Philosophers here—or *there*, in the undersea, believe that some leviathans drag beings under water because they feel it as an act of love. They feel that the place above the water is some sort of hell and they must spring breathing things out of it.

"But up! The nets took me. I writhed and I twisted, but the more I writhed and twisted, the more embroiled in the trap I became. Helpless I was as the light grew, and this servant hates daylight, it burns wherever it touches me. Wherever it touches me! Struck blind, shoved against the sides of a boat, burning alive, captive. I cursed and bared my teeth, hating the ten men that must have dragged this net— for it would take the strength of ten men! Imagine my shock to find it was only a young, barely grown boy on a rickshaw of a boat staring down at me.

"I cursed him and hissed, but we both stilled when we heard the other boats nearing. They had heard the commotion and were rushing that way to see what had caused it.

"And this boy spoke very sharply to me, and I, having been a philosopher in the court of the undersea, had known all the languages of men and yet had never been so directly addressed, stilled when he said, *Be silent! If you are silent I promise that you may yet live!*

"And silent I was! Quickly he threw canvas over this burning body and cut the ties that fastened net to ship, and there I was, barely hidden from the boats that bumped near him. When they asked him what had happened, he said a shark had gotten tangled in the net and ripped it away in escape. They laughed fondly at him like he was an unlucky fool.

"The boy took me to quieter waters and astounded me by freeing me. He turned his back and began to leave.

"A kindness unpetitioned! What was there to assure him that I would not have sunk his boat and eaten him as soon as I was freed? And to leave me without a word!

"Isolation does strange things to pride, all things it cheapens have now cheapened it. I wanted to be talked to again. Better blind than to be deaf or dumb, a mouth needs to utter prayers and to speak, the ear to take in conversation. It must, it must, or the mind, the spirit, dies. And what use is a body then?

"I showed him where the flounder gathered to breed and helped him drive schools into nets, protected him against lurching waters. He was my friend and one cannot bear to eat those! Certainly not when one has so few.

"As Ali grew older, we hunted farther, better. Oh, if all the fish in this sea would die! And I saw him grow into a man until one day, to my astonishment, Ali brought a small child to totter about.

"How strange, how small in shape, it waddled and then it walked, and then the father taught it how to clean fish, how to salt it and cook it and every day it came with my friend. And he would say, my dear friend—for this servant's name cannot be properly pronounced by the mouths of your kin and nevermore above the water, the acoustics are all wrong on dry land—I have no brothers if you are not my brother.

"And how touched this soft-butter heart is, till the words glow along the ribs of this entire body, and this entire body is all ribs, my dear! To be called brother! Such long ribs, you feel it completely.

"I watched the child and waited till it slept—as it usually did once the sun had reached its apex; there is a heavy, drowsy stupor that addles the brain. *Oh Ali, are you not my brother?*

"He was whittling a wooden bird and laughed heartily, *Of course, we are!*

"Might we not be brothers for true, then? Give me the child as a bride so that I might make a home for all of us under the sea.

"I smelled blood and watched it drip from the thick, rope-calloused meat of his palm. He had slipped with the knife and its blade was so deep in the root of his thumb, another flinch would have severed it completely.

"Injured by his astonishment and his horror, this head ducked beneath the water and begged forgiveness for presuming too much.

"When Ali returned the next day it was without the child. I was relieved, for I thought he might leave me forever. But I was stung deeply for all that Ali called me brother he could not bear to treat me fully as one.

"But what can this heart do? It must bear it, it must bear it! Love is all teeth, my dear, and we must forgive one another, and this heart endeavoured to forgive this man, because it is what this heart must do—I did not want to argue or to chase him away, but that day a whole third of this heart was eaten—when you love someone they often make a meal of it, but what else can one do, what else?

"Soon he did not want the breeding spots of the flounder, he wanted farther and farther, in waters dangerous even to me!

"But what could I do? I took him to jellyfish, to the secret sleeping places of tuna packs and long-tooth merlin. I would herd fish into the net and protect his boat, and Ali would send me my share—cleanly gutted and neatly diced. Though this servant could eat a tuna whole without such help, it enjoyed these attentions.

"I would herd in ten fish and Ali would give me five. I admired him for this—every day I would whip this body through waves and herd swarms of fish and I would ask him once he'd pulled in his net and began to count his fish, *How many have you caught today, oh brother?*

"And though I always knew, he would call out—ten, fifteen, or thirty! It was to make a game of it and Ali would divide the catch between us.

"One day I herded fifty parrotfish into his net, and as usual I asked, *How many have you caught today, oh brother?*

"And Ali said to me, *Forty.*

"This servant had heard a lie! And from my brother! I said nothing, even as Ali threw me twenty fish. He did not know that I did not need him to keep count.

"I did not hunt with him to feed myself, for that I can always do, but for company. And this heart must forgive, what does this servant know about the economic needs and workings of man?

"So I never asked Ali why he lied. I waited, for surely he could confide in his brother? But the lie endured, and this heart, its next third was eaten by this—that my brother would not open his heart to me. Two-thirds of my heart your father has eaten and neatly has he made a meal of the final portion!"

Overtaken by emotion, the creature could no longer speak, but Aisha had suffered this story with such great feelings, felt compelled to beg it to continue. The man it had spoken of was no doubt her father, down to the livid scar in his hand—and it caused her great pain to hear of him and what he had done.

And to hear of herself in the story. She understood, as tears smarted her eyes, why her father no longer took her out to sea, and though she could not regret his decision to keep her away from such a suitor and could not fully forgive the entitlement of the creature's proposal, she could also understand the injury done.

"Please," she cried out. "You must tell me what happened!"

"Oh, how can I? How can I? He has betrayed me and done so with full knowledge."

"Then know, oh friend, that if it wounds you—you are speaking too in a language that hurts me! But I must know, I must find him."

"Farther and farther he desired to roam!" the creature returned angrily, its shrill, reedy voice shaking. "But it was always fish that were hunted, always only fish." The creature wailed, long and high, raising all the hairs on Aisha's arms. "Oh, but he had not had enough! He wanted to go to the undersea. Brother, I said, you cannot reach it for you are only a man! He said, *Brother, what lies beyond such and such a horizon and why do you not go?* And I warned him: that is the sea of sharks and sharklings, and beasts like them. Ali nodded, and then he said, *Oh brother, will you not take me there?*

"Ali! I said, hoping that if I spoke in jest he would leave it alone. And what will such as you and I do there? Those waters are dangerous to us, you cannot hunt there! And I cannot go there, I begged him. Those you mean to hunt are not only dangerous, ever so close to the undersea, but they are my kin. This servant, even in his isolation, his loneliness and his disgrace, has never dared approach them, or speak to them. Even though they would kill us both, they are my kin and you and I cannot go there.

"If you bear any love for me, brother, you will leave that place alone! You will die before you reach it. I cannot accompany you on a mission to kill mine own relations who would kill me just for being in their sights. You must not do this.

"But I could see that he had made his mind up and that he never loved me at all. Or that if ever he did it was a pale love, dimmed by a greater love of something else. And he took his boat and he went. He left!"

The creature was weeping. How could she console it, inconsolable herself? What might she say that wouldn't feel like an excuse or a lie? And yet she was desperate to know. "I know you grieve, oh friend, but you must tell me what happened after!"

"I saw him leave in the same direction in which your boat of bones goes. After that I can say no more of what has happened to him, other than that which I suspect. That he is sunk or eaten, and that you will be too, should you continue!"

"I must go on, I must find him!"

"This servant has warned you. Go if you must, only leave me be. I no longer wish to speak on this."

Aisha felt in her heart a heavy misery that ran through the very marrow of her like cooled black lead—a sadness so deep she felt that she, like the slippers, would plummet forever, through the very core of the earth, through the other sky, and fall through the mouth of the world and breach into the never-ending blackness.

The strange smell she could not place was the heavy warmth she associated with kerosene flame. Burning sick yellow holes, pinpoints of weak light, illuminating too little in the night-time and the sea that enveloped it. And in that flame, the feeling burned away, eating itself until it was nothing. Like smoke it lifted, floated away, and Aisha's body cheap in its own meatiness, its leanness, a vessel extinguished.

"Goodbye, goodbye," she whispered. "We leave you in peace. Thank you for your help."

The sea creature sighed, its shrill breath like the exhausted whistle of wind through the highest branches of the baobab. "Peace unto you. Thank you for the words, the worn soles. Dear fishling, never say I did not warn."

"God willing, we will both find good."

"God wills what He wills," her father's friend agreed, bereaved. "If you are eaten may it be in one swallow and not in thirds."

And the serpent, with these good wishes, sank back into the water. Its eyes disappeared. The water was clear and black again. Stilled.

CHAPTER NINE

Nothing moved, no knife nor seam to split it with. Aisha moved slowly like an old machine, her palms returning to the smooth bone curves of the oars. She had even forgotten her companion who had kept such silence, who had offered neither interruption nor aid. Wise but cold, inanimate and unfeeling.

She pulled her arms back and pushed them forward, rowing the boat again. "You did not speak."

"It would have been poor to speak for the sake of hearing one's own voice."

Aisha's heart hammered once, hard. Angry and shamed that it perhaps implied a certain mental vacancy in her, a vapidness. Defensively she clenched her jaw, grunting as she rowed. "In loneliness, in darkness, in fear—a voice offers comfort."

She scowled at her feet so she would not look at him.

"Then a voice is just a noise, but you are mistaken if you ever presume that anyone is alone. God stands between us and a devil too. If you have no conversation then pray, did you not study in the madrasa?"

She had. Her blood boiled. A shallow education in it, the kikotho's lash a long, searing burn in the meatiest part of her palms . . . a shallow education in it all, but she knew it. "Are you preaching at me?"

"The prayers of a cat are different from the prayers of a man. I cannot give you khutbas on salahs that I do not myself perform."

"How does a cat pray?"

"Any way it can."

"You know much that I do not, not simply on prayers. We stop to ask for directions you already know. For histories and truths that you yourself could have shared. You know where he is and what has happened to him. Rather than tell me you make a performance of it!" Her voice was raw, shrill, on the edge of accusations, she feared. "Are you so miserly with your knowledge that you would use it to cut the weak? Does it amuse you to torture me? Did I wrong you? Do you trap me as my father would have trapped that snake? Eat me or drown me, or kill me, but do not make a game of it!"

Her chest rose and fell rapidly, shallow breath, scraped raw. She had stood up at some point. Her throat weak, her tongue coppery. She had screamed at him. She had never screamed at anyone. Not *ever*.

The cat blinked slow cat-blinks. Unperturbed. "To hide knowledge because I determine only that there is a lack of worth in another is to be a traitor and a liar, no better than Fir'aun. I am a speaking feline, no sentient god, I know much but not everything, I share what I know with you as you have shared your meals. You fed me, even at your own cost—I cannot feed you in the same way. I accompany you so you might learn your own truths and determine yourself what to do with them.

"That knife," the cat said, and Aisha's hand jumped to the sash, clutching at the place she'd secreted it as if she might clutch at her own heart. "What did your father teach you with it?"

Aisha studied the cat's flat yellow features. The luminous eyes. His stillness. "To gut fish."

"Ah? To open its sides, to clean it well. And your mother, to cook them?"

She rubbed her lips together. No, she had been too young to be let near the hot oil but she had been allowed to watch her sometimes, when Shida was well enough to tolerate her. She stiffened, to keep herself from discomposure. "No."

"And do you know how to catch a fish?"

"I have seen my father do it."

"Let me rephrase . . . have you ever caught a fish?"

She hesitated, silent. She remembered with a sickening sudden-ness her father's finger wriggling through the gill of the frightened, wheezing catch so long ago. How his face had fallen. How Aisha had been frightened and alarmed about the splatter of scales, its struggle to breathe. Worse than the thing beneath the boat, that blind, thundering panic of being tugged onto the dry deck, to be immobile—and her father's laugh, not cruel in sound, but encouraging, sharing with her what he loved—that he could even for a moment teach her what involved playing with what he killed, that she could be so visibly, vulnerably alive—

She couldn't catch them. She watched her father do it, but he only spoke to her and guided her hand in cleaning and filleting the meat. In those days the fish he brought her were always already dead. It was easier that way. She could split it, debone it, unperturbed by blood and gore—she could do nothing about the killing of them, but she could determine how they were eaten, how they were cleaned and cooked and served. The empty vessel in its deadness did not frighten her so much as seeing the vessel being emptied. She cooked, coconut and ginger, golden turmeric, sweet, glistening onion, and the pearly gleam of rice, swollen, bright. Beautiful in an appetizing way. But never so beautiful as they were when they were mobile, swimming, *alive*.

"And has your father taught you how to kill a fish?"

She was not sure what she felt, as if she were to be ashamed for a failing she was not sure belonged more to Baba or herself. Had she been unworthy of learning or was her own lack of willingness at fault? She did not know who to blame, she didn't want to always have to wonder if she should blame anyone at all. It wasn't fair to anyone.

"Aisha, whether it is the knife, or the boat—or even the navigation course," the cat said, "there are some things we must learn ourselves."

In the following silence, Aisha forced the wound her rage and fear had slashed to knit itself; practised little hands stitched back her composure efficiently, as they had done thousands of times before. Then, shutting the door of her heart closed, she sat down again.

The cat could give his education, but Aisha was wasting time pursuing the matter or looking too closely into his motives. She had fallen into this endeavour as though in a dream, a vacant desperation clouding her—above all she needed to find her father and not allow the cat's philosophy to deter her. There was no more time left to loiter. She did not even fear some betrayal, or that the cat might have nefarious intentions. What did it matter? Better to die at sea than return to Mombasa with her arms empty, to die like everyone else, slow and unlived.

She began to row again. The boat moved smoothly as though pulled by a string, its ribs made faint lines in the water, running creases and neat cuts that immediately vanished, flattened without impression. Her bare toes rang, twitching and curling in a water suddenly colder. She tried not to shudder at the feeling.

The cat spoke no more. Aisha chanced a look back, shoulders huddled up to protect her neck from the eerie chill that plagued her in turns. Aisha swallowed as the cold slid down her back and sank into the notches of her spine, a chill now ensconced between her vertebrae too tenaciously to dislodge. The shore-line had disappeared. Forward and back, a seamless dark, the sea and the night-time were one body, laid out cold without breath. Dead and very still.

It was an unnatural sea. In Mombasa the sea had had life in it, a movement. This was the sort of sea that blew no wind or sail, the kind of sea in which nothing moved.

She rowed and the oars made no noise, nor the water she put them through. The sweat was turning cold down her back.

She addressed the cat flatly and with forced civility. "Is this the undersea?"

"This is another sea between your sea and it."

"It doesn't feel . . . right."

"It shouldn't."

She frowned, touched with uncharacteristic impatience, like a flame to paper. And then she heard it. Her body recognized it long before her mind did, or her heart discussed it—it hit her like the corner of a table slamming against her elbow, the electrified numbness, the unwelcome shock. Fear is prehistoric, instinct the immediate insight, terror comes later.

She heard the glide of fin through water that had refused sound all this while.

Aisha's palms creaked around the oars and she didn't dare look to her side for fear of what she would see and what curiosity might invite. Dread balled up in the pit of her stomach—the cat watched her, something of alarm to his stillness.

A yelp cut in her throat when the feline leapt onto her knees. His nails dug into her skin, skittering up her lap, biting into her arms—

The acrobat perched on her shoulders and she shuddered when the end of his tail flicked against the root of her skull. "Are you afraid?" she whispered. There was something swimming alongside the boat. She screwed her eyes shut, jolting when the water lapped over her ankles, a wave in the wake of some creature's motion.

"No," the cat said, "but I protect this neck, this throat."

Aisha swallowed thickly, nodding as the tail brushed her left ear. He sounded calm and she could take courage in that. The cat would not give her comfort in his silence but gave her his small body. How could a cat protect her against the monsters of the sea and her own fear? What could a cat do? And yet, she took strength in the weight around her neck, in his closeness, and did not need to ask questions. That was trust.

Whiskers tingling along her cheek, he whispered, "Row, child of Adam."

Her eyes shivered open. The night did not move. Ahead. She did not look right, she did not look left. She picked up the bone oars and took a deep breath, she looked down and a luminescent, ghostly long shape shone in the deep, dark water beneath her. Beneath the ribs.

Aisha held her breath, looked ahead, and began to row.

Water sloshed alongside the boat, the sounds of bodies flinging themselves through, above, and beneath the surface, following. And every time they came up she heard the croon. *Baba wa Papa, Baba wa Papa . . .*

The splash and the sung warning of a child's voice. Aisha lunged forward and back, pulling, pushing, so absolutely trained on the task, as though it could keep her from peripheral danger.

Every time she swung forward, the cat would go with her, head and body rocking, as if he perched on a swing. His tail curled, anchoring around the curve of her left ear. When she swung back, his claws dug bracingly into her right shoulder. He protected her neck and her throat, and the children sang through water, and a great body moved beneath it. *Baba wa Papa, Babapapa, BabaPapaBabaPapaBabaPapa. Father of the shark.*

Luminescent, transparent, the creatures flew—like flying fish, glowing at the corners of her vision. She heard a long, echoing croon, the long whine. It was a sound she had never heard before and she was struck by its strange, nameless beauty. The spectres scattered and the flowing shape beneath the boat plunged, escaping into the deep.

Wondrous, frightened. "Is that . . . whale song?"

The cat flicked his tail thoughtfully along her neck. "Is it familiar to you?"

Not at all and yet . . . something in her wanted to answer it. The ghosts were gone, frightened away, and the deep echo came again, like the ache in her heart.

"I always wondered how it might sound . . ."

"How does it sound?"

"Lonely. A person in an empty hall, singing to a thousand locked doors. By themselves, to themselves."

"Who says that the creature is alone?"

"I hope that it isn't. I do know often that something so big, so entire usually exists in a sort of aloneness."

"What gave you that idea?"

"God is by Himself because He is God. The angels and the birds sing around Him and we pray to Him, but He is all that will remain after the third trumpet. I do not compare anything to God, but the whale is proof of His grace. Even if we pretend we do not hear Him, He still speaks, still moves through all that He has created. He is beneath me and above me, on my left and on my right, in the ground and in the sea—and He sees me, I am listening."

The cat, who had listened for so long, spoke after a time. "You are clumsy," he said, "but you have the beginnings of a poem, absurd feeling anguishing in translation. Though I should not wish the soul of a poet on anyone—they look for divinity and beauty and ornament for meaning, meaning for ornament. They grieve for grace, they destroy their hearts with their own hands, eat their hearts."

"My mother was a poet."

"She was crucified by it."

"Grief and grace?" Aisha asked quietly, a little bitter. "Ornamenting divinity? Blaspheming for beauty?"

"No," the cat said, "by a longing too great to properly name. That which pulls you, pulled her—but she was already fastened to the floor of that place by her feet. So she sang and she died."

"She was sick . . . in her blood. The sickness killed her."

"It was not the only kind of sickness with her. When your heart is full of birds and you cannot fly, they peck at you until you are nothing. Until you are vanquished."

"Was it my fault?" Aisha asked. "Was I what fastened her feet?"

"No, Aisha." For the first time she heard sympathy in that voice. "You are what pulled her."

She had not realized how long it had been since the last wail. She had stopped rowing when she'd first heard it, and now she shook herself awake. Aisha swiped beneath her eyes before she grabbed the oars again.

She continued, back and forth, shoulders rolling. The first monster's words niggled at her; what danger lay ahead? She remembered the sharks in the market with their black, doll eyes. Their stark white bodies . . . sometimes she used to imagine their gills moving, like they were alive.

Babu wu Papa . . . the cat's decision to curl around her shoulders, to protect her neck and her throat told her to anticipate something she could not possibly be prepared for. There was a great danger and she felt the usual fear, but with it a sort of emptiness that had its own clarity. That the worst thing that could happen, perhaps would. Perhaps the tenants of the water would rip her apart and destroy her.

Hababa would wake up and find her gone, Hababa would cry with no more kin. Both son and granddaughter lost to her.

Aisha's throat caught, hooked by a sudden swell of emotion. The idea of Hababa crying always squeezed at her heart.

It is a selfish thing I've done, she thought with some pain, but soldiered on, refusing it foothold. *It is the necessary thing.*

Baba wa Papa. Danger ahead. A knife she was forced to consider as more than tool, as weapon. As if it had betrayed her. She didn't know how to use it in that way, she didn't want to, and she realized with a building panic that she could not use it. She could not bloody the water, she could not be her father, a hunter, a practical killer but still a *killer*.

And to use the knife, that which was most known to her, in such a way—it would sully what little of herself she had left to herself. Her heart ran, a loud drumming in her throat, hateful but true. *Coward.*

She was a coward.

The cat's voice cut through her. "Here."

Aisha dropped the oars, her movements undecided, as if her body and mind were arguing with one another. The air stoppered in her throat. "I've nothing left to give the water."

The air was getting much colder and she was startled to see the faint plume of her breath in front of her. The tips of her fingers rang, tingling and a little icy.

The knife. She was ashamed of her relief, that she could offer it up. Her hands shook in their haste, scrambling for the weapon in her sash. She held it in her lap, the blade so cold it seemed to steam against the air. She looked at the worn handle, the blurred metal, her breath fogged on it. So many scars she still had from her clumsiness. It was only an ugly knife, the only good gutting blade in the kitchen small enough to properly control. Old and well used. It had no great workmanship or discernible history, and it was a knife. A knife should only be a knife. It had become hers through use, through the means she decided for it, it was her gutting knife, her cleaning knife. But now, in this sea, it had to be a cutting knife, a killing knife, the kind of knife that *took*. It was true, it should be both things to her, but she could not bear the other thing. Yet to part from it pained her. She handled it with the gentleness of one cradling their drowned child. It tore her heart to keep it and it tore her heart to give it away.

The water wanted what was dearest to her. The knife was dearest to her, but it was also now dangerous to the very essence of herself and she was afraid that the water would realize that the gift of the knife would be false, for sacrificed it would be given away, and it would give the giver greater ease than to keep it now, no longer ignorant of its uses.

Aisha weighed the blade over both palms, she licked her cold, salty lips and raised the knife above the water, and then she lowered the knife. The icy surface skimmed her knuckles and with a gasp she tipped her hands forward, the knife toppling over the scored whites of her palms and into the water.

"It is a curious thing," the cat said, flat, cold, "that when given the choice you would rather die than fight."

The words went through her with agony. She was unable to reply or grapple with the humiliation of being read so easily, or being known so exactly, and been found disappointing. She watched the water, watched nothing happen. The surface remained still. Aisha faltered. Was she wrong?

She'd wasted a knife. It would not accept the gift. She was in the middle of a dark sea in a bone boat with a speaking feline and the adventure had ended. The quest jeopardized by her own folly. She would rather die than go home empty-handed. What would she say to Hababa? How could the sea let her go? How could she go back?

Her face frozen, mouth raw and cold. Clinging to the boat's sides as if she could not decide if it was what kept her from following the knife or a launching point from which to throw herself into the very water after it. God, the prayer soundless, but for a wheeze between her teeth. She felt as if she might die. *God, please don't let it end this way.*

The water rose, the boat with it. She swung back, unbalanced, scrambling into the bottom of the cage of ribs. She screamed but the cat's tail whipped sharply and slung around her throat firmly, protecting this neck, this throat.

The sea-water swelled, fabric being pierced by a large needle—the tallest mast of the largest ship of her dreams. With it the rest of the vessel ascended. Hysterical familiarity bubbled and blocked Aisha's throat as she reared back. The mast was *still* rising. The vessel was no fisherman's work or traveller's dhow.

"A warship," Aisha gasped. When its hard belly finally came up, water streamed through gaps and missing teeth, through vicious holes where cannon fire once blew through. Scarred and chipped, the dredged-up boat had, strapped to its sides and stacked beneath it like children's building blocks, other ships. Ships made of metal, ships made out of bone and blackened gold. Salt mist bristled off the flanks of this great beast of boats and the largest black sail Aisha had ever seen. Tarp heavy, it gleamed, crow black. How horribly it might have once bloomed and swelled in a favourable wind, though it was hard to imagine it could be any more fearsome.

The sea dragged up old battleships from their graves. Roman fleet, Phoenician ships, German submarines. The old, magnificent, and once powerful—the gouges in the metallic paint of their sides, the garrison that might have stood on crumpled starboards, the might of them!

Her heart grew unbearably dizzy as if to take flight. The beast had risen, and water caved through the gaps in the bone boat, washed over her ankles before settling into stillness. The last drop clinging to the sails, pinged sharp like a coin, resounded so through her she flinched. The icy spray clinging to her as fear clung to her, Aisha spread her arms, the cat's weight on her shoulders. Tenuously balanced, quaking with the cold, her teeth clicked together, ice heavy in her bones. There was a kind of nakedness about her in terror, in her awe, in the violence of silence and cold.

She called out first. Her voice was loud, shook. "Are you Baba wa Papa?"

There was a familiar smell, the smell of a small cold room with nothing in it. Like a wet, abandoned storeroom in a house during the monsoons. A suppression of any other odor, the faint acidic scrape of metal, ungalvanized, sharp beneath the nothing.

Her nose and throat felt bloody, coated in ice. Her breath was loud, a trembling wheeze, her very ribs rattling, bristling. And beneath the nothing was the red scrape and drag of the knifing rust in the pit of her lungs. It hurt to breathe.

And the voice was many voices overlapping, booming through her, above her, beneath her. It reverberated through her heart as if it were the hide of a drum. Voices of thousands, children and soldiers and the drowned who had peopled these wrecks. The voices of all the drowned dead. "Who *dares* address me?"

Her body shook uncontrollably, the voice going through her, vibrating through marrow, through bone. "A girl"—she held on hard, lest her fear bow her—"looking for her father."

"A girl," the voices corrected, with laughter and scorn, "who disturbs my sleep with blunt blade and worn hilt?"

She stood braced, knowing it could carry her away, kill her. Her feet fastened to the slippery bottom of the boat, the cat's tail around her neck, his neat claws puncturing her shoulder, his silence.

"Forgive this one," she called out, her child voice with its uncertain tremble, a child's careful, empty bravery. The cold knifed along her cheeks and her skin felt like marble. "It was not my intention to cause upset. A fisherman passed through here, I—"

"That vessel. A rare ship. Those are old bones, fishling—know you this?"

Aisha, stumped, hesitated. She felt like a courtier petitioning before a king. "I am . . . not sure. Though I am certain that one such as you knows much." She felt she should bow, the careful confusion giving way to the harmless, well-meant flattery she'd learned and breathed in the majlas growing up. "And would in mercy and benevolence educate this one who knows so little."

Launching into inquiry as she had with the first creature was not the answer here. Not yet. The ship of ships loomed, bristled with broken masts and pointed prows designed for gouging and sinking all it met. She began to shiver now, not knowing how much longer she might be kept in this cold. Her toes were icy and she feared they would never thaw. It was a cold unfamiliar to her. In Mombasa the cold was that of the coming rain; in *this* sea it was the cold of a great, infinite crypt.

"Flatterer!" the voices snapped. Aisha winced but did not change her open, reverent posture, as if she awaited crucifixion.

Aisha flinched, but the vessel had not sunk her. The voices tore at her ears and she bowed her head, frightened, yet still alive—she must preserve that. She spoke smoothly, in the voice of a well-loved courtier. "There is flattery, true, but praise as well." She tried not to squeeze her eyes shut, hating her desperation. "This small one is an ignorant one. I am laid low," she said, "before the King of the Drowned, the Master of the Wave, the Sinker of Souls." And she was silent, as if in reverence and veneration. Her heart drummed in her throat, and she was torn by the waiting, the waiting to see if she was still a fool.

"What does this fishling want with this king?" The voice was pleased and haughty, a rumble of pleasure when it tasted that word. "*King.*"

Aisha opened her mouth, the truth crouched at the root of her tongue, metallic, bloody. She was looking for her father. Aisha screwed her eyes shut, her face twisting, head bowed from the monster. Flattery before sympathy. Seduction before request. *Entertain it, praise it, revere it.*

The truth can be made to bend. Aisha bent it, her mouth opened and at first nothing came out, her brow riddled, her mind whirred, snatching at opening lines, at the proper words, ill-prepared, stumbling for strategies. Aisha's lips curved as she blew through the truth carefully, a glass-blower to bubbles of sand.

She crushed her own bitterness as she would an old skull beneath her heel, and she spoke, almost spitting, as herself. "I am a keeper of histories. A recorder of legends. I have heard of the creatures of the sea and set sail with this feline—my aide and companion, and this boat, sung out from the deep so I might find you, oh king."

"And what gift is this? Is this what you offer a king?"

"It is all that this servant has," she said, affecting the lamenting, respectful croon of the first creature. "Though this is to my eternal shame and I should be drowned for the offence. Know, king, that this servant is disgraced."

"Perhaps you will be yet. Tell me . . . what have you come to write?"

"Why," Aisha said, as if astonished, "I come to write of you, and of Baba wa Papa."

Immediately she knew she had said the wrong thing. The air boomed with the launch of a thousand cannons. There was a high-pitched ringing in her ears in the wake of the boom, and, disoriented, it took her several petrifying moments before she realized that the next ball of gunpowder had not ruptured her or the water.

It was only the echo of the old sounds, the ghosts of fire.

Gunpowder burned in her nostrils, singed in her chest, her throat. Was this another illusion? She yelled, "Forgive this one, oh king. Forgive me!"

"That . . ." the voices cracked, nearly fearful, like a child from its hiding place, careful of moving out, "is not a name spoken. Take it in vain and you take your own life in vain."

"This servant heeds your words."

"What historian follows a fisherman?"

"One in love with story-craft," Aisha lied, as if humbled by her imagined accomplishments and embarrassed to speak of her imagined aspirations. "He is a character in the story. I follow him and I must find him so I know how that story ends," she added. "Though this servant would be grateful to listen to you first. You who know much and surely have more to offer!"

"And what am I in this story?" the creature demanded.

Aisha allowed no external show of faltering and said, without skipping a breath, a beat, a moment more: "Why, my king, that depends on the story you wish to tell me."

CHAPTER TEN

Aisha stood in the blistering cold, foolish and grand. A salt-struck pretender, wet cat curled around her shoulders. Her teeth rattled, her fingertips stung, and her ribs felt bruised from how hard they shuddered around every breath. They were surrounded, covered by sunken ships and the vessels that trapped the drowned dead. *You're alive*, her heart pounded as water trickled into her eyes, ice-touched. *You're alive right now.*

From the water rose a ghostly figure. Aisha first thought it might be the singer that had followed their boat. But had not whale song exorcized it? She steeled her joints. It was a child, small and skinny; under the surface it glowed like luminescent marble. Its head breached the water, then its neck and shoulders, and it rose like a wax candle and stood on the black water as if on a steady floor. A boy made of white marble, catching all the light that was not there. A ghostly moon. Aisha swallowed. He could have barely reached her shoulders and his features suggested that he was only as old as one of her little cousins. But where her cousins whooped and ran, Old Town shaking with their yells, there was infinite stillness to this child. His mouth was stone, his eyes were stone, the short fuzz of his head was stone. He stared ahead of her without pupils, around his hips the pale drape of stone carved to wrap around him, looking as light as a kitenge, as if it might move had the air made the slightest movement.

She held her breath and gritted her teeth so hard she thought they might shatter. The cold air was sharp as if it were her own blood in her mouth, the bright rust of metal cutting her lungs. She took a breath that nearly carved them out when the Sunken King spoke next.

"A pretty song from so plain a girl." The words came, but his stone mouth did not move. It was the many overlapping whispers of children, wispy and scraping that chalky shiver along her arms like a scythe over stone. "Might be I should eat such a vessel, wet cat and all."

The cat's claws were in her shoulder, anchoring her to the present.

"I have not had a bone boat in centuries, nor do I care for the taste of scholars or the taste of cats, but you have lied to me. That is a courtesy in itself. I shall tell you the story so old I scarcely remember where I myself truly began. There was the sea and Mombasa and a contract dissolved. Man created fire, so what? The most fearsome discovery of all was when man realized that wood could float.

"Man boarded boats and went conquering. They drew fish and mined coral, they crossed to conquer other men, and though they dove deep it still could not touch the scalp of the tallest leviathan, never mind that of the sea bed at its deepest.

"Man has no legs here and still yet, they came hunting. Perhaps man should have been more afraid of the water, there was much swimming in it already, hungrier than even they."

She heard in his voice old wrath, old blood, old resentments. A king of rot, a keeper of graves.

"Where do the old contracts manifest? In the old time, in the long days, before Mombasa had a name such as your mouth could pronounce the coast was *wild*.

"The land and the sea had no great separation, they were apart only as two brothers are apart: shared blood, an understanding. There was a language between them. The shore-line was not a slash upon which the two were severed—but the very seam, parting only as a mouth does. These two were joined.

"In the old time, in the long days, the jinnis of the sea moved freely and spoke and lived among the jinnis of the land. Sea and land and sky, merely provinces.

"And then *Man* was created, and what a new thing man was. Newborn, interesting, a blood clot hatched. So favoured, yet so burdened. Your prophets came with their flocks spread, they sought living spaces, built and explored and procreated, they sprouted other prophets and were honoured. How soon did they turn our dwellings into hunting grounds. The coast was wild, the lands whistling, whistling with us.

"Man built villages and lived. In those days it was not so strange nor so rare for Adam's kin and mine to converse, trade, marry, and swear to labour together and for one another. No place was more full of contracts such as these than Mombasa. One family in service to another, one family vassal of another, the alliances if you will, the fealties . . . were the culture and the tradition.

"But as your *religions* spread, when *Islam* came especially, many such contracts tore. Partnerships formalized millenniums ago, *dissolved*. The sea jinni returned to the water and those of the land departed, looking for far-flung hidden hovels to haunt.

"So we savage fled to this sea. We remember the contracts. I held no love for the land, sheep they made sacrifices on their vessels before they set sail, blood bought passage. Do you know what it is like to be at the heart of a prayer, fishling?"

Aisha, who had listened intently, realized she was being addressed in a way that expected an answer. Hurriedly she bowed her head. "No, I do not, oh king."

"Of course not." The flat superiority unnerved her. "How could you?"

She shut her mouth, and the cat maintained his silence, his wet coat an orange bristle against her icy cheek.

"Some of us were servants, some of us gods. Which of the two relinquished their positions with better grace, do you think?"

She understood that most of all in this, though the monster had addressed her directly and awaited her answer, in truth, hers was not a speaking part. She ground her jaw to keep her teeth from chattering.

"Aye, I came to the deep blue and your ships passed me as yours does now, they would interrupt my peace so I would drag them down as I would have dragged you down had you not paid me the courtesies, poor as they are. I took for myself vessels of war, pleasure, beauty . . . I took gold, jewels, for I can taste that metal in the back of my snout the very way a shark knows blood. I adorned myself with your dead, I wear their skins and eat their drowned, those first to give up to the tide. These are far waters, for anything less than a king's ship to swim above my eye would be insult, and your father was the biggest insult of all. A fisherman's skiff! Torn net and flimsy sail, and no gold on him—no gold on him at all! Why, I broke it between my jowls and I spat it out!"

"You ate him!"

"That would have been too gracious," the children's voice demurred, a saccharine snarl. "I drowned his skiff and watched him swim. The fool."

"Which direction did he go?"

The laughter that answered her was dark and cruel, discordant in a thousand voices. "Where do you think, fishling? Toward that *horizon*."

Lies, it was all lies. He had eaten her father, and if he had not then he might as well have done. If grey idols and sleek ghouls who sang of the horrible father of sharks existed, then what else swam beyond that would let her father make his way unharmed? It was too far for him to make for shore and yet . . . he had once more risked the unknown. Her father was a strong swimmer, but it had already been three days.

Aisha's eyes filled with tears. He was dead. Hababa had no body to bury. She would probably be waking in a few hours—or already had, time did not seem to pass naturally here—she would be going to the khadi to arrange it, and perhaps to the soko to buy goat meat and grain. She should have been helping Hababa with the funeral preparations. People ate with the most gusto at funerals; they'd wiped their plates clean and complimented the broth the afternoon they buried her mother. Her mother was dead, and Aisha had had to kiss her cold temples because it had seemed something Hababa would approve of, had wanted done. She'd thought, *It's only a body. She isn't here really.*

She never had been. Until Aisha realized that the rooms no longer echoed with her coughs and that there were fewer clothes and linens to wash and the pallet had to be moved and folded away. There were different chores to do and there was more space in the majlas than there had ever been before. It was vast enough to kill.

Baba was never really there either. He was always gone. But evenings had there not been the loud slosh of his bucket when he brought her his catch? Or the sound of his knife peeling back driftwood to find the bird buried beneath? Those would be gone forever. There wasn't a body. It wasn't real if there wasn't a body. Something to bury. If she didn't bury him then he hadn't died and if he had not come back it was because he was lost and she had not found him.

The fish had eaten him. She had run out of gifts to offer monsters. Everyone had already had their share. *Except me.* She remembered the words of the first monster. *If you are eaten, let it be in one swallow and not in thirds.*

Aisha curled her fists. "Give me back my knife."

"Oh?" the monster mused. "Are we done with flattery and courtesy? Mombasa has gotten bad form if these are its children."

"It is you who are discourteous!" Aisha shouted. "I gave you a gift and you repaid it by gloating over my father, the one you endangered!"

"Does lightning give the tree apology? Or the lion beg forgiveness?"

"You are not God. Neither can you pretend to be above the judgement for thinking your cruelty the very acts of God. Compare you to lightning? You are just a sad, ugly wretch who hoards misery and nurses its own wretchedness. You lie in the sea and think you have a right to it. This sea is not yours and it is not mine. You petty cowardly relic! You preen when I call you king and yet the name Baba wa Papa makes you afraid. Give me back my knife, monster!"

"Coward, she says! I can taste intention. This knife you beg back so self-righteously is one you gave up all too willingly. *You* are the one afraid. You come here in a bone boat with a scholar's skinny cat and tell me what is and what isn't? Oh, with weapon! With vessel! Companion! None which belongs to you that you did not disgrace in

89

deserting. You swim over *my* eye and breathe *my* air and taste *my* salt. You met the first coward and thought me the second? That I would *confess* to you and play the same game? Will you attempt more *conversation* with a third? Is that all that you would have braved? You are fit for none of the things that you have parted with. What sacrifice was in it except for the weighing of sentiment? You are not fit for this knife, small island girl on an adventure. At the end of it you will still be a small island girl, too afraid to make a blade a blade, or a ship a ship, or a companion whose loyalty you are worth. You made no vows nor contracts because you are too weak to honour anything. To have virtue or vice. You only want to sit in a boat and pretend that you are tired. Go now, fishling, before I eat you—vessel, cat, girl, and all. *Coward.*"

With this the Sunken King descended, shooting downward so fiercely that the waves rose, a high wail rung up like a hundred dogs with knives striking suddenly through their sides. A hundred children's twisting cries tugged on all the strings of her soul, a shrill claw that scythed beneath her diaphragm and *pulled.*

Aisha staggered back, all the boats plummeting. Her shoulder tore beneath the cat's claws and she opened her mouth when the dark wave, taller than any building she had ever seen, shot up. It fell on her, rammed down on her bones.

Salt choked her scream.

CHAPTER ELEVEN

Aisha floated on her back as the choppy sea resettled itself into a flat plate. It lapped around her and stung her eyes. She spat up as water shot from her, wanting to be purged. Awake, an offering no one wanted. She heard the cat. Her eyes burned, her heart was scraped empty. He must have been the one that called her name. Hamza sat on her chest with his feet tucked beneath him, wet and sorry as a soggy brick of bread.

"We must go back to the boat." Water clung to Hamza's whiskers and slunk away from his huge yellow eyes. "The children will float back and eat you."

Let them. If there's enough of me left for eating.

Remember, Aisha. Everyone must have their share.

Cat and girl floated there, belonging to no one. If she moved even a little she'd tip herself over and have to decide again whether she had the courage to swim back to the boat or the courage to die.

There was no urgency in Hamza, his utterance calm. It was all absurd. Water twined through her fingers and the sea calmed. There were monsters below and an extraordinary fear. It was true, she was a coward. *Something I did to myself, because I couldn't carry a knife, because I couldn't love without hating—because I am an empty nothing of a girl.*

"Do you want to be eaten?"

No, she might answer and would not know if she was lying or not.

"Then you must remove yourself from between the jaws, not make your home between the teeth. Swim on, Aisha."

Had Hamza said her name before? *They want to call my soul back into my body. Why is everyone so cruel?* With all their gentleness, still cruel.

"It doesn't matter." She did not know anything anymore, but she'd drunk and waded the sea to no avail. "He's gone." Long gone even before he'd died, before they buried Mama. Everyone went and never cared to take her along. She had never been able to keep him, she let him bring her eels and fish, she shed their scales and they ate—an arrangement, a habit.

Poor Hababa. Heat coursed along her cheeks, and she realized with a numb, removed surprise that these were tears.

"I'm tired," she confessed to the awful sky, so empty of stars. It deceived her; its wholeness and absence told her she was present when she was not. "I don't want to go home."

"We are so very far."

"It's a game, it's a trick. It's a dream. So is he? Alive?"

". . . answers we must find for ourselves—"

"This game where you teach me to be wise"—she saw Hababa's back and swallowed the brine in her throat, a sulphur now forever in the lungs—"is a game I'd wanted to play. I thought for a moment that I could be one of the girls in the stories, that I could be brave and certain and true and *more*. In the stories they're guided by some force that makes them righteous and honourable. But I am no such person. I ran away, not toward. I'm just a poorly made thing looking for a father who doesn't want to be found, to bring him back to a place that will eat us alive anyway. There are no songs about girls like me, neither magic nor miracles."

The cat was silent for a long time. "There is still a journey to finish."

"Don't you know?" She laughed, but it was a sob. "All journeys end in Mombasa."

"Morbidness is a self-indulgence you can no longer afford."

"I'm tired of suffering."

"Then pray for death and swim deep."

"I want to be taken back, I want to not have been made."

"And what wonder you would miss! I might envy you, I who will turn to sand on the last day."

"Even the sea won't take me."

"Swim deep," the cat reminded her. "And if it does not take you then, then you must stop. For someone who resents the idea of being eaten alive, you put yourself in the very trap. If you care not for your own life—which I assure you, you do—think of my small life which you would doom. We must go forward, we cannot turn the boat around. See, I can sing it from the water but I cannot move the oars."

"Is he dead?"

"How do you want the story to end?"

"I want the story to end."

"Then go and meet it."

She turned over slowly and the cat went over her shoulders as she did, laying his paws over her head, his hind legs and tail snaking along the water like a rudder trailing above her back. Her legs swept and glided the flat water away. Her eyes burned but the tears were gone, as if the function, so rarely employed, had closed itself off as soon as it was noticed.

The bone boat was a little way off, and though she kept waiting for something to brush up against her shin and pull her down by the ankles, Aisha kept on in a clear direction, pushing her body through with seriousness. She was cold and weary, and by the time she reached the boat her arms had grown heavy. Somehow she managed to pull herself over its sides. The cat leapt up her back. Aisha sat in the boat, freezing and exhausted.

Shaking himself off like a dog, the cat settled again on her shoulders, tail a wet scarf around her neck.

The jarring motion of her own tired body was like the rock of the cradle as she rowed, a halting saw. Her eyes grew heavy. "Where have they gone?"

"They're afraid to follow."

"Why?" Exhaustion made it sound like a song, a children's rhyme. "Because we go to that which monsters fear."

"Baba wa Papa." It sounded like father of the father, but that wasn't right. It sounded made up by a small child still learning to speak. Her mouth tasted the name again and she could not explain why it made her afraid, this child's nonsense of a name.

"The King of Hunger, Baba wa Papa. Even the fish made dumb by nature know how to quiver the lips and speak such a name in fear and warning. It whose kin is the shark, whose mate is the shark, whose children are the shark—it lives among them, lies with them, rules them, and eats its own children, and they are of it, the mute, coal-eyed things."

Hababa had laughed when she'd seen how much Aisha enjoyed shark. Such a stinky, dried fish—a husband would flee from such a smell, she'd been warned. Then Hababa would fill both their plates twice more and show Aisha her turmeric-stained tongue.

In time she'd learn it was not the delicacy she'd thought. They sold the only precious part of it to foreign merchants—the fin. Why should they not want the rest of it? Foreigners threw it away.

At home they salted, sun-dried, and smoked it. Aisha had once gone to market to see it freshly split open, felt for a moment wondrous, a student. Too big for her to do it at home. Baba promised to bring her a small one if he ever caught it, but had been so bemused by her enthusiasm, for her zeal so rare. It was not easy to know what could succeed in invoking it.

The old man had passed a knife deep along the shark's spine, split it through, and flattened it down. Scored its flesh, rubbed it in salt. It was so beautiful.

It's a poor man's meat. Her father had smiled and yet seemed somehow alarmed. But it was their ancestor's meat, poor or plentiful, and they the descendants of the Waswahili, and the Omani and the Hadrami, who had leapt the inland rocks to sail oceans, not even knowing how to swim.

You should be proud, Baba. She'd felt sorrow for his sorrow, hurt by his shame. That he should think her deceived and in need of enlightening. Shark was not to be belittled; it tasted sweet in coconut.

It's a gift, it's a blessing. Say a prayer over it, let the blood from the old dead—usually so estranged to me—warm. When I eat what they ate, I am for a moment more than the little I am, I am the present because of what was past. I am blood. I have a people.

"Should I pray?" she asked as she rowed.

"If you've faith enough," the cat said. "And even if you don't. There is no place that can be made empty of God."

"Will it be dishonest?"

"It can become less so," said the cat. "With an earnest enough heart, we can learn sincerity, faith. Know what you are singing to and trust that you are heard, even if your voice trembles, even if your hands shake. We go on breathing even though we do not see the air; somehow it is present. You make the prayer, do not fear the answer."

Her chest was aflame, her skin icy as the air grew colder and colder, her wet clothes chafed, the bone beneath her naked soles prickled. Every now and then water would slosh over her toes; her ankles thick in the cold seemed to congeal. *It's ice,* her breath plumed in a white fog. *The water is forming ice that the boat is interrupting.*

The ice yielded, breaking into hard flakes, glassy and fragmented. Every time she pulled the oars something in the flat unmoving waters would break and split, lurching past the skeleton ship.

It was colder than an icebox. The muscles in her arms began to quake; she had passed her limit. How did the fishermen do it? Zubeir and the other shark hunters bringing themselves close to the bottoms of cliffs. The foam of the wave like clouds, like gunsmoke, *like Chinese snow* . . . the whip of white linen on a line. They would disappear for days and come back with sharks, stingrays, the underwater deep-sea predators. All of these men were lean, lithe, and dark from the sun, even old Zubeir—he must have been seventy at least and yet he had the strength of ten men, his body scarred from running, burning rope, and commanding his men without even having to speak. They were strong. *I can . . .* her teeth chattered, joints locked down in shaking so severe she thought she'd break. *I can be strong.*

Her eyes fluttered. She sloped forward into a sleep and then dragged back into wakefulness. She was drenched in sleep, in ice, and yet, she had to go forward. Back and forth. A saw.

I'm cleaving through ice. A black ice like blood, buckling beneath the winged oars. To go to the King of Hunger.

Yes, the King of Hunger. *What do I go to do there? To die?*

To die. No father, no knife—a coward nothing of a girl, and a cat. "A scholar's cat," she said suddenly. "Why did it call you that?"

The cat did not answer but the silence that greeted the query was a hum, a dream itself. It was like trying to sleep on the hot days in Ramadan, the heat of sunlight so intense that it flooded every action with time, dragged it down and made it slow. You thought only in vibrations, stutter and stop and mind-numbing heaves. Hungry, tired, and the acuity and sharpness fasting brought out, a higher thought, a sharpness—a groundless elevation of the mind, which itself was a ringing dream.

And then hunger made you sharp, awake, a blade.

The King of Hunger would be no drowsy fool.

"Aisha," the cat called, his murmur feathering like palm leaves along her ear. "We have arrived."

She slotted the oars back, asleep. She was not hungry—that had been her flaw from birth—she was weary, not sharp. Moons weighed down her eyes, cold had sunk numbing poisons into her sinews. She wanted a story to end, sleep, darkness. She wanted an end to want. Icy slurry, slinking through the ribs, a razor shaving and scraping inside her throat, the kind of cold that tastes like blood.

No shoes, no knife. Clothes, she thought, blind with cold, what would she do then? Stand naked before monsters?

"I've nothing more to give," she said, her mouth so slow it could barely form the words. She felt the cat slink from her shoulders, his claws controlling his descent into her lap, tugging at the fabric. He sat on her knees.

She managed to look down, his large yellow eyes, his short coat dark and nearly orange, his whiskers clinging with frost . . .

The world was silent around them. The cat's stare hooked her, keeping her there, awake.

"Do you remember when you were a child in Ramadan?" the cat said. "You would put a plate of fish guts and cold tea out on the step for me, you wanted to pet me."

It was the desire of any child, truly, to touch small soft things who do not speak. She raised her palm hesitantly and just as quickly dropped it. A scholar's cat would not appreciate something so patronizing. "Did I insult?"

"You did not insult," the cat said. "It was kind of you. Ah, but there you are—you flinch. How does one's heart recoil in the face of kindness?"

"I wanted to keep you."

"Is that so terrible?"

"It was selfish."

"No one can be kept, not in their heart, if they don't want to be kept. Will you hate egg merchants because you fear their expectations? Do you not have the strength to deny others what you keep to yourself? Do you belong to the generous and the dead? You are so stubborn, Aisha, and so very hurt, to turn living into a transaction, a business of debts one cannot escape from. Do you want to escape? You think you can belong to yourself by being so cold to yourself?"

"What do you know of my life, to preach to me of living?"

"Adam's folk these days read and memorize and graze beneath a roof called 'God' like bleating sheep. Before the truth they worshipped idols because their fathers did, they *inherited* belief. Is one a believer in inheriting the true faith like a brass pot? Do you not think for yourself how to be improved by it and to improve it? You pray, put His names in your mouth and still have them be nothing to you. Is paradise prayer alone? Being is to be alive, awake—to believe, *not* to roll under the world as it is. Are you alive if you do not question the world? If you do not go to war with yourself in deciding how to acquaint yourself with it or challenge it? At the end of all worlds, will you show how neat your miserly kept book of sums? Or will you have had the courage and say *I did deeds good and bad, I disagreed with the world around me, I was awake and I believed and I doubted, but I was not immobilized. I was alive, to the best of my abilities, I was alive.*"

It sounded impassioned but she only wanted to weep. "You are not a girl, you do not know."

"I am a scholar's cat, a cat of the House of Rust, where I know knowledge alone is nothing. You are only passing through this world but you must be awake for it, you must believe."

"I want to believe."

"You think you believe in nothing?" the cat remarked. "When you have shaped your world around one pillar? Your entire soul tangled in mathematics, in an equation you heard once as a child—and did not question, only obeyed and in being shaped by it, worshipped it?"

"There's wisdom behind it."

"If one looks hard enough one can make a forgery close to wisdom and pretend it be that."

"It was selfish." Her voice broke. "Why were you silent all these years? Why do you speak to me now? Do you think you help me now? By teaching me a lesson? I have nothing to give monsters or cats or egg merchants or anyone else. I am finished."

Two frozen things in a frozen eternity, outside of time and thus outside of mercy, outside of end.

The cat said, "I have behind my ears an awful itch. My body is cold. Let us complete your equation and repay a small girl for her kindness."

Tired, she did not move. The tears had long dried, frozen salt on her cheeks. The cat waited. He had injured her heart hopelessly all those years ago, trying to court him, to bring him back, to give the love she was in mutilation trying to learn. To be gentle, to be tender, to practise this alien thing called affection. To be kind. It had been labour and fruitless, her offerings taken rarely and very often spurned, but she had kept at it and habit had made it ritual, and ritual had given it meaning, and meaning gave her disappointment grace. Her father would laugh sheepishly at her, her mother's silence was often displeasure, but Aisha would continue.

Kindness is a debt to be repaid. Perhaps the cat's rejection had been comforting, to know that there was a creature in the world that she did not owe.

She did not know what would happen to her father and she could not bear to think of sums. The cat was skinny, his head as scrawny as it had been when he had been a skeleton in a thick skin of short fur, slinking across the roof, around corners, disappearing like a magician. He had looked dirty, the neighbours called him ugly in his leanness, in his directness of stare, his aloofness. Ugly because he could not be kept and ugly because he was too quick to trap for punishment. He was alive and indifferent to them, which was in itself a defiance.

A cat can decide when to enter and leave a room, from whose palm to eat, it can decide how to be wild, who it will love, who to be loved by . . .

But she was a child then, being told she could never return to sea, hearing her mother bang pots in the kitchen. A child hidden beneath the step, wanting with all her might for that skinny ugly orange thing to come close, just a little close.

Her throat closed up. Lifting her palm, she placed it on the cat's head. It was skull, the fur stiff with ice. She felt awkward like she didn't know how to go about it. She could hardly think the cat was real, all these years just seeing him without being allowed . . . a small, small skull. He blinked up at her. Hesitantly she passed behind his ears, felt the small, alarmingly protruding blades of his shoulders, the hollow of his nape.

The cat's eyes slipped shut. Aisha scratched gently, carefully. She did not want to hurt him. She squashed her lips together as a sob bubbled in her throat; she stroked along his wet, freezing back, his poor, breakable body. Freezing in the middle of a far, remote ocean. She sniffled, gasping tearily when she felt the vibrations of his ribs, his *purr*. To be gifted this touch she'd wanted for so long, the only touch she'd wanted.

"It is time, Aisha."

A wet laugh burst from her lips and shakily, she smiled. "I've nothing to give."

"You gave to me a long time ago. And you gave and gave and gave, you did not hate me when you gave. I did not hate you when I accepted. A traveller I was, it was kind to have a meal set out for me and know that you loved me nonetheless. Did you not love me?"

"Yes," she wept, marvelling at finding a truth. "I did, I *do*. But it is a poor love, a version of love. I was pretending, I must have been."

"Did ever I tell you that I could taste it still?"

"No."

"It was very sweet," the cat said. "Very sweet."

And he bowed his head, so she stopped, attentive to this end. The world was noiseless around them, her blood ice and her hands nearly numb, but she felt the rasp of his rough tongue when he bent his head and licked the back of her hand once. His yellow eyes reminded her of the sleek, shining sheen of the tiger-spotted shells on the shore. Of sweet Achari from Malindi. "Remember, Aisha," the cat's murmur struck through the cold fog of her soul, "everyone must have their share."

Quicker than lightning then did he wind away from her. He bounded across the boat and leapt into darkness.

She threw herself forward, screaming, but his tail disappeared into the depths and the water was already still, beyond shattering. "What have you done!" She shrieked, animal and alive, her raw words cracked with weeping. "Hamza! Hamza! Come back!"

But he was gone.

Her strength vanished. She was an empty skein weeping salt water. *Alone*.

But for the movement of fin, skimming against the boat, a knock against the ribs that had her gulping. Lazy knives so subtle they felt nearly innocent. Shark. Moving in a slow circle exactly where her companion had disappeared. She swallowed a yelp and scrabbled at the oar but its slippery winged prod would not move out of its socket no matter how hard she tugged. She thought wildly about leaping into the water, but she was no fool, for where there was one, there were many.

I would see blood, thrashing, if they had him. She stood stiffly. But the water was so dark . . . could it be possible? To dilute its blackness?

Another fin followed the second, then another, and another, they were like the blades of a paper fan unfolding. She fell to her knees when she counted ten, ice in her throat. She nearly reached for the sides of the boat to cling to but feared for her fingers. She feared for all of her, scrabbling onto the seat with her knees drawn up as the dark world beneath her ran with slicker bodies. Through the ribs of the boat, the sharks were squirming. She huddled her knees tightly, breathing hard. Their numbers were multiplying still, and their dancing circle lost its neatness to crowding and deepening chaos. *They aren't undulating, not like a flower or a fan.* No, she realized with horror, they were being *pushed.* They thrashed with growing frenzy, and she saw their heads, their empty round doll eyes, the eerily white snouts like dead flesh, foolish faces petrified with their own teeth. The water boiled white with them, and they squeezed and spilt over one another, stabbing and alarmed. A tide, a whirlpool of fangs, cracking like icebergs breaking.

They would spill into the boat, overturn it, worse.

She wanted to curse. Her teeth were chattering fiercely now; her skin burned with the frost. The wet, noisy mob. Beaching themselves over one another, a whirling white hole of death.

So sweet in coconut, she'd thought once, but she felt only icy, only death. *Hamza,* she nearly called out but dared not speak, hypnotized by what unfolded. The boat rose and groaned beneath her as wet, sleek hide slapped and splashed around her. She flinched at every stab of water. Her head spun, all around her, everywhere, there was no calm water, no dark water. It was all white, all thrashing.

Boiling with sharks, hundreds, thousands, whirling in broken frenzy—dancers whose heads had been climbed inside of by ma'rouhani spirits. More sharks than water. Luminous, as though someone had smashed the moon and left it bleeding in the water, sharks rushing through its slurry to feast. These corpse-coloured wraiths with their mad, round stares. Rolling up to garland in death their king, their keeper, their killer. A ceremony of death for their hungry king. *Baba wa Papa.* The unspoken name touched marrow, its slick death a cold, freezing current. As blood calls to white snout, did her terror call it.

And rising with her terror, Baba wa Papa grew tall.

And she stood once more in the dark shadow of a pitiless king.

CHAPTER TWELVE

Baba wa Papa burst up jowls first, with such force and speed Aisha's ears popped. Teeth tall as houses, rows upon rows, and tangled between them what had been caught in the trap.

Blood clouded the sudden spraying mist as the sharks thrashed, blind frightened things impaled upon the fangs. The monster's body followed the pried-apart trap of its mouth, the sickening white underbelly of the mjiskafiri. Baba wa Papa swung, rushing as it rose in place, and still it shot up and up and up—

It could swallow a moon!

But the monster lunged to a halt as soon as Aisha thought it. Yanked like a rope with no more slack, curving its bulk over her like an upside down fish-hook, taut and at the end of its reach.

Baba wa Papa was a fanged, pointed skull with the filmy eyes of a blind lantern-fish. Great whites squirmed and floundered amid its wildly taloned teeth, sharks wriggled on the bed of his jaw. Iron clouded the sea-water that dribbled and splashed from its mouth and over her head, skittling heavily on the children trapped around its body.

Aisha had turned to ice, half crouched in the boat. Shoulders soaked in salt and shark blood. She felt death then like feeling rain in the air, promised by the flutter of black moths.

"What a skinny fishling." The monster had a voice like thunder, a boom caving in a roof, an unnatural echo that displaced her with violent vibrations. If the Sunken King's voice was cannon fire, Baba wa

Papa's was the twisting stab of a spear, whose exit pulled out all her ribs. "To come before me . . ." Its eyes glowed, blind and filmy white— the maw of a dead fish. ". . . with a boat of bones. Why do you disturb my waters?"

The voice was a terrifying purr. *My friend*, she'd called the first creature. *Oh king*, she'd addressed the second. Flattery and mimicry were no education. She was without friend or weapon, as all will be when death comes.

But he is not death—this savage devourer. Grief blazed Aisha, maddened from rage, too hot in the ice. Sickened, the blood thick of it was in the roof of her mouth, and her stomach twisted at the slick wrestle and twist of bodies slithering over one another, silent in their torment, deprived of escape.

That pale, bloodless body was poised over her, playing with her. A hook to hang herself upon.

Aisha's fist curled. "Where is my friend?"

The sharks undulated violently, like a stomach spasming; alarmed, they thrashed even more wildly. The great white pierced on Baba wa Papa's front fangs tore in two, landing with a horrible wet thunk on its brothers, fins still jerking.

The monster was *laughing*, roaring with laughter. The sharks turned on their brother, tearing at it, feeding even in their horror.

Bile flooded her mouth and she lurched to her feet, her defiance meaningless to the monster but amusing in its worthlessness. Aisha stood akimbo on the seat, shrieking, "Where is he?"

The rope wriggled, all belly. Within it a sloshing, like a distorted current breaking in a cave. Jiggling as though her pain were the sweetest music, Baba Wa Papa commanded: "Stupid little fishling, you dare question the father of sharks? Do you question my hunger? You have bought my audience with a scholar's cat but your wearisome, boorish childishness guarantees you a seat within. Now . . . how shall I eat you?"

"You selfish, unfeeling thing! You've no brains but to eat and eat and eat!"

"Oh! Does the fishling mean to play with me as she has been out-played by another many-toothed thing? A little bone taking airs—a first, a second, a third? I am not a third, I am the *final*, I am the end-all, I am your fate and your end. Now, *bow*."

"Where is my father?"

"Do you still not know in whose court you step?" the monster crooned, its voice like the scrub of steel wire scraping the bottom of a pot, dragging shivers down her spine. "Do you come to seek an in-vader? Your petty, useless father has overexerted himself."

"What have you done to him?"

"Oh ho! Does a fishling seek truths? To avenge him, herself upon me? It was your worthless father who came hunting for me, who paid me the insult of a net, a spear! It is he who swam here, who had lost his vessel, come to find me, to catch my children, my wives, my prey—mine. My water, my dark, my moon, *mine*. Where do you *think* he is?"

She gritted her teeth.

"Imagine my delight to see this fool tread water above me, disturb the ice and move through this freezing vein. I could smell the blood in him. He swam so very hard. Which way, little bones, do you think he went?"

It hovered over her, the hook of its head lunging down closer, closer, till its foul breath clouded above her skull and frosted her eyelashes.

She stood there, a stone resounding, struck. Barely aware of the periphery, the vibrating circle. The voice was a hammer and she had felt its blows severally until her body was hardly real without it. This twisted, scornful truth wanted to swallow her whole at all corners. Just how little her father loved her, just how foolish his ambition and hers for trying to call him back. He was dead, eaten, gone—and even if he wasn't, what did it matter? *I could drag him back to shore and pin him to the bed-rock and still, he would come here, run away, fear death less than how little he'd loved me.*

She was a washed stone whose gleam was wet from tides, worn down from being taken anywhere by the weather, by boats and cats and other deciders. Locked in by negligence and the owing of things, creating barely a sound and with no desire except to sever this ugly monster the way it readied to sever her. To divide her, to eat her, to own her.

She was a flinty tongue darkening with the taste of the blood, the pain of it like a blooming flower. "You are no king. You are not even a worm. You are a belly filled with rot and hatred. You are a petty, dead thing and your lord will call you and death will enshroud you and on the last day you would be so lucky to turn into sand. God keep you from me—put Him between us else I wrest your soul and rip it to tatters. Father of nothing, king of the *eaten*, loser most great. *God keep you from me.*"

She was an angry, drowned thing, alive in a land beyond name—on a borrowed boat, with a borrowed cause, with a borrowed hurt. But she had a name and it was not fishling or girl or Shida, it was not bones and nothing. It was neither spell nor curse nor ritual. It was hers and not a thing to be given away or a cup to sip from.

Hababa was waiting for her, with sunflower seeds to roast, and Zubeir with his secrets and the black moths, and even Hassan who would never be beautiful to her. There was much for her to return to.

"Oh?" The monster slurred water like it was honey. "God? Who has conspired to bring you here? Why not love me instead? I love all my children. You can be beautiful for me, little husk."

"You're a liar. You don't love anything or anyone," she said coldly. "You don't find anything beautiful. You only love those you can easily eat and you find the weak beautiful because they are brittle to you. You only love that which you can crush, that which you can devour. You want to be an old god and pretend that your blood is divine, is grace."

"But I will eat you, fishling." The monster bared its teeth and its eyes rolled and spun, the thick jelly around them quivering and shaking. "As I did your father, as your cat. As all brittle, weak, enterprising things." Its voice brightening felt like the glance of a knife against her throat. "You buy audience, but nothing will buy you your life. Not god, not cat, not kin nor dead nor friend, living, unliving. Neither love, nor daring, nor cleverness, nor prayer, nor ghost, witch, or wedding singer."

"Only me," she said to herself. "Me alone."

"And what a small, little *me* it is—poorer than bread or Eucharist."

"You have given death and misery," Aisha said. "And you will have your share." This thought settled on her, a rich mist she absorbed before it could disperse and fade. It did not strengthen her like a meal so much as fill the empty, stinging skeins of her lungs with razors. The sharks thrashed, the monster loomed above.

She took hold of the ribs of the boat and pulled with all her strength. The hook of its body lowered, dancing above her. The bone snapped like a stalk of sugar cane. Aisha struck forward.

"Here is your share!" she shouted and drove the rib and the entirety of her arm through the beast. Its skin tore and flapped around her shoulder and the blood spouted from its body as the monster shrieked like an angry rook. She shoved her arm through the cold slurry of its guts. It was acid and rot. The beast thrashed, but she dragged the rib along, running around the edge of the boat, and fell backward to see the huge slash she had made in its corpse-bloated flesh.

She had slit it through the belly with a rib from the boat. The blood soured her to her neck.

But the cries of wrath twisted into scornful laughter. Aisha lay heaving on her back, arms sticky, lips fouled with rust. Baba wa Papa laughed, jostling side to side, its pale teeth snapping and its eyes rolling. Blood rained on her, sea-water, failure.

"Who do you think I am?" it roared. "Who do you think I am, little girl?"

Sharks thrashed and swelled like a tide cresting to fall on her. Sharks rising like foam as Aisha choked on her kicking heart. They rose, the monster's laughter a swelling thunder.

And then it yelped.

Aisha clambered as the hook shrieked, bending on itself, twisting out of its pointed curve. Its dismay and surprise turned into a thunderous scream of pain and rage. Aisha spilled herself away, finding her feet.

The sharks! The air slammed out of her chest in a gasp. Pouring out of the slash of its belly, sharks! And the sharks opened their jaws around it, snapped and tore at the flesh. They had turned on the wound, eyes rolling, and the monster screamed and rained blows on them, its great jaws shredding down, thrashing sea to blood and chum. But there were thousands of sharks and the blood in the water only added to their vigour. Ravenous, they fell upon the beast. They were eating it alive.

The monster's strength was unforgiving. It contorted in rage and agony. It roared forward, eyes white as foam. It lunged to snap itself over the boat of the bones, but there were too many sharks swelling between them. She saw them prise apart the wound she'd made till it was a gash as ghastly and huge as the monster's jaws—the flesh parted and the sharks tunneled into their father's belly.

The monster fell back into the water. It was going to swim deep! But this was no hook with a line to snap; they were inside it like rats eating through flesh. She had thought them animals without consciousness, but by their viciousness and uniform intensity, Aisha wanted to think that they were avenging themselves upon their king and keeper.

The water foamed red as ruby and the monster resurfaced with a grievous wail, the shrill of distorted screams like parrots trapped in a burning house.

The blood was turning stiff on her arms and her heart pulsed shallowly in her throat. Aisha could only watch the King of Hunger be devoured by those it had enslaved and starved, by its children and its mates and kin. She felt no sick satisfaction; horror had hollowed her. Tired from the surge, vessels burning as though she had only just survived lightning and survived it badly. She was cold and faint, scooped out. And yet she was filled with the sound of the world in a way she had never truly been before.

Grief would come, and tears. But now her head was silent, absorbing insensibly the sounds of ravenous eating—and her feet cold from ice, her arms tired of rowing. Tired of thinking and fighting.

I want to go home, the phantom sting of her eyes. Swaying infinitesimally where she stood, burning, ice-sheered knee-caps. But she could not sit down, could not be taken down and it sounded far away again, not entirely of herself.

The night was dark, the ocean oily, reddening the pale bodies with their frantic, nonsensical eating. Iron filled her nostrils but she was not sure whether it was the blood of the savaged or the bite of the cold.

She felt nearly nameless then and it did not make her want to weep. Her weariness overtook even sleep, but she did not want to die. Did she want to go home?

The monster had stopped screaming. The sharks' movements were almost lazy now, like water circling a drain as it left the bath, slowly sinking their king. She saw its bones, now pulled clean, as though the meat of it had always been melting away, decomposing.

Aisha's head bowed, finished. Listened to her own breathing, the hush of it, in and out, barely conscious. She had survived, and barely felt the guilt she'd feared. She didn't feel brave or ashamed. She only felt the air she breathed out, the ice on her skin, the bottom of her feet growing icier, sticking to the boat.

Earlier this night she had vanished, but she had not disappeared, and in the darkness, in the middle of the court of hunger, she was not afraid. And she had been a girl of many absences, but never a girl for a moment without fear.

Her eyelashes were fusing stiffly to her cheeks by the time she heard the water open. Sharks parted from the bloated mass that floated to the surface. Had the monster returned? She hadn't the strength or presence to even flinch at the possibility.

Yet it was not a corpse but a net. The sharks parted like reeds bending away from a panga, though what led the net was not a blade but a small, wet body, skinny and ice-bristled—small, so small. It padded across the water as though it were a glass floor and between its teeth was the broken white shard of a rib.

The sharks nosed the net toward her, each touching the floating bundle as though it were a sleeping child carefully passed along.

Her face was hot with tears, her nose ran, she laughed. "How?"

The cat leapt into the boat. Perched where she had broken the rib, he reattached the piece. And only then, with his mouth free, did he lick his whiskers and look at her. "Hurry and help me while they are still peaceable."

She swiped at her face and followed, grabbing the net when it bumped against the boat. She did not understand, but struck by Hamza's urgency, she obeyed. The net was heavy and Hamza could not help, but prowling by the lip of the boat and standing on his haunches, he would peer over only to settle back down impatiently. She had hundreds of questions, and was teary with relief, but she had to bring the net in.

When she finally managed to roll it in, her arms were ringing, barely attached to her shoulders. The shape of it was odd. She pushed at it and it moved. A shallow breath escaped her. Aisha pushed at it again a little more. Quickly she untangled it, pulling it apart.

A crab scuttled away and a starfish opened like a rose. Her heart stopped mid-beat. Ali lay in a nest of seaweed, in the net—she touched his chest, springing forward.

He was breathing. He was alive.

She wept.

CHAPTER THIRTEEN

On a white wave of shark did they surge on, the fishy bodies rolling beneath them like the wheels of a juggernaut. This envoy of teeth, this retinue of devourers.

She drew her father's head into her lap and bowed over it, trying to stroke the sleep from his eyes. He would not wake. Death clung to him as salt and sand clung to the eyelashes. She called him by all his names and he did not stir.

Hamza perched on the very end of the boat like a sullen yellow flag, not looking back once. Shrunken, iced body as bold as a little alif. An ink stroke that would not allow itself to be lifted or erased, only pronounced.

The night rushed past them as the wind streaking past her cheeks, tangling bony knuckles into her hair and dragging at her scalp and skull. She shivered and held tight to Ali's shoulders, shielding him from the world.

His mouth was grey-blue, pasty from the cold, pruned up like a soaked date, skin clouding away, half—bled out by the water. Rubbing her frozen hands, she cradled his face, his cheeks, trying to warm him up. How many years since she had last held him? She tried to work the blood and colour back into his body, but he remained drenched in sleep.

Fins scraped at her through the boat's ribs. Land would be the remedy, would leach the wave from him. He would be whole there.

She had to believe that he would live. The cat had brought her here, facilitated this journey for a *reason*. The lesson could not be death, could not be losing her father forever.

Beneath her breath, she prayed what prayers she knew. In the Arabic she little knew and then in the words of her town: *Protect him, save him, keep us.*

Suddenly, white. Ribboning ahead of her, spearing out and over the water. It twisted like escaping snakes, smoke made flesh, struck by lightning and fleeing. It was the shape that had been beneath the boat before. That had taunted and sung at them what felt like years ago.

The sharks leapt forward like hunting dogs and she heard a high, wailing whine—the squealing whimper of warring rats, wounding one another. She saw white flesh caught in the teeth of the invading sharks, like torn strips of cotton, fibrous and without blood. The ribbon could not fly fast enough. It rose from the sea and bloomed ahead of the boat, skipping like a stone over the water. She saw its shape now: a winged white eel, with eyes all along it, eyes. Pale human eyes, iris blue like rotted flesh and whites grey like cloudy stone.

It fled, both vapour and silk—trapped in its panic, bouncing between states, material to immaterial, half-set ghost fused to the mould. But beneath the teeth it could not be vapour; they ripped at it to make it flesh.

The boat was racing now, the water relinquishing its ghostly stillness. It was as though a curse had been lifted. The sea was alive, keen on the kill.

The ribbon soared up abruptly, willing to sacrifice its tail like a wily lizard. The sharks did not rip it to pieces then, but bit down like dogs. Aisha saw the beast yank to a halt, at the end of its reach.

Then she saw it spear downward into the water like a diving bird. Was it over?

The sharks slunk forward, their dorsal fins flipping water as they gently rolled downward, hunting deep, giving chase.

By either side of the boat the white flesh was coiled in the teeth of hammerheads and the fat, bulky great whites. The flesh knotted around their teeth and heads and bodies, winding around their teeth and prising them out, crushing their bodies, unwilling to release the noose. Their skulls smashed and crumpled, but more took on the task, replacing the fallen, launching a charge invisible to her.

It was madness. "Stop," she could only whisper. She wanted to go home—the taunting creature had done her no harm, perhaps because the singing of the leviathan had frightened it away and interrupted any such attempt—she wanted to go back to land and see to her father. The sharks' skulls caved in, their glassy eyes broke and oozed a dark, bloodied gel, but the sharks did not let go: their viciousness told of delayed justice. They were avenging themselves upon all the sly creatures, all the cunning liars who had kept them bound or been too indifferent or afraid to intervene and free them.

With a thunderous rumble, the sea exploded, showered upward. A hundred prows broke, a thousand sails snapped, as the Sunken King slammed through the surface. Around its rotten spires was coiled the white-bellied, pale-winged serpent; like a trapped lizard, its heart was solid through its pale stomach, and several of its eyes were now wounds, torn or gouged out, leaking an odd grey milk of pus or blood, the colour of stone. Aisha dreaded and pitied it.

It was her lot to address the boat once more, she knew. The cat had never spoken to any of them. Aisha lowered her father's head from her lap and the net beneath his neck before she stood. She stepped carefully along his body, but her knees were weak and she stumbled. The sides of the boat dug beneath her ribs, carving the breath out from her. It was time to speak, only that the roiling white bodies beneath her made her dizzy and she did not know what to say.

What was left? What could she say that would not be cruel to either party?

The Sunken King rocked on the water as precariously as a child's toy, but it could not shake off the white many-eyed dragon that clung to it and doomed it. The creature was white guts twisted around a flute, its force such that the prow buckled.

"The fishling has returned." The voice was as a thousand dissonant whistles wheezing through a punctured throat. "Alive, bloodied, with an army to bloody *me?*"

"Baba wa Papa is dead," Aisha said. "His children are free."

"Free to kill me? You cannot command them. I have acted within my nature. But you? Great Triumphant Innocent, what lies there in your borrowed boat if not a decaying corpse?"

Her silence was worse than any rejoinder she might have made. The sea rumbled under the Sunken King but cut itself short, for the water beneath her thrashed and boiled in reply as though in threat.

"They do not love you. They are blind, deaf, dumb things who have no long memory, only instinct. The grudge will fade, their peacefulness toward you vanish. And they will rock you out of the very boat they have carried on their heads."

"So they have made meat of their lord and will make meat of you if you don't give up the snake."

"Is this how to conduct yourself, fishling? Will you run aground avenging yourself upon the world? They cannibalized one another, no different from man in that regard—you are lush in the blood of their kill and you know to cook them in coconut, don't you? Have you not eaten as they were eaten of?"

Aisha was tired of grand games. "Vow that you will hurt no one again."

"And? You can keep your father from me, but can you keep me from him? When he returns I will greet him with all my teeth."

"*Give me your word.*"

"Action is what matters, but words on water? Mean nothing. They vanish. "

The prow broke, tumbling forward. The snake could not squeal or scream as they fell upon him. The Sunken King escaped back into the water, and the waves bucked to cover where it had once loomed. Aisha had to scramble backward to hold tight on to her father. The water was cloudy with a thing bleeding smoke. Torn eyes bobbed in the water, blinking grey tears, scarcely able to film over with death before some mouth nipped them away.

An eye nudged against her ankle. The slimy beak of its pale lid pecked at her skin as it blinked in clicks. It edged closer, sticky, seeking her skin. She drew her leg back with a hiss. Hamza darted into sight, landing with the plop of his dancer's feet, and took the eye between his small glinting fangs. The cat bit down, thrashing his head, and gel erupted down his scraggly yellow chin. Hamza flicked his head to shake off the grey excess and returned to his perch without another word.

Aisha wasted no time checking her father for signs of those eyes, knowing now how they sought skin like parasites. She dragged him up onto one of the seats, keeping him above the cloudy starch blooming in the ink of the sea. The boat juddered over the broken skulls again, sending her stumbling, and they were rushing at an incredible speed, the sound of the lines and Vs whizzing in the surface from the point of her ankles like the cane vibrating through the air. She panicked at the suddenness of this voyage, the renewed, accelerated speed, and realized with horror who next would be on her path and in their way.

She secured her father as best she could and tottered over to the cat. "Stop, they'll eat everything. Even the innocent."

"The innocent," Hamza mused.

"They'll eat the first creature! It *helped* us."

"Hm," Hamza said. "I'm just as little captain as I was before." The gelatinous goo made the scraggly hair on his little chin gleam.

Aisha's fingers tightened on a rib. She beseeched with her eyes and then her voice, but no matter how she commanded, firmly and then increasingly desperately, that they stop, no matter how she shouted and begged, the gnashing jumbled wave did not heed her. She clapped her hands and stood on the highest point of the boat that she dared, but their ferocity did not flag.

She saw from the pinkening slash on the edges of the pale dawn that the sky would soon flower with the threat of day. Her heart ran ahead of her. "Stay away!" she shouted, praying her voice would reach and warn away the creature they were heading toward. "Stay off the path! They're coming, swim deep! Swim deep!"

Slowing to a stop, the sharks became a circle again. A lazy rotation of fan propellers, licked by a hot breeze. Aisha felt her heart being yanked.

The circle opened, revealing the strange pistil. Day had made the sight of this night-time thing a dangerous thing. The boat edged in. The sharks nipping on the flicking tail coiling around them.

The first monster was like a child absently teasing a feral pet. Lightened, the water was a creamy blue. The monster's eyes shone like bright pickled lemons in the sleek black of its shrunken skull.

She saw through the rippling water loops upon loops of its body, an endless rope, undulating like fire smoke, hazy through the shimmer of heated air.

She put her hand on her fast heart to slow it. "You said they were dangerous to you, before."

"They are my kin," it blubbered, a reed underwater, a flooded pipe. A tea-pot in a basin. "Dangerous, if they are given cause to be. A tail grows back." It neared her, pressing its slick, slimed face against the ribs. Peering into a cage, or looking out from it. It watched Baba breathe for a long while.

Like a skinny metal clothes hanger, its sharply bent arm reached down, caressing the edge of Ali's half-curled palm. Aisha allowed it.

Then it began to tug and Aisha slapped at that skeletal limb. "No!" she cried out as it began to weep again, and tug in earnest until she hit it hard. "No, no! Don't touch him!"

It wept terribly then. "It was always him and me, you'll try to keep him, you won't let him come back! You awful girl," it sobbed. "He'll come back—you won't be able to stop him. Give him to me, I will keep him safe. *Give him to me! Please!*"

She was horrified and incredulous. Baba would go, wouldn't he? He would rise up from his bed soon as he was well enough, and go running. The creature wept, upset, and she watched, holding tightly to her father, transfixed by its misery and its audacity. "No," she said stubbornly without her lip wobbling. "You didn't come for him. *I* did," she realized aloud. Her childish voice twisted into something smooth. "You have your kin, leave mine to me."

She held her father's scrawny body tight to her, as if he were her child, as fickle as a heart. She had to keep him.

A red glow crept across the glassy sea. The pink shards had melted and ebbed around them, nibbled and suckled and gnawed like a new-born. "He will find me," the creature said persuasively, pettily. The sea sniffled in petulance.

"No," Aisha drawled coldly, looking at it from above her father's head. "You will not be so unwise, will you? If you live as a fool, I will shorten the time."

She had shocked both of them into silence. The sea around them still murmured with the slow propellers of shark fins, snouts butting against each other like blind kittens clambering drowsily over one another. Her skin was still tacky with the stain of death, of terror survived. She held her breath.

Hamza was a silhouette, a charm poised on the prow with his shadowy back to them, whiskers fiery, profile calm. He might have been a wood-carving for all it mattered.

Was this who she would be now, a maker of bold threats? She lied, jaw hard, she lied. She held no dominion here, but what was it to be laughed at now? She'd been laughed at all of her life; the sound could not hurt her, she had hardened herself to it.

Would it challenge her bluff or turn its kin on her—surely they were not equally powerless when it came to mobilizing all these teeth.

Through her palm the too slow stumble of a heart, the long slender rib. To die now, to lose him. She lied. Jaw hard, she waited. If the first creature attacked, would the cat intervene? What would the cat do, if he even bothered to do it?

She stared adamantly into its half-submerged, kerosene eyes. Its body a long shimmer, a cloudy snake through water, miles long, ancient.

"You're too young for the art of slaughter," it said finally.

"I've been practising," she said, and listened to its affronted silence. "I will gain skill, if that is what you want."

"What cold eyes . . ." it trailed off with the disdain and disapproval of one of the other women, women like Hababa Hadia who sneered at her, their eyes telling her what soft places she lacked for a knife called "husband" to carve her to his liking.

"And what foolish eyes." Aisha jerked her chin. Anger made her bold. "Never drag a man to your heart again. Never again seek daughters as though they were livestock to trade between you, as if it is what you are owed for the farce of friendship. You were selfish with your request, and I was kept from my father and the sea because you wanted a child bride. If I hear that you approach man with such requests in future, you will suffer. Do you understand?"

Its head rose, indignant. "This servant—"

"Will understand now or be *made* to understand."

She accepted its silence with a nod of her head. "Swim deep," she said, unwavering. "Swim very deep."

If it was malice in her heart, then let it be. Steadily, she watched it sink. She had found within her a small thing that would not yield—that only God could break.

Good, she thought, *if it be malice. If he must hurt so that we are free, I hope he bleeds forever.*

The disorganized assembly broke, as though taking a cue or following the smell of their meal. If it was the first creature's will that it be eaten, that was its right.

Once they'd disappeared, her head dropped forward—the ocean cleared, the surface had returned like a lid over a boiling pot, but she knew what lay ever simmering, murmuring underneath, and it was not trapped, only veiled.

For an endless minute, her temple bowed into her father's. His heart was still too slow, too slow. She lifted her head and swallowed thickly. "They're gone."

"The reef is near."

And the army too great to cross it. Day's dawning had broken the pause of time, a current brushed the vessel forward, the water bobbed through the ribs. She could close her eyes against that sweet hush, the sky marbling, splotching orange yellow pink like the skin of apple-mango—she couldn't remember her last sip of cold fresh water. She heard in the distance the gather and swell of rain clouds that would cover the sun like wet cloth over rising dough. Longing dragged through her. She wondered at it, at the strength of *feeling* anything at all—and even in this dangerous sea she almost smiled.

When she was younger she'd never been able to sleep at this time. Before fajr prayer she'd creep through the darkness and watch the grey shape of her mother in the corner of the majlas—her shoulders moving, her chest rising up and caving in, a peace and calm not yet stained by wakefulness.

Then, small as a bird, Aisha would hop up next to her and quietly, carefully curl so she could sleep next to Mama. If she was lucky, her mother would not wake until it was *just* before the time she might risk missing the prayer. They would pray together, Aisha following her movements, her thigh pressed to her mother's hip, her head barely reaching her waist. In sleep, in prayer, had been the moments Aisha was close to her.

Knitting her fingers over her father's heart, Aisha bowed—the land was nearing, inching toward them as she'd inched toward Mama—but she couldn't sleep and if she'd tried, she wouldn't have heard her name.

"Come with me."

She looked up. Hamza, faced away from her, still looked the same, indifferent animal he had been a moment ago. The rain clouds gathered ahead, covering up the apple-mango blush, chasing the sun out.

She'd heard a great many things, been asked a great many things, but never that—it took a while before she could remember how to speak. "I don't understand."

"Come with me to the House of Rust—you will know everything that the lord has not forbidden. You will go wherever you want and ask whatever you want, all the poorly hidden things and the deeply buried ones. You will know why it is that a cat speaks many tongues and carries many names. Everything you only half saw because you half imagined it will be fully seen, will show itself to you."

"And my father? Will you heal him?"

The silence that answered her held no yielding in it, not against time, not to a plea, not for mercy.

The old blood stung like lacerations. She knew the answer. Every raw wound turned prickly as sleep lost its power over her—she knit her fingers closely over her father's heart, tighter, tighter.

The waves propelled them forward unhurried, unchangeable.

The cat faced landward, away from her.

"And my father?"

Hamza's head turned to mark her repetition. This time she refused to feel like a fool. "He has made his path," the cat said. "And runs the circuit many times."

"That's unkind of you to say, and unfair."

"It is only true."

Her eyes burned. She could not argue, only swallowed. "Why?"

"You asked what drew your mother and what bound her feet. Sometimes these are choices."

"You would question my courage?"

"You must question yourself. Will you refuse and say you remained because you loved your father? If I said let us take him, you would then say *and what of my grandmother?* And what of her? What of any of them?"

"It was you who said to hoard knowledge was criminal and dishonest."

"Oh?" He turned, facing her primly, eyes serenely a stranger's. "Do you return to educate? Will you be righteous?"

"There are dangerous things in the sea—"

"There are dangerous things everywhere—they will call you a witch or you will make them hunters, and everywhere blood. In the House of Rust you will be wiser than you are afraid."

"*There are some things we must learn for ourselves,*" she recited with finality.

"We must learn to let ourselves learn them," he said. "I will not ask again."

"There is much I would need to prepare!"

"If not now, then never. If not you, then no one. This is the hour."

"That isn't fair!"

"It is the reality nonetheless," the cat said. "Neither fair, nor kind."

"Then . . ." shakily, she swallowed her tears. "Then you will not ask me again."

Hamza's chin lifted and beneath his eye she felt all parts of herself present—it thrilled and horrified her, the book shut on her, the hall with its thousands of doors, all slipped back into their frames and whatever leviathan's songs had filtered away into resounding silence so absolute it became a ringing in her ears. *Please.*

Don't give up on me.

The rain clouds murmured close, silver lanced over his skull, silver and grey. "The debt is settled."

The ribs split open like a badly built bear trap. Aisha clutched her father, refusing to shut her eyes. She would look, she would not be asleep this time. The spine of the boat halved with the crack of a machete cleaving a coconut. Waves splintered up, salt lashed at her eyes, the floor crumpled beneath her—she held on tight as the ribs toppled away, bones swallowed by the sea.

The long-toothed prow sank last, its captain perched with stoic grace, watching her fall, not caring that they drowned. White blinded her eyes as the waves toppled over her and she had to twist to get her feet out and kick. She gasped and choked, crushing her father's ribs, eyes wild, but the undercurrent was strong, trying to drag them down.

She blinked the fire from her eyes. Hamza was gone—water walker, thing colder than a saint. A sob broke behind her clenched teeth. She kicked and kicked, the storm racing toward them, the ocean a freezing froth dragging at her ankles and twisting her joints. She thought of teeth, of claws, of a thousand reaching things. The sharks were not far, and reef or no, some must have still prowled. Aisha kicked, her father a dead weight, she pulled and she kicked, viciously opposed to dying— not here, not after everything.

The waves grew stronger, thrashing at her. She kicked, they clawed. She twisted, they dragged. The storm rumbled overhead, its freezing shadow creeping over her eyes. Her father's flesh grey. She kicked, they tried to tear him from her. She held on and her hands rung to her elbows when he was torn from her. She spun head over heels, the force of the water unspooling her, the surface broke, a mosaic of grey shards, a cloudy mirror into an unsinkable eternity. At the bottom of a boiling pot of sugar water, she couldn't scream, couldn't breathe.

Then Aisha was in the air again, wind a whistling howl about her ears. She searched wildly, but could not find him. She dragged air into her lungs and dove deep.

He was a shadow in a smashed mirror; there was no sound. A slow falling shadow the grey light could not lance. The sea caught her by the ankle and hurled her downward, and Aisha spun herself a turbine as she kicked. Her shoulder joint rolled and she threw out her arm, her fingers brushing the edge of his shirt. She grabbed him with both her arms and wouldn't let go. She crossed her arms over her chest and screwed her eyes shut and kicked.

Her legs were weak, the strings in her thighs and calves burning and snapping. The waves had twisted her and when she looked she didn't know if it was up or it was left or right or down. They floated in a sky with no earth, no sun, no moon, no stars.

Her lungs would burst, her eyes too. She couldn't breathe and she kicked, a bird stripped of all its tendons and bones. She'd make it if she left him, she knew. But she did not let go. She twisted around him like the very net that had drowned him, and yet, kept him one unbroken mouthful in the belly of a beast. There was no science, no sum. No fair or unfair. Her father. A name, a body. A dream. She kicked. Baba, her heart. She kicked.

CHAPTER FOURTEEN

Consciousness trampled Aisha and she spat up water. Something hard cleaved her shoulder as she rolled up, and the wound bloomed like hot tamarind muddying the brew. Ali had nearly slipped from her grasp but she woke in time to catch him again. She realized that she could feel the rain on her face, that hard coral had nearly broken her arm. Rain, hard rock. The shore.

The sea had lost its interest in battering them, for now. Aisha shot a wary glance backward, but it was churning itself away. Tightening her hold, she swam them shoreward while it was distracted.

This was not the beach she'd set off from. The rain blurred it all out, all except the shape or shadow of a man. She heard a name on the wind, thought it might be hers. She swam on, felt splashing ahead of her and struck out at it, but it was Zubeir, angry mouth and sad eyes. She twisted her arms around Ali and would not be parted from him. Zubeir had to drag them both onto land.

Only then did she roll away so she might find her father's heart. "He's still alive," she blurted, teeth chattering. "He won't wake up. I've tried everything . . ." She let Zubeir shoo her off, watching him place his hands over Ali's chest, press his ear to it.

"All right, Aisha," Zubeir decided. "Come on." He rose and with surprising strength hauled Ali over his shoulders. She had to scramble to her feet to catch up, following unsteadily, half-numb from the cold.

"What will you do?"

"See the extent of the wound."

A rainy drizzle darted at them and the trees began to swing. Clutching her throbbing shoulder, Aisha trotted after him.

Ali was nothing but a grey net over his shoulders, a lump.

They did not go up into the town, nor fetch a doctor. Zubeir moved with the gangly spryness of a spider. Aisha ran, trying not to look back. *The extent of the wound . . .*

There'd been no blood but hers and only at the end; hers and the false god's.

The hut was rust and tin soldered together; a careless fringe of flaking palm leaves roofed it. Aisha tripped over the threshold and after a shout from Zubeir, shut the door on the rain.

She helped lower Ali onto the table after Zubeir swept away old mismatched cutlery. The legs of the table were short, the surface lopsided. Ali's chest caved in, without air. His skin was paper, his lips grey.

"Go call your Hababa."

"No," Aisha's voice shook. "That won't help. We don't have time."

Zubeir drew a dagger, curved and small enough to fit in his hand snug against the heel of his palm. She stiffened. He floated the blade above Ali's mouth and nose—it was ages before the blue steel misted, clouding with breath.

"Get out, fetch me salt water."

"Stop trying to get rid of me. You can't chase me away. What do you mean to do?"

"A horrible, necessary thing. A man with a broken heart . . . there are many solutions. But for a man with a heart like your father's, there is only one. If he is revived he will return to what calls him. What he has seen had broken his heart and yet even his longing now sinks his heart. It is too painful to be awake."

"Old man Zubeir," Aisha growled. "Speak directly. I have had enough riddles in this one night to last me several lifetimes. *What do you mean to do?*"

He considered her, but she did not look away. "Shut all the windows, block them with cloth. Let there be no opening."

She didn't ask anymore. Aisha hurried to do as she was commanded. Zubeir gave her old rags, which she stuffed beneath every opening. The hut was a hurricane of motion; she stoppered every orifice and returned to him.

"Since you are here," Zubeir said, "I have to ask. I am to sever something your father holds dear, a beloved anchor—it sinks him and yet it is his. Are you settled, that I will scrape his dreams from him?"

"What do you mean?"

"It is no riddle. I will scrape the sea from him, that dear thing killing him. Will we take that choice from him?"

"I want him to live."

"Is this about what you want, Aisha?"

She was taken aback. "If it breaks his heart, shouldn't it be destroyed? If it's killing him, shouldn't it be severed? If I don't, won't he die? What kind of *choice* is that?"

"Will you or won't you, fishling?"

Aisha swallowed. "That isn't my name, don't call me fishling."

"He's fading fast."

"Then do it."

He bowed his head and pressed the blade at the base of her father's throat—he gave her one last quick glance and she stared back, petrified. He slammed his palm against the hilt and broke Ali's sternum. Aisha bit her lip hard, taking her father's hand, holding tight. He didn't even make a sound. She had to be strong and that meant not looking away.

Dead blood spilled away from the blade as slickly as from the sides of her gutted fish. Zubeir split her father from sternum to navel. Her mouth twisted, her sight trembled. She covered Ali's temples, slipping her hand over his freezing eyes. She fixed the old man with determined warning. If her father was to die for the trick of a knife . . . what she'd do would not be kind, but deserved.

Zubeir prised open Ali's ribs, and between the two tongue-like lungs, red-veined and fleshy, sat her father's heart. Pale moonstone, puttering like an unsheltered candle. Aisha fastened her hand over Ali's eyes.

Zubeir paused, deftly turning the knife. Sweat beaded on his brow, his mouth a focused seam. He split her father's heart, as careful and practised as Hababa splitting manda.

Ali's heart burst open before Zubeir was finished making the cut—and she thought they were tiny, sharp-pointed sparrows, launching like arrows darkening out the sun. Yet they were not birds but fish, frothing out and exploding through the slit—the beat of their gift-paper wings wild as they poured out of him—beautiful and silver.

The fish beat at the ceiling, spinning round and round in the air, tugging at her clothes. She was blind, salt searing down her cheeks, breathing hard from tears. All that he loved, with a heart so full.

A heart emptied like a skein onto the earth—it was like fireworks lighting up the day's sky with sulphur and strange, beautiful smoke.

This was the most wondrous thing she had ever seen. She looked at her father, her ribs closed, her throat tight. It was the song of the hard rain on the ocean, of the birds he made rise from driftwood, that scarred his hand forever, of all the love that had dragged him away—her love for him could not keep her from doing this.

His full heart, her father. It was a cruel and beautiful crime. She hid her temples against his shoulder, trying not to cry.

Zubeir gathered the bird-fish like an old woman gathering locusts, sweeping them into an old sack. He showed her how to cover Ali's heart with both hands so that the fish could not go back in and undo his work. Her palms reddened, blood welling between the grooves of her tightened fingers. The ceiling whirled with dancing: a marriage of underwater grace and the franticness of birds, breaking their bodies on the promise of escape.

A false promise. Zubeir gathered them in gunias, batting them down—comets, they were but flies all the same.

Icy black water seeped between her fingers—a poor band on a punctured engine bleeding oil. As freezing as the sea between hers and the undersea, she tasted without quite understanding how; a chrome yellow moon, a tiger eye in the deep. It interfered with her pulse, sent it in flux—Zubeir was busy flinging the feathered fish and the scaled birds into the small stove, which, spluttering, changed colour. The flames blazed as green as copper ore.

What could she say? Sick with dishonour—she had made her decision, a hard choice she'd had no right to make—but it embraced her with crushing force. Her father's face was mute as though faded by moonlight—he bled and bled ocean water, a ceiling swilled in colour being given to the ashes . . .

She pressed down hard. The bleeding would not cease, it was not a bubbling mouth, loosening its seams.

"Old man Zubeir!"

Zubeir swore, curses and godly oaths, a tangle. Water had flooded over Ali's chest cavity, spilling over the table onto the floor. The abscess of dreams that needed abandoning. Zubeir hovered over the cut but made no move to close it, hands floating, waiting upon something to escape so he might leap upon it. Water rose up her ankles, to her knees. The birds rattled in the sack; the thought of taking over that task made her ill.

At this rate they would drown. "Old man—"

"Quiet, Aisha!" He snapped but was not angry. "It's only water—" but it was filling up to her calves with stomach-turning familiarity, dark as that other sea. "We can't let it reach the heart again. Open the door, let it out."

She was already splashing toward the door even before he finished speaking. The water pawed at her, hungry and demanding. She held her breath, panicking, and she didn't know then what she caught her foot on, only that she fell and the sound of her body hitting knee-high water was the slam of a building into concrete. She fell below the surface, bubbles rising up ahead of her. She was a hundred feet submerged. The bubbles disappeared. Her heart was hard in her head. She floated in the veins of time iced over. There was darkness all around her; she held her air in her chest. Zubeir's little shack had disappeared.

A luminous shape moved ahead of her, and Aisha forced herself to be still. She was sure her heart was a drum, calling these things to her. She tried to slow her heart, but it became more difficult. The shape was getting nearer, meandering through the dark in a slick, buttery way—

The swimming bones—bones again! Was it the boat? Her fingers shot open where her arms floated, sending a current through the water. The shape twisted in her direction—she saw it now more clearly, a long skeleton, racing toward her.

She had made a mistake.

Zubeir tugged her up, but when her head broke the surface she was thrown. The current raced out ferociously, and she tumbled out with it, torn from Zubeir's grasp. Her brains sloshed around in her skull, and she leapt to her feet as the water emptied out onto the sand. Zubeir shouted her name just as she felt something whizz past her ear like a dart and she turned to him as he tossed her the old jar.

Aisha bolted out after the spluttering fish. It flew like an injured moth with a torn wing. It was escaping! She wrestled off the lid and leapt after it. She jumped and twisted and when she caught it she slammed the lid on so fast, it snapped the injured wing. Blood fled her face; she was agonized by the high whistle of pain it made. She had not meant to hurt it.

She ground her jaw on her blistering shame and returned to the shack to find that Zubeir was already sewing her father's chest shut with long inky thread, unwieldy as the wood-wire of a hard broom. He pierced the skin and bent the wire through like a basket weaver. Zubeir's hands were busy, so she put the jar next to the table leg.

"Is he all right?"

"He'll wake. Maybe tomorrow. Unless he decides not to. But likely he will wake."

"I don't understand."

"Don't say that all the time. You think you can get away with looking stupid? It's not as convincing as you think. You say you don't understand when you mean to say you don't know how to feel or cannot accept it. Ask me another question, silly girl." Zubeir tied off the final knot, biting the wire with the edge of his strange knife. "Or look for yourself."

Tentatively, she stepped closer. Ali's ribs rose and fell with shallow breath. Aisha's eyes swam until Zubeir became a blur moving about the room—she hardly heard him until he repeated himself, touching her sleeve with his tough hand. He was going to go to call his men to help carry her father back home to her Hababa's where he would be tended to. He told her not to go too far.

She was still the same fool she'd always been. When Zubeir left she ran out into the rain and dropped to the sand, her knees lowered and then her temples—she bowed over in sujood, in gratitude, in sorrow, in triumph, and in shame. She wept as she had never before wept. She gave thanks, pelted by heaven, and asked forgiveness most of all.

The cleansing rain shrouded her, pouring away the salt and the blood and the clinging dreams—and her heart slowed when she found she could cry no more. The rain reminded her of her mother and she stayed there, freezing and yet calmed, drifting toward sleep.

Dizzily she sat up again, heart tired and shivery and raw. A lump on the beach gave her pause. She focused her stare, so she could not blame it on tears. Rain washed out her sight, the fogginess seeping out of her eyes and down her cheeks with the last of it. She rose and approached.

It was Ali's tangled-up, torn-up, net. How it had managed to float to the shore she did not know. She unfurled it carefully and then recoiled, springing away.

Blinking up at her, wriggling at the sight of her, was a pale inverted eyeball.

Hamza had destroyed the last one that had tried to leech onto her. She stared in revulsion and anger that something so small could repulse and threaten her so. Never a squeamish person, she could not now abide feeling abhorrence with her body. She had never shied from filthy work, had taken pride in it. To feel disgust so viscerally now felt insubordinate. The thought of smashing it with her heel nauseated her, and the thought of it rupturing in slime again turned her stomach even worse.

Making up her mind, Aisha ran back to the hut, searching for something, and saw the trapped bird-fish, rattling in its prison.

An old bottle? That would do. Newspaper. A spoon on the low stool, yes. She raced out to find that the eyeball had been a hardy traveller, wriggling frantically out of the net and . . . toward the sea.

Her whole body lit up in a great refusal and she blocked its path like a titan.

It paused.

Then it crawled toward her.

"No! No! No!" she told it shrilly, as it went rolling speedily for her heel. She squashed a squealing yelp, kicking up sand, shoving up a wall with her foot that it struggled to circumvent. It renewed its efforts, unflagging, and Aisha did squeal then, quickly acting and jabbing the spoon at the ground. She airlifted a crumbling spoonful of sand and shoved the eyeball in the bottle, where it stoppered itself in the neck. She gritted her teeth, wanting to squeal again, grabbing handfuls of sand to pack in, forcing the eyeball to drop into the bottom with the plopping sound of a grape. Disgusting! She grabbed more sand, half burying it and then stuffed that with the old newspaper, before stamping on the cork many times.

"Yuck!" She jumped a few times, shaking out her arms. "What is wrong with you? I hate it, I hate it!"

Then she marched around it, trying to dissolve her excess of revulsion-driven energy. Truly disgusting! How could she have allowed in herself such a reaction? Pitiful!

Aisha forced herself to hold the bottle properly. In the hut she put it down gratefully and picked up the other prisoner. She folded the mutilated wing back inside before screwing the jar shut again. Taking a deep, bracing breath to clear herself of all frivolous overreactions, she took both captives and went back into the rain. Aisha placed both at the foot of the tree and dragged the net in as far from the water as she could. She checked the net carefully again and found nothing in it.

Zubeir returned with four of his men. They looked alert, solemn, and ready—likely none of them had returned to sleep after the dawn prayer. "What do you have there?"

Aisha held the bundled net protectively to her chest. He laughed so she knew she must have scowled for him to do so.

He sobered quickly, but his face was still soft. "You must burn it. It's unwise."

"Then I don't care to be wise."

His brow twitched in intrigue. "Not even to save your grandmother from fretting?" he hummed. "Run ahead and tiptoe back to your pallet. We will bring your father and wake you and your grandmother both. Run along, little girl."

It was better than *fishling*. Giving Ali one last pained look, Aisha glared at Zubeir and then ran home. She ran to Hababa's and tiptoed into the house. She'd have to change. But Hababa was already stirring and Aisha had to crumple, plumping herself artfully onto her pallet just in time for Hababa to roll over and blink, her irritation accompanied by a confused struggle with wakefulness. "Aisha?"

Aisha gave an exaggerated yawn, squinting rudely—she would never be rude if she was awake. As someone not yet out from under the shadow of sleep, she was lent to a sort of shameless grouchiness, politeness not yet having settled on her—it was a lie, but one understood as sleep. She hummed impolitely and made her hum rumbly and deep with the very same sleep she'd had none of.

Hababa shot upright. "I slept through fajr? Have *you* prayed?" A pause. "No, you have not, you wicked girl! You should be the one waking up an old woman if she has overslept! This never happens, I always—get up, come on, we've missed prayers! In all my years I have never once, God keep me that way. It's you for making me talk so these past nights. Come on, go make wudu."

Aisha dragged her feet and made a show of looking tired, which wasn't difficult at all. Exhaustion was starting to overcome her, sleep a weight hovering over her that would soon plummet from a snapped cord to crush her. She did as she was told, then muffled her yawn against her arm, changing her clothes while Hababa sloshed around in the bathroom. Blood could negate her prayers. The rain had washed it away, but one could never be too sure.

She decided to wait for her grandmother so they could pray together. Hababa had bad knees and settled on the stool. It was quiet, united in their motions—every time Aisha's temples touched the floor she felt herself fighting a peaceful, sleepy sigh. When they were done,

Aisha let herself loosely slump against Hababa's legs, resting her cheek on her thigh.

Hababa murmured duas. It was unlike Aisha to lean into touch or ever ask for it, but Hababa took it in stride after only a small pause, stroking Aisha's scalp, knitting her fingers through Aisha's short, boyish hair. Peace soaked her like a cloth swelling in a bath of warm water. Hababa's prayers ended, but she kept her hand on Aisha's head. Her silence had been peaceful until it had grown contemplative, and then Hababa said, "Aisha."

Aisha tilted her head to look up at her grandmother and her smile, while sleep-addled, came more easily to her than it ever had before. After all the terror and the exhaustion, her love had nowhere to go, her love had deepened. She hummed, contented.

She heard the crease in her grandmother's mouth. "Why is your hair so wet?"

A rapping on the door saved her. Aisha was on her feet like a good, obedient girl. "Ah, who could that be!"

Hababa's hand shot over her heart, having suffered the indignity of an awful shock. "God protect us. At this hour?" She snatched Aisha's elbow and pulled her down with alarming strength. "Stay here."

Aisha didn't listen, following Hababa's patter to the door. Grandmother scowled at this perplexing disobedience, before sighing and lifting the metal scrap that hid the eyehole. After peering through the eyehole, Hababa threw open the door with a sharp inhale. Zubeir's young hunters stared up at her like hounds. Incapable of alarm, they greeted her blankly. "Peace," they said and adjusted their burden. Ali was laid on a stretcher like a small old man. Hababa clapped her hands over her trembling mouth, but that just made her hands shake, too. Her eyes trembled with a glassy light. She stepped aside so they could kick off their shoes, keeping their gazes low and respectful, waiting for orders and directions.

Tears streaked Hababa's face—her breathing wet and wheezy. She made them put him on the bed and touched his pale face and his dark lashes. She wept like a child beyond comforting. She whispered and gasped God's name and Ali's. Aisha's throat closed up, but she didn't turn away, didn't leave her grandmother's side.

The shark hunters turned to leave, their work done. Hababa stopped them. "What's wrong with him? Where did you find him? Why won't he wake up?"

The oldest one—she assumed—spoke with all the gentleness of a son taking his mother's hands, without once moving toward Hababa. "He's tired. All he needs is some rest. He's been fighting a long time, that's all."

Hababa wept openly. "Where has my boy been? How did you find him?"

He smiled gently—the other shark hunter looked so nonchalant that the brief, deliberate glance he sent Aisha's way seemed nearly a thing of her own imagining—there was a pause here, for her, she realized. If she wanted to say the truth.

Aisha lowered her head an inch and shook it slightly.

He spoke warmly, soothing and kind. "I think he might have lost his boat," he said so naturally even Aisha might have thought the whole of last night to be but a dream. "He washed up onshore, the old man looked him over. He'll be all right. He only needs to get warm and rest. Ali is a lot stronger than you think."

Aisha wondered who *that* was meant for. Hababa smiled tearily and launched her assault of hospitality. They declined her gratitude and her generous attempts to get them to stay with the grace of princes. They all knew how ill prepared she was for such things now.

You silly woman, Aisha thought with anguish—watching Hababa swipe at her eyes like a child bravely fighting tears. *Your heart is ready to burst and you're fretting over tea-cups for your guests.*

Aisha's heart felt ready to burst, too. She picked up the stool, gently steering Hababa by her father's pallet, and made her sit. It was a sign of how unsettled the old woman was that she allowed herself to be herded.

Aisha saw the boys off. They ducked their lanky frames beneath the overhang and averted their gazes respectfully.

Aisha made some tea and brought it back into the room to see a mother stroking her son's temples. Hababa had stopped crying but every so often she would be overcome by sniffles, mouth wobbling and her breath hiccupping.

"We should let the neighbours know he's safe."

"Tomorrow," Aisha said.

Hababa blinked at her straightforward tone before shaking her head to clear it. She sniffled and bit her lower lip.

"I was going to bury him."

"Drink some tea." Aisha made sure Hababa took the saucer from her hands. "Don't call the neighbours," she said, and kissed her grandmother's brow. "Let you and my father both have peace for a little while, no guests, no interruptions. Just this once."

CHAPTER FIFTEEN

It was still early, a few of the usual characters milling about the street. Aisha wove between them, a dull green blot in her robes. The drizzle showed no sign of stopping, and it would keep the sky overcast and looking like dawn until asr prayers. The people ducked back into their homes or bundled underneath the roofs of their stalls—they looked wet and small, like crows made sombre by the rain.

She returned to the beach and lifted the net. The captured remnants of the bird-fish in the jar and the eye in its bottle were still there, evidence that she'd not dreamed all of it. Like a sand worm, the eye had wriggled little lines of air upward, but had encountered the obstacle of the newspaper, which it could not creep past despite its most enthusiastic attempts. It still twitched a little like a tadpole, but appeared to be tiring itself out. Eventually she'd have to take the cork out and move the creature somewhere else, though she wondered how she'd manage it without having to break the date-brown bottle. Suspicious of this tenacious eyeball, she stripped off the long dry finger of a palm leaf and wrapped it around the mouth of the bottle, further securing it. The small wing of the bird-fish fluttered at the bottom of its own jar. She couldn't bear to look at it, and accepted her cowardice in wrapping both of these up in the net where she didn't have to see them.

Reluctant to return home, she sat watching the water, grey and white. *What an adventure.* How lucky she had been to have had a part

in it. How sorry she was to have squandered it. She had been ac-
cused of cowardice for staying and yet she could not regret her reasons. Better a coward than a hypocrite.

How could Hamza have asked that she leave, after all that talk of
knowledge and that hoarding of it? Yet how could *this* knowledge be
shared?

*They will call you a witch, or you will make them hunters. Then every-
where blood.*

No one would believe her. Her strangeness itself was something
only barely tolerated—a thing whose correction they postponed but
ultimately thought inevitable.

Hamza hadn't corrected her, not really. Not even guided her toward correction. The cat had given her the tools, a means, a way. The
will had been hers. That had been vital.

She'd lost out on the House of Rust, hadn't she? It was an impossible choice to make. Of course she couldn't have said yes. But her
mind whispered with the ghosts of many what-ifs. The last she'd have
seen of her home would have been night's shrewd shadows, Hababa's
lonely back—the last of her father would have been his death-touched
face, sinking grey, drowning. She never would have been able to forgive the girl who made the choice to go.

But it existed, this place. Imagine if Hamza had left without letting her know there was *more*. Things she'd never be able to blame on
imagination, the curse and luxury of adulthood, the destruction in
forgetting.

She pressed her bundle to her chest. An eye plucked from a hidden sea and an insect from the heartache she'd helped bleed out of
her father.

By now she knew the shadow that fell on her quicker than she
knew her own name, its gangliness like an old broom. Zubeir settled
beside her, mimicking her posture, huddling forward as if to ask if
this was to be their bodies' arrangements now.

"Have you run away again?"

Aisha glanced at him. "Why didn't you come to Hababa's house?"

He scowled as though she'd now finally exhibited some new insolence he did not approve of. "The others did as I told them to, did they not? It is a poor hovel, mine, but someone needed to make sure it was still standing."

Aisha turned back to the sea to forget him.

Zubeir bristled at this dismissal. "And why are you not by your father's bedside?"

"Do you think he should have woken up?"

"Eh heh!" He shuffled and huffed, trying to look annoyed. "He was still asleep when the boys left and you know very well your grandmother will need help with guests soon!"

"If you care so much, you can go fetch the tea things." When Zubeir sucked his teeth in bewilderment, she softened. "They won't yet descend upon us. It's early yet."

"No. Perhaps. It is how it is, you know."

"Why must it be?" Aisha wondered. "To be a good person you have to be a good host, correct in both heart and manners. It's not meant to be a burden but there are always too many people all the time. The kind of importance we place on always readying to give welcome, to lie about how well I am, it's ceremony, sometimes I don't want to be kind or say that I am well. Manners and expectations that are so selfish, giving kindness the wrong name. I can't stand it sometimes."

"Have you changed at all, Aisha? It would be admirable and a pity both if you did not."

"I haven't changed," Aisha said. "I've simply revealed myself to myself. To do the terrible thing that I have done . . . How do you live knowing you can cut a heart open and take it—take whatever love is inside?"

"I created necessary distance. In my defence, it has been a very long while since I cut a heart. I only exorcize that which eats it."

"What right did I have to let you take the sea from him?" Aisha's eyes stung bitterly. "I did to him what they've tried to do to me. If he wakes he'll hate me for the loss. Or not know the loss and not hate me at all, which will be even worse!"

"Everyone who ever came to me has come willingly or was brought by a loved one, or wiser ones. I have cut out of them their lovers, wives, children, grief—the dead flesh around it, the missing itself. I had never before cut out a sea. I didn't expect it to bleed so much . . . but Aisha, listen to me. Love was punishing to some of them."

"The punishment can never have been to have loved," Aisha said. "Are they still the same after? Doesn't it undo some vital thread that unmakes them?"

"Are people so delicate?"

"Do you hear yourself?" Aisha glared at him. "My father was defined by his love—I have cut him out! In his heart, are we even there? Did we bleed out with the rest of him—or were we never there? What if he didn't love us?"

Zubeir was silent in the wake of her outburst, which only made it worse.

She swiped at her eyes. "If you cut me, would I just be empty? Would I forget?"

"You've answered your own question," Zubeir said. "To forget, there must be something to forget. To cut love out, there must be love to begin with."

"What if . . . some people just can't love anything?"

Zubeir inched closer, ducking his head to look at her like an inquisitive child.

"What if—if I opened my heart and there was nothing?"

"And everything, too?"

"Either, both—it's terrifying. If I had nothing and everything to lose." Aisha buried her nose against her joined arms. "If I was still empty after everything, or if I still had something secret that you could snatch away. That could break me in half."

"Do you want to know something?" Zubeir asked. "You may already know, without having spoken—may have felt it like a rumour—so let me speak it. As a young boy I used to hear them say: keep your heart open, but the heart of your heart closed. Do you understand?" he murmured. "It's deeper than anatomy, deeper than body—we keep closest to ourselves that which is most dear. Deep in your heart—beneath the sea, beneath the lantern-eyed, many-toothed things, beneath the flying feathered fish and the many-eyed serpents, beneath the sunken boats and beneath even the bed of that ocean—there is another heart, and in that other heart, there is another name. Everyone has that other heart, a buried thing that cannot be killed, for to strike at it would be to rupture a wound beyond all wounds. I would have gone elbow deep into that cage, I would have gone swimming, I would have drowned before I ever could have reached that heart. Give him some credit. If he went, don't you think it wasn't only love, but shame, too? That he felt unworthy of you? Sometimes we keep love, real love, right next to our shame. Your father, that fool, loved you—and loves you still."

"I don't believe you," she whispered. "If I did, what does that change? I have done an ugly thing. I have severed him. I asked it done. It was wrong."

"Maybe, but it let him live. That is not the end of love; nothing is truly an end to love. There's always more. Even when you think there's nothing left. You find the sunken chest, and the sunken name. And it is still there, it will always be there, and truer for it."

"Did I love him?"

"Aisha," he sighed, "you idiot. Love . . . is like courage. It can make you leap to your feet or stay your sword, it can make you a fool, but it does not paralyse. If it is only cutting you and cutting you, then it isn't love, it's just something you call love so you can pretend a wound is beautiful. Love is not an eternal prison, is not a wound, is not a poison. It is an exchange, it is always returning. It nurtures and binds." He flicked sand at her. "Does that make sense?"

"It doesn't."

"Ha! Never mind—you'll marry one day and understand, and wish you didn't understand."

"I don't want to marry."

"Oh!"

"You're not married either."

"I'm a man," Zubeir said. "Your Hababa married, your mother married. That is the way of things."

"I don't want to do things because that is simply the way."

"That's fair enough. It will take strength, courage, and, yes, even love, to forge your own way."

"I don't want to understand it the way you say that I'll one day understand it."

"Then what do you want?"

Want. That word, she'd never really had an answer for before, or at least one she'd dared let herself understand. There had been that great sea, and now the return.

She wanted to know her own heart. She wanted Baba's forgiveness, to love her father, and she wanted him to love. She wanted Hababa to be happy with her and proud of her, she wanted to be the best that she could be for her family.

She wanted to go back, to see for herself what the whole world was like. To speak to the sea things and go to the House of Rust, and to feel Hamza draped over her shoulders and to tell him that she understood. That she loved him still, even for what he made sound like a betrayal. She would tell him that she had not yet been ready to learn the secrets of the world, but she would be soon. She would not need him this time, or be afraid of fear.

She would have the courage to go back to the sea, to leave home and forge her own way, the love to admit everything to them and the strength to build her own life with her own two hands.

"I don't want to pretend to be a sweet girl so that I don't alarm. I don't want to forget, and more than that . . . I want to never regret again. Better I hate that I leapt than to bemoan that I never did. I want to go back, Zubeir—and I want you to promise me never to cut out my heart."

"Even if you beg me?"

"I will never beg," Aisha decided. "Not for that."

CHAPTER SIXTEEN

Hababa's head lay against the wall. Aisha drew out the mattress and pushed it next to where Ali slept, before coaxing her grandmother into it. She tried to stay awake as well.

But she was dreaming she was submerged in the water that had spilled from her father's heart. Ghostly serpentine ribs shucked through the dark, rattling like metal springs. She held her breath but bubbles escaped her mouth, rippling up. This disruption alerted the creature and it turned now toward her in dangerous lethargy. She held her breath, she heard her name.

"Aisha," Ali said, "please, some water."

She was fully awake now. That was usually what people asked for, right before they died.

Her front was damp where she'd spilled in the hurry. He drank down one glass and she refilled it four more times. He gulped and gulped and then gasped. "Don't do what I just did. It's three sips, then a breath, right? I'm very tired."

"You sound like Mama. Telling me not to do what she was doing, but to do it correctly."

"I did, just now? Imagine."

He played with the glass, coarse thumb pulling clear notes that smeared at the end, like the music of a slippery disk. He looked young in his hesitation, and she hated the pity that welled in her heart. "The worst thing my father ever did was not be God. He was like the mountain that cleaves the land in half and diverts the stream. I was like the stream, something that obeys, but wants to be a mountain, too. I was frightened of him the way the imam wants you to be terrified of God, but he was just a man—flawed, prideful, yet sometimes kind and unjust like a man. I negotiated who I was allowed to be because I wanted him to be proud, not curse me. But I could never slot myself into place. I couldn't stand to demean him with my pity and trying to hate him only made me sad—I told myself he's only an old man, what I want from him is . . . in some other language he doesn't know. He had a father, too, someone who made him look to his own future fatherhood as an effort in correction. I couldn't hate him and didn't want to shame him with my love, so I kept that to myself, too. I won't be like him. Do you pity me, Aisha? Do you hate me? How I have failed you, how you must succeed."

"No, Baba, I could never hate you."

"I wasn't running from you. I know it's what your grandmother always says, but I wasn't. I used to run before, but I don't anymore." His face closed with pain and she watched him clutch at his chest and muffle his groan. "Sacrifices made my father tough, and my mother tougher. This toughness hurts Mama. Don't ever be tough of heart, Aisha."

"What were you thinking, travelling so far? We want for nothing that we can't borrow or earn in time."

"Now you sound like your mother."

"Why did you go?"

"I wanted to see marvellous things."

"Why didn't you try to come back?"

He couldn't lie, so he stayed silent.

"Did you even think of what would happen? Losing you would have destroyed me!"

"You're strong like your mother."

"*You* are my strength! You and Hababa. I am too young to leave you, or to be abandoned by you, not in that way."

"I was weak. It was all a trick—the sea was cold and deep and dark and wet. I'd committed myself to going forward. How could I come back with my hands empty? I'd have brought grief with me. I am that fool. I should have died."

"You're lying."

"No. I am a coward and I should have died."

"I don't believe you."

"I am a weak man with nothing to show for my travels."

"Don't speak of my father that way!"

He fell silent under her orders, then laughed so he would not weep.

"I met the monsters," Aisha said. "The first who loved you, the second who sank you, and the third who ate you. I was hated by all of them. The first was jealous, the second was cruel, the third was a liar. None of them helped but to tell me *go forward and die*. But I went forward and I did not die. *We* did not die. If I hadn't come . . . the cat must have known everything all along. I know why you left better than you think I do. There's a great world out there with so much to see and survive, it must make you feel small. But I don't feel small anymore. Baba, I'm sorry, you wouldn't wake up so I had . . . I had Mze Zubeir cut your heart!"

". . . my heart?"

"He said you were dying of heartbreak. Did the journey break your heart?"

"Yes."

"It wasn't what you thought it would be?"

"It was," he said. "But I was sad."

"Why?"

"Because I'd left you."

"One day I'll leave you, too," she said, forgiving him. "It's all right."

"You'll marry someone close. I'll still see you."

"No, Baba," Aisha said. "One day I'll go. On a boat, looking for someone of my own—but not a husband."

His hand tensed in hers. He understood her meaning. But he did not protest yet.

"I saw strange things as well on my journey to you. Do you want to hear the story?"

"I want to hear whatever you want to tell me, Aisha."

So she bowed close and told him, beginning to end.

~

The day after Aisha and her father returned, after she had commanded him not to call her *fishling*, Zubeir made a decision.

He had always walked past Swafiya's house without looking at it. If he'd seen her on the step he'd greet her with the same warmth he gave everyone else and no more. That day Zubeir slowed. This time, Zubeir brought his scarred, tan hand to knock.

He waited there for the stubborn girl to open the door. She greeted him with surprise, and relief. "You're sweating, Mze Zubeir!"

"The heat is really awful."

Aisha had grown bolder. Her face, flat and unexpressive, communicated the great irony of his words as she extended her arm out into the air, the drizzle splattering on her skin.

She had not called him a liar, so he could not berate her.

Zubeir sighed, eyes rising to an overcast sky—the colour of old ash. With the brim of his hat opening his face to it, water darted into one of his eyes, making him sigh again. "Did you lose your manners in the sea? What did the doctor say?"

And behold! A smile! She was a beauty in that singular moment. He made a note to bring it up later to anger her. "He wasn't very worried, it should be all right. A lot of rest is needed," Aisha said, more collected. "Baba woke up, but he's gone back to sleep."

"I expected there to be a crowd."

"People have dropped things off, to help us. But since Baba needs rest, they've been told to stay away for a while. They've obeyed for now."

"You're surprised."

"I should have a better opinion of others. I expect Hababa would grow angry if I turned you away. She'd berate me endlessly."

Zubeir swallowed, his throat dry. If he hesitated now . . . whenever he took an action, he was sure of himself.

Aisha waited for him to come in so she could close the door. She told him to wait, darting in to ask her grandmother if she was ready to receive him.

Ali lay on the bed, looking only a little less corpse-like than yesterday. He slept on his back, arms folded over his chest like one as well. Zubeir wondered how the wound was doing, felt a rush of pain to recall it. Strange, it was not regret, or even guilt—he saw Swafiya's precious boy, and could not separate the two.

Swafiya rose, and he noticed her then, shaking himself awake. "Mze Zubeir," she said softly. Her eyes were circled with silver, her hands were humbly folded over one another. "I heard that it was you—"

"I beg you do not."

His fingers curled into a fist even as he forced levity into his tone. Aisha had not told her grandmother the truth, else Swafiya would rip out his eyes for letting her granddaughter run into the sea, and for cutting open her son. He did not mind either. Aisha's eyes were wide with warning. He could not betray her in this, a man's truths are his own—he was here to speak his. He forced levity into his voice. "It was not me who found him, or saved him. Please don't waste your thanks on me."

Swafiya pulled at her fingers, and he restrained the overwhelming urge to close the distance between them so he might cover them with his hand.

"Your granddaughter told me that his health will return."

"I'm praying for it."

"I am, too." Zubeir smiled gently. "And you?"

"Come again?"

"How are you, Swafiya?"

"I'm all right."

"Forgive me, but I had to come see you. May I sit?"

He could see her go to war with herself, her gaze alighting on her granddaughter, her son, him—measuring how to cordially refuse him, to limit the witnesses, to stop him from causing any scene. Oh Swafiya! Always wanting things to proceed within a previously agreed upon design. Swafiya and he were never unkind to one another, but they had naturally never spoken together as they'd spoken when they were younger. She was worried, she was suspicious.

She opened her mouth, but he interrupted her. "Let the girl stay, I'm not hungry or thirsty. I didn't come here to shame you with the past. I know you have never liked to be alone in a man's company. May I sit?"

Swafiya was still worried but she sat down herself, which allowed him to settle on the floor.

"It is too late, I always told myself. You are hammering at cold iron."

"Mze Zubeir—"

He did not like the title from her. He shook his head gently. "Now you will call me an old man?" They were bitter words, but he spoke them with a warmth. "Yes, soon, we will die."

Looking at him, he saw in her eyes the indescribable feeling that she had to watch him, she had to keep her eyes on him at all times—as if he were an unchecked fire, a breeze winding itself at the highest tight rope, she had to watch him, she had to stay awake.

"Zubeir, what have you come here to do?"

Zubeir grinned boyishly at her, brash and brazen as a man forty years younger, far too handsome for his own good. And then that handsome slyness evaporated and he pulled his hat away from his head and bowed his eyes. "I love you."

She was, perhaps for the first time in twenty years, robbed of speech.

"I love you, Swafiya," Zubeir said, speaking from a badly buried place. "I've loved you since you were ten, bossing around the young ones and catching beetles. I loved you when you loved your husband—in Old Town, in Kibokoni, on land, in the sea. I loved you with your long hair, and then with your short hair. I loved you when you covered it. I loved you, strong even before you had to grow up. I loved you, cussing out the children and turning sunflower seeds over. I loved you when you were within my sight, and I loved you when you left it. I loved you in the war, when everything was on fire, when everyone was dying. I loved you after you refused to have me. I loved you when your words put strength in me. I loved you when you weakened me. I loved you with your belly swollen with the son you loved. I loved you when you lied to me. I loved you when I ran from you. And I love you now, too." He spoke to the earth now. "Swafiya," his voice strained with a true and long-carried pain and tender sweetness, *"you are my entire heart."*

Swafiya's lips went frightfully thin, and tears glimmered in lines down her cheeks. "You were cruel. You hurt me."

"I was wrong. I let you hurt me, you are the only one who ever could." He bowed his head in pain. "I thought I could cut you out, but I could not bear it. The punishment was not to be hurt by love, but to forget it. I could not forget. I never wanted to."

When they were young, Swafiya was easy to anger and just as quick to cool. She had the same way of swelling now, full of the fire of womanly indignation. "What do you mean by telling me all these things?"

"You hag." Zubeir laughed, but it was wet with tears. "Haven't you been listening? I love you."

"What is love *now?* It is unseemly—"

"You love a scandal, Swafiya—but I won't indulge you that. Here is our chaperone, dead to the world, but it must matter to someone so we'll forget that technicality. I want to be a husband."

"Ali is asleep."

"I am not asking your son to marry me," Zubeir said. "I am asking you."

"You insolent old fool," Hababa protested. "I cannot marry you!"

"Why not?"

"Ali—"

"You want me to ask your son's permission as I asked your father's?" Even her protests were helpless. "You are a free woman, aren't you? No one is listening anymore, no one will pinch you and berate you for pretending you are the perfect girl, unspoiled and unheard. He is a little chick still. You are a grown woman, married and widowed. With her own mind, her own heart, her own will. I will not ask another if I can have you. I ask *you*, Swafiya. I ask you, will you have me as your husband?

"I am barren."

"You think I come here to you as though you were cattle to sire me children?"

"I will not wait on you hand and foot!" Swafiya hissed in outraged hope. "Not at my age!"

"That you have been a wife and a mother is a part of you. I will love those parts and not speak against them, but these are not the only places where honour and grace lie. I'd love you if you burned water and poisoned my food, breakfast or no breakfast. If you never cooked or cleaned at all. I can feed myself and clean myself. I've lived alone too, Swafiya. I want to care for you now as well as I'd care for myself."

"I am haggard." She hid her face with her leso. "My body is worn out, I am not a beauty."

"Are you looking for compliments? How sly. I am handsome enough for all of us."

"You were a child—"

"You were not much older."

"I am an old woman." But she was crying, and her protests were no use. There was no more escape, and therein there was freedom— she could not be imprisoned anymore, for he would not allow it.

"And I an old man," Zubeir said.

Hababa was angry but grateful for his audacity, and she still hid her face, shoulders shaking, but he had heard her. She called him a fool, a wastrel, a cruel demon—but he had heard her say yes.

Aisha looked at him with wonder.

But these two crazy old people, they laughed, even as they wept.

CHAPTER SEVENTEEN

Ali did not go back to the sea. He returned one day from walking the town to tell them he had gotten an apprenticeship with a carpenter. His face had glowed with a shy, boyish happiness. Hababa had really cried then! How relieved she was that her son had finally come to his senses and sought what was better and safer for him.

"Don't you worry about me?" Zubeir had demanded at the after-wedding lunch when he was told. "I face dangers, too."

"You are old enough that it won't be a waste."

"Oh ho!" Zubeir gripped his heart. "Will you sit ida so carelessly?"

"You're right. Don't inconvenience me by making me lose four months for nothing!"

Aisha choked on water and two people pounded on her back until she was well.

"That's unusual," Ali said. "You're usually very careful when you eat."

Hababa withdrew her fist, worry shuffling into irritated disapproval. "You know it's said that when someone is discussing you, you suddenly choke. I wonder what they're saying. You must start being more ladylike, Aisha."

"Yes," Zubeir agreed, having observed her walloping. "You must eat as neatly and sweetly as a kitten. *Are you mad?* Let the girl eat how she likes!"

"She needs to think about her future," Hababa countered, with an unshakable wisdom stubborn enough to ward off all challenges.

Zubeir sighed. It was a logic as apart as the stars. "I'll pity your husband if he gets a bride with no class."

"Don't listen to her, but nod," Ali said. "She's feeling especially proud of herself that she can say these things because she got married, so she's having airs."

Aisha finished clearing her throat, but she was still a little wheezy. "It's true, Hababa, newlywed girls always get very bossy and haughty about their marriages—and talk down a lot to girls. Even if they are age mates, they behave as though they are no longer peers and start sitting with the older women and acting very strange."

"Marriage safeguards a woman's honour."

"Look at this sagely wife," Zubeir marvelled, unbearably fond.

"How dare you all mock me! It's true, Aisha you'll know one day."

"I don't want to get married. I'm going to travel the world."

Hababa, with astonishing openness, nodded. She reasonably accepted this request, then put her hands up in prayer, speaking intensely. "God," she said piously, powerfully, "please give Aisha a husband to travel the world with."

Ali laughed into his glass. Aisha decided not to frown. Getting into this kind of fight with Hababa, today, was poor strategy.

Hababa cracked one eye open when no one said *ameen.*

Zubeir's grin was cheeky. Ali's look was one of such supreme nonchalance it would have inflamed violence in the most peaceful of saints, and Aisha did begin to frown.

Ali decided then to raise his palms in prayer, rice grains glistening on his fingers. "God, please give us *all* what is good for us and put us on the path of *kheir*, for indeed only you know what is best, and what lies in it *kheir*."

"Ameen." Hababa drew the word out with a kind of suspicion. The others echoed the sentiment, approving this circumvention.

Mze Zubeir pinched Hababa's hand. She only stopped laughing disdainfully at this meek berating when he lifted her wrist and bit it lightly. This embarrassed her, which more effectively suited his purposes.

Ali's smile was full of joy and pain too. He ruffled Aisha's head, full of nervous energy as Hababa crowed at the impropriety. Zubeir soaked in this nagging like it was a warm bath. Aisha smiled at her father, to tell him she loved him, and when she moved to begin clearing the plates he shook his head. "There's no rush," he said. "Let's sit a little more."

So she stayed, and father and daughter absorbed the antics of two happy fools. Baba had insisted on being Wali to the marriage, now he was well enough. The religious authority who had overseen it had seemed confused the entire time, that two people would marry at this age. This private affair was sure to inflame the mouths of the town with new gossip. Hababa would be the woman who starred in a fresh batch of lies, but she did not seem to mind. She had relayed many stories and myths in her time, so it fit that she was at the heart of her own.

~

Ever since Aisha had tripped into the deep dark sea of Baba's heart she saw and did not forget so easily.

In the day she did her usual chores. Now that Baba had recovered, she was shocked (and a little embarrassed) to find him even helping her. By afternoon, when she was sure he was out and before Hababa could force her to lunch at hers, Aisha saw to her two guests.

Bird-fish Ndoto now lived in the big box tin that used to hold halwat hania. A gift from one of Jedh's old friends. No matter how she washed it, when she popped open the top, a perfume of crystallized sesame sugar still emanated from it. Its corners were going to a muddy rust. Aisha cleaned it, filled it with sea-water, and piled some pretty rocks to make an island. She pierced holes in the lid before transferring the creature into it. Its short scales like sharpened feathers, Ndoto had pulsed in the cradle of her hand like a slowing heart. Lowering it in she waited a little, to see if it could swim by itself, or if the stress of all these happenings was going to kill it for sure.

It felt like hours before it stirred. She opened the loose prop of her fingers, and it wriggled slowly, seeping into the surrounding water. She talked to it as she did these things, informing it of every step before she executed it—perhaps for her own comfort, perhaps to be as gentle as possible. She told it she did not yet know what she was to do with it, despite these unfortunate circumstances.

She could not kill it, but she could not let it slip back and rot Baba's heart. It did not speak and did not leap for escape whenever she popped the lid to slip it crumbled-up bread. Perhaps still too weak to go? Certainly too weak to refuse the name she suggested to it.

Ndoto. Dream: as pretty as, as impossible. Its lushly winged feathers had stripped away, and the brittle scales underneath those feathers had been chipping away too. But sometimes when she opened the lid to speak to it, to feed it, it glowed emperor gold and glassy, grass snake green, then the deepest pink, tangerines, and crimsons of sunsets. The time of the day, as they would look, glowing choppily on the sea.

"A dream is not a pet," Zubeir had said when she'd showed him in his seaside shack. Aisha did not want a pet. It was not right to keep anything locked up like this. But she could not free it, for wouldn't it go back to Baba?

"Why did you bring this to me?" Zubeir had rubbed his mouth. "Aren't you afraid I'll throw it into the fire?"

"I want to do the right thing."

"Were you thinking of doing the right thing when you caught it?" He had called her reckless, as if he were calling her brave.

The tin went under her bed. Turning away from the thick, blinking thwacks of the hidden eye, she listened instead to Ndoto ever winding and unwinding through the water, in peaceful murmur. It was the sound of the sea.

Hababa and Zubeir quietly married, and nothing changed except that Zubeir would come to sleep there in the evenings. He still spent the majority of his time at work on the sea, at the port with the shark hunters, or in his seaside shack—which he dragged Aisha into helping him clean. Hadn't he inherited a dutiful granddaughter? They got rid of all the old newspapers, relocated colonies of crabs and mice—and even fixed the roof. It was becoming homely enough that it might lose its reputation as a house of terror and become a tempting accommodation for the wastrels and restless wanderers of the beach.

"What will you do now?" he wondered. "What is your future like?"

Life had reassumed its shape, dimensions slightly altered. But even the slightest adjustment in the body of the globe will drastically change its spin. Time would have gone on as usual if she had not noticed the air's flavour. There was a deepening of senses, as though Aisha could feel through her feet the thrumming of the earth's heart.

She had seen too much to continue as before. Zubeir had seen things. He told her about how his father had been a heart cutter, how his mother's grandmother had been a princess, back when Mombasa had had its wild kings. It was comforting to hear him speak of these things. He had decided not to pass on the art, for he had no children, and cutting hearts brought all sorts of troublesome characters. He was too old to set up a practice, he said. Subtly, he had asked if she wanted to know the art—but how could she? It was not her legacy to inherit; her future was shaped differently.

She found the thread that would start her journey by accident. She decided she would find Hamza. She would need direction, a vessel, a weapon. More than anything she would need experience. She had told her father the entire tale of her journey beginning to end. He had nodded along, but ever since he had found employment on land, she knew she could not ask him to return to sea. She looked for her education by herself, studying the beach and tagging along with Zubeir and his fiercely shy shark hunters. Blood all up their arms, gutting sharks and addressing her feet whenever she visited.

It was fighting with Hababa that led her to her revelations. Hababa had tugged on one of Aisha's brittle, lank curls. "You've had a busy day running about with Zubeir, I see! You really should stay out of the sun, and do something about this hair. We'll grow it out and strengthen it."

"It's too hot for long hair," Aisha said. "And mine is always falling out."

"Don't be lazy."

Accusations upon accusations! "I don't want to get married, Hababa!"

"Have some pride as a woman."

"I don't like anyone! And don't praise me for that! It's not as though I do it in service of something else. I don't like anyone at all like that, and I'm too young besides!"

Hababa would never make Aisha marry before she was ready, she always said. *But I must make myself ready, mustn't I?*

"Aisha . . . what do you want me to say? Have you no dreams? If you were interested in academics, I'd sell my teeth so you could become a professor. If you sought religious knowledge, I'd go begging up and down the street so you could go to Saudi Arabia. If you wanted, if you wanted anything," and she began to cry, "but you're like your mother—you never *tell* me anything, you just look and look, and stare empty-eyed, like you don't feel anything at all! It kills me to think you unhappy. I want you to have a house of your own, a life of your own, a future with someone who loves you! You think I'm being cruel by wanting you to be pretty? I want a good man to come for you!"

"That's not what I want!"

"What do you want?!" Hababa laughed bitterly, swiping at her eyes. "Travel the world? You think your father spends money so you can sail? You're living in dreams! What are you meant to do now, an Arab daughter, sailing the high seas? For *what?* It is cruel of Ali!"

"He isn't cruel!" Aisha exclaimed. "He's the only one who could understand what I want! I'm arguing with you, with everyone, telling me that not knowing what I want is indecisive and weak, but thinking to sway me when I *do* know what I *don't* want."

"You're keeping secrets, like your mother," Hababa said. "I never forced her and I won't force you. I can only guide you. I don't want you to regret being lonely. And I know she wasn't happy but I was trying my best!"

"Hababa, I'm learning how to go to sea because it's something I'm interested in! It's something I *want!*"

The truth would kill Hababa, if she even believed it. It would spoil everything, make her warlike from misunderstanding. She would blame Ali for being a poor father, Aisha for being strange, and Zubeir for not stopping her. Then she would cry, wounded by them. There was so much Hababa didn't know. Keeping her in the dark would be unkind and yet . . . she had just recently become happy, with a son who had decided to pursue a less dangerous livelihood, with a husband who had been her childhood love. Knowing anything at all would ruin *everything.*

What could Aisha do to find her own answers? Would she need to find the House of Rust in order to find Hamza? What *was* the House of Rust, beyond the abstract little she'd been told? Who could she ask, if Zubeir didn't have the answers?

And if she was able to gather all the things she needed, could she leave home without telling Hababa the truth? Could she leave without destroying this peace?

Could she tell the truth and trust Hababa to give her blessings?

Zubeir brought the interruption, taking off his shoes and singing his greetings. Aisha swallowed, Hababa lifted a brow. He settled next to Hababa comfortably, leaning back on the throw pillows. "What's going on?" he wondered, humming.

"It's this granddaughter of mine." Hababa grumbled. "Mannerless."

"*Hababa,*" Aisha begged under her breath.

"She has no ambitions, and no sense. She just wants to meander foolishly, and be like the masterless mombe of Mombasa."

"Hababa," Aisha closed her eyes. "It's *ng'ombe.* Not mombe."

"It's neither of those," Zubeir drawled. "It's *mbuzi.* Folk look after their cows, they're too expensive not to jealously guard, there is always a herder nearby. It's the *goats* who belong to no one. Don't be like the masterless mbuzi of Mombasa."

"Being masterless is supposed to be terrible?"

"You must have direction," Hababa decided, suddenly tolerant.

"Serve God and be true," Aisha agreed heatedly. "Yes! I can do that anywhere!"

Zubeir rolled his eyes at both of them. Aisha was ready to fight him, too, but . . .

Masterless.

She lowered her fist.

Belonging to no one. Like the cat who spoke the language of men . . .

There was a way, she realized, to have all her questions answered.

And that was to ask her questions of the same kind of odd folk who would have business knowing.

"Aisha," Hababa warned, suspicious of this sudden end to anger.

But Aisha had forgotten the argument entirely, occupied by other things. "Let me make some tea, all right?" she said, and went to do so, before she could be further distracted.

She could think of no other name for the eye than "Jicho," which meant . . . eye. Certainly he felt as ever present as one, never sleeping, always watching, absorbing. As unabashed as those shrews at the weddings, devouring all the details of the guests, with no care as to decency or kindness. A superior, cold, and unceasing staring that made her apprehensive.

Jicho, in understanding his captivity, was a cleverer hostage than Ndoto. He did not eat bread, but meat. Lids unfolding forward like the trapping beak of an octopus, rolling onto his prey and growing on it. Enveloping, twisting, trembling, wriggling as if he were ever digesting. Blinking up at her when she watched—it was like watching a shark grow a tongue—and to see that tongue licking, sucking at his teeth, wanting more . . .

She kept him in a big glass pickle jar, which despite cleaning still stunk of the briny carrots, sharp lemons, and green chillies that had soaked in it. She filled only a third with sea-water and floated in it a tiny plastic bottle cap where she could safely deposit the food without fearing for her fingers. She ran a glob of ghee down the sides of the tub before tightening the lid. He was a sneaky animal, always trying to slip upward toward escape, climbing stickily to where he was determined to go. She poked three holes through the lid using the thinnest meat-skewering stick. Not merciless, Aisha stood a brick in the jar so he could have somewhere dry to rest after his exertions.

When she scolded him, Jicho had a watching and waiting air that raised all the hairs on her arms. This was a creature full of cunning.

Jicho anticipated her and responded when he was talked to. And attempted escape less, as though to prove to her what an obedient and unhostile captive he was. She could not fault that strategy or feel particularly annoyed with it, seeing as she was playing the role of dungeon keeper.

From him she felt a self-aware being, readying himself for something.

As she could not play favourites, her own reasons for keeping them captive being murky, she sang and spoke to both of them. She would pull the tub from under her bed, feed Ndoto, and sing to him. Then she would put him back and go get Jicho to do the same, though with a little more reserve.

Aisha was never one for singing, not even as she worked. Singing was something Mama would do only at weddings. When Mama worked, she'd do it with soldierly toughness—making the bed as if she was ironing out steel. Moving about in the kitchen as if she would break everything that did not obey her.

No, that's not right. *Sometimes, when you were sick, Mama would sing to you.*

When Mama was praying, there was a songlike quality to it as well.

She sang old wedding songs, which were always nostalgic and a little smug, and a little warlike—they made her grin sometimes, and she found she could never be annoyed with them. They were too haughty and too much fun. Sometimes she made up her own words. Hamza had said she had poetry in her, which had shocked her a little and made her a little happy, and a little ashamed. *I am still your daughter, even if only a little.*

The feathered fish seemed to do better under her bed than as Jicho's neighbour.

Sheathing the jar in an old pillowcase, she put it away, hoping this would shield him from anyone's sight and shield her from his. The wood of the cupboard muffled its abnormally loud blinking. Even sitting still, Jicho blinked. Blinking, blinking, blinking—it was enough to drive anyone mad.

When she showed Zubeir, she had wanted more guidance than what he gave her. "I don't know what to do," he had confessed, thus unburdened and growing more boldly relaxed with himself. "Yes, I don't know what to do. You're a grown woman now, aren't you? You'll have to decide what you want to do with the things under your mercy."

Aisha hadn't wanted anything under her mercy. Before she had fed Jicho meat and sea-water, Aisha had shown him to Zubeir in the iodine-brown bottle stuffed with newspaper that had been his first prison on land. Shrivelled as a zabibu and dried up like hard lime, wrinkled and unappetizing—his appearance had been corpsewrinkly, the dry leatheriness of his lids blinking testament to his being alive. The odd sound had made even grown old man Zubeir recoil with a hiss, as though cockroaches had erupted over his skin, crawling over all of him. "Salala! What else do you have in that bag, odious girl? No more!"

She told him of the serpent that had followed their boat, singing its threats. How the cry of a leviathan had frightened it away. Had it been simply warning them, it might have been forgiven. But he was a servant to the Sunken King, taunting them, weaving underneath, threatening to jump into the boat. The serpent was the many-eyed umbilical cord from which the stone boy that had interpreted the Sunken King's words grew, and he had taken his nourishment from the very same monster. In the end, the serpent had wrapped around him like a dog seeking its master's protection.

"But the Sunken King sacrificed one of its masts and the serpent of eyes *fell* into the water." She paused and said, solicitous as she set the bottle on the floor, "I will show you how."

"I'd be blessed."

"Like this," Aisha said and threw her arms up outward, kicking herself to the side and leaning on one leg. "Wah! It fell. And the sharks began chewing, chewing it up."

"Mm hm."

She told Zubeir of his many eyes, sticking on everything. That Hamza, breaking one in his mouth, warned her not to let him touch her. She explained his gelatinous consistency, like a huge passion seed. Like faluda seeds but also more disgusting, like a boil. Not pleasing at all. She'd *had* to capture him else he would have rolled into the sea.

"What if it's like a seed? Like in December when it's so hot and seeds are all on the wind and the grass and the paths, and whenever you walk those tough little brown burrs stick to your clothes like ticks, just wanting to be carried and be born somewhere."

"It happens all year round."

"Well, that's when I start noticing all those clots on the back legs of the sheep and goats."

"It's the hottest time of the year. Maybe that does odd things to that brain of yours and makes the mundane extraordinary."

"It wasn't hot in the sea when *I* went. And it *rained* when I came back."

"Oh ho, so you bring blessings now?"

"That wasn't what I was saying. Do you mind?"

"So this one . . . is more *outrightly* villainous."

". . . yes."

"You have doubts."

"The cat deemed him dangerous but never explained why. I can't release him into the ocean lest he do some other person harm or grow into a serpent with even *more* eyes! I've hidden him in the cupboard where he's dying like the other dream—but Mze Zubeir, I can *hear* his strange, dry blinking—like the leathery thwack of a bat's wings. And I don't like it. What if Hababa comes in? When she visits us, she goes into every room to sniff at its lack of tidiness—she will definitely know there's something there. What am I going to *say* to her?"

"I tell you again that this is your problem to navigate. You're curious about a lot. If you have questions, seek answers through observation and come to a decision. Is it permission you want?" Aisha's jaw dropped. "Well, then, don't ask it. You've asked for advice, I've done what *I* can. You do what's best."

"What if it's wrong?"

"Do your best," he patted her head, "and figure it out."

Jicho's hungry alertness, his rapt focus when she spoke, unnerved her greatly. But she did her duty no worse than she'd done with Ndoto; she sang to them both. Fed them both, and then returned Jicho back into the cupboard.

She did this, her chores, and travelled Mombasa. She walked a lot. From Tudor to Nyali, Sparki, and Kiziwi. Travelling the land in search of information, Jedh's old satchel by her side, filled with corn and peas and fish-bones wrapped in newspaper. She went places where people would be less likely to know who she was, trying to discreetly escape notice and gossip. She was already remarked upon as an eerie girl; she didn't need to distress her family further.

At night, she quickly checked on her captured guests again, and then lay down to sleep. There were no mosquitoes in her room anymore; even the mjiskafiris who usually slithered on the ceiling were gone. Usually she'd stay awake, angrily, tensely waiting for one of them to drop down and thwack on her face. Those malicious creatures . . .

Were gone. Aisha curled on her side. With Ndoto under her bed, her ear, pressed against the dry cottonseed pillow, felt as if it were pressed against a sea-shell—waves swirling and eddying, wakefulness racing from her. Jicho's blinking had kept her awake for many nights, the old bottle a chamber, augmenting the suctioning echoes of the eyelid. But with the jar in the cupboard it was not so bad. And with Ndoto under her bed, she could hardly hear the blinking. Perhaps that was why Ndoto was doing better, because it preferred the dark, without such a shady neighbour close at hand, staring at it.

Aisha fell asleep quickly. She had her usual dreams, most of them forgettable, but she always had one dream that did not feel like a dream at all.

Deep underwater she floated in a darkness so complete that she felt as adrift as the moon in a starless sky—anchored in place, waiting for time to revolve, but incapable of movement herself. And like the moon, she felt the light of a blistering sun at her back, the glowing presence of a larger being.

With difficulty did she turn, not of her own will—but by the water's capriciousness, turning her gently by her shoulders, her feet swinging slowly as her hips twisted away first.

There was a familiar skeleton, swinging through, and as she turned, so did its eye come to attention.

She looked up and saw endless dark; she looked down, right, left. She was surrounded by the cold, clear, dark.

It was turning toward her, its tail twisting. It raced toward her, eating distance, its procession fast.

She tried to hold her breath longer, fists closing tight, brow contracting, crushing bubbles that floated up between her clenched fingers. A perfume of flowers, bright and blooming, knifed at her lungs, coating her tongue.

She tried to hold her breath and let it meet her, but the air would run out and the water would rush in and so would the light. And above her was the shadowed ceiling of her room. Her lungs burned from the sudden rush of oxygen, cramping up and blistering her throat. The smell of flowers, as though there were petals crushed beneath her pillow, would fade away with wakefulness.

Sweat would rise on her strained body, speckling her like seawater, and her ears would pop from pressure like the diver's.

In the day, she taught herself to hold her breath for longer. Between her tasks she would sit and focus on her lungs, her heart, and hold her breath until she felt dizzy.

She had to train her lungs, train her body.

Something was coming to meet her.

She would meet it.

CHAPTER EIGHTEEN

A troupe of goats, white and busy, chomped at the grass around the cemetery. Twitchy weeds rolled between their grinding jaws. They stepped on headstones, collapsed themselves against stone angels and weeping saints. Yawning, they butted against the black bars of the boundary, occasionally becoming fixed on the fencing, stuck.

Aisha's advance into this busy ring went unnoticed, even when she jumped the fence studded with stuck goats, until she was done picking up her third goat. Then news of this stealthless creeper went among the rest of the party in a confused jumble—and they skipped in dismay around her while Aisha set the third kid down to heft the fourth one up. She greeted it seriously. "Habari ya leo," she rumbled sternly, and then, "Have you heard of a scholarly cat?"

The goat wailed in protest. Receiving no further answer, Aisha carefully set it back on its hoofs as if it were a chair she'd knocked over in the middle of the night, quietly and quickly. Moving on to the next goat, she apologized for the inconvenience.

She continued in this straightforward manner—businesslike, executing the bizarre. "Does anyone know how to speak the language of men?" The warbled moan of the truly oppressed. "Have you heard of a cat called Hamza?" The weeping of the bereft and the stepped on. "Or a cat that has called itself Hamza?" A chattering, gummy show of teeth. "Yes, I am very sorry." This one sat in her arms, legs dangling stiffly, playing statue. "Sawa, haya sawa! Where is your chief?"

The goats grew agitated, rattling around her in a distressed dance. She still had the youngest in her arms, or at least the smallest. She was a hardy girl, she'd been told with a sigh. She'd like to think she was, but her arms would get tired soon. This lightest one, realizing he was not going to be put aright like a vase, tossed his legs about and let out the most plaintive of cries.

His cry rippled through the rest, baying yells vibrating their tongues in answering congregation. Aisha, pitiless, and becoming slightly sour with these dramatics, adjusted the anarchist on her hip, clicking her tongue in admonishment. "Heh-weh! I know we are near the Little Theatre"—the production house that was as gothic as the cemetery it faced—"but there's no need for such dramatics! Come on, let's look for him! Let's look for your chief!" She clicked her tongue again, in a determined attempt at gathering authority over their panic. "I've no intention to eat you, so you can please stop. Let's look."

She walked deeper into the cemetery, patiently half turning toward them to indicate her desire to have them be reasonable and follow. They quietened a little—or *were* quieting before a disruptive yell sprang out of one of the goats.

If there was a talking cat, then perhaps there were other talking cats? Did it not stand to reason, other talking things? Strays she'd chased, wrestling them into audience had seemed to cost her more than anything. Aisha liked to think she had in the past developed a neighbourly rapport with the wild animals that roamed their streets— a civilized tending of boundaries where she respected them and they ignored her as tolerance. She fed them on occasion and they never menaced one another. Destroying this diplomacy was agony to her.

The neighbours were finding her odd again, only it was more unbecoming of her age—Hababa would soon learn of her shenanigans, gossip would hurt and inflame her, and it would become a Whole Matter.

Mindful of conducting her investigations too close to home, Aisha ventured out looking for some creature who would speak to her. She mulled over what Hababa had said and after bothering the cats of Old

Town, arms stinging mildly from the day's clawing, she'd thought, *Of course!* It was so simple she pinched her tongue between her teeth in exclamation.

The masterless mombe—*mbuzi* of Mombasa came in many herds, shades, and sizes. They are usually more than ten strong and unusually (but not to a local) have no herder close by, if at all. One might think the people of the coast are so lazy that they sleep on the job and care not to guard their livestock. That is a foolish one.

No one ever stole from the masterless procession—well, no one ever stole them for long. Goat thieves would return the kidnapped kids very quickly, and seek out other humans to stammer and confess the confused crime and the mind-bending reversal of their convictions.

When you heard their tales, you had to pity the poor thieves for not knowing any better and comfort them.

No, you did not dare bother the masterless goats of Mombasa, it was simply known.

You did not steal them, kill them, eat them, pester them. They were harmless and it did you no good to interfere with them or harm them. What would you achieve?

Aisha watched her step, muttering apologies to the dead she trod over as the goats followed, having no such reservations. She needed to find the Big Billy.

He couldn't be far. Every herd always had a Big Billy: a male goat the size of a young cow. Had he been in the herd, would he have attacked her? She would have jumped the fence immediately. With that getting farther and farther away, she could . . . climb a tree? Leadership would know better how to answer her questions.

The worst of the year's heat was over, the rains having returned, and today was one of the few sunny days. Mild, even pleasant. Aisha worked up a sweat nonetheless, weighed on one side by satchel and on the other by kid, navigating the graves as best as she was able, dewy, manicured grass scratchy on her ankles.

The Big Billy lay against a great graphite angel, rolling cud in its mouth, regarding his surroundings with blasphemous irreverence.

His gaze drew toward Aisha as she arrived before drawing past in continued dismissal.

"Peace," Aisha greeted, making her voice strong.

She was ignored.

Her brow twitched, dislodging a bead of sweat that dripped into her eye. When she was not addressed in welcome or to be chased away, she turned toward the rest of the goats seeking a recovery. "I understand why you would be upset and I apologize, I'm putting this small one down."

Unhanded, the kid turned to fully absorb her idiocy, so she might fully absorb his disregard. A sharp cry from his mother had her giving Aisha one last pointed glance before she trotted away.

Aisha scowled. If it was ever her intention to truly take a hostage in the first place, then she never would have let him go!

"I'm sorry." The sharpness brought on by her indignation undercut her sincerity. "I have a few questions. You'd help me greatly by answering whatever you can." She said more solemnly: "I'm sorry."

They had not run away, but, no longer restless, were halfway through forgetting her already. To lose her audience and her argument . . . Aisha sighed, and glanced just in time to see the Big Billy blink one heavily lashed, slit-pupiled eye to unseat the fly that had been resting there.

She soon had a sifting of uncooked sunflower seeds in her right hand, and a carrot in her left. "Excuse me," she hemmed politely, and waited for the billy to intervene. When he only burped, she approached the herd, tentatively armed. "Sunflower for all of you, to apologize for coming upon you like this."

She let the closest goat sniff at her palm, then bury his face in it. There was more wet sticky tongue than the scrape of teeth, unpleasant but not frightening.

The next huffed at her other hand, but her arm shot up, holding the carrot high in the air. "Carrots!" she gasped, "are for those with answers, sorry!"

She might as well have been speaking to goats. They were slow to take interest in her again until they noticed their brothers eating, thus the commotion restarted itself. Aisha couldn't refill her palm fast enough, shaking off the slobber webbing her fingers—nor could she hold the carrot high enough!

They began to chew at her clothes, nip at her satchel, wanting directly what they had intelligently surmised as the source of this bounty. "Bad manners! Haven't you any shame?" Aisha scolded them, jerking away from another tough-skulled bump.

Neither.

Wrestling her satchel to her chest, she hid the carrot. Aisha huffed, dumping the satchel back on the ground and sitting on it, arms folded and jaw set.

They could not get at it, so they settled in to wait, biding the time by chewing on her collar and drooling along her ear.

She glowered at nothing so she would not glower at the Big Billy, but she huffed finally, twisting around to study his profile. He was large enough lying down, horns pointed, at an angle—grey and a little dull, but still dangerous, if she made herself more than just a tolerated nuisance.

Goats were strange-looking animals, monstrous in some storytellings. Their eyes like subtraction symbols—to hear one's eerie braying in the night-time had demonic connotations. They had seemed gentle to her, minding their own—for every witch-like association there were several godly ones. That had to be respected.

The goat gnawing at her sleeve saw that her new position offered new avenues, and began chewing on her hair. Aisha's eyes slipped shut, searching for calm, or calm's more dignified sister: patience.

She found only summery dark and the back of her neck growing sticky from slobber.

She opened her eyes, forging on. "Do you know anything in regard to the House of Rust?"

Silence.

". . . no? Then a cat called Hamza. He spoke the language of man, do you know of him? Can you speak the language of man? Have I

167

offended? Will you answer yes or no questions? If yes, blink your right eye. If no, blink your left one." She waited. "I would be grateful if you helped. It's a bit important to me. Very important. I'd really, really like your help. Do you understand?" ·

The Big Billy responded by *falling asleep*.

Aisha clapped her nose between her hands, bowing her head in wearied plea for grace in the midst of unreasonable circumstances. Nothing happened. Aisha sighed and stood up. Now her nose was sticky. Great. She had never been one for sighing so much! She picked up her satchel before it could be chewed at like some old root.

Five carrots, no sunflower left. Guarding her bag by stuffing it between her arm and side, she went about breaking the carrots into small pieces; she did so rather roughly as she had not brought a knife.

The goats that had patiently been chewing on her got to their feet, keen on these snapping sounds. None of them had given her the answers she had come looking for, but she distributed the orange chunks around anyway.

"With faith, all right?" she sighed, leaving them. As she scaled the small fence, two crows swept ahead of her, gliding low and scything high, pointing her way home.

CHAPTER NINETEEN

The weird girl had gone to and fro with a mysterious bag. A university student's worn-out cast-off given away before it could shame. The accessory competed with her in unstylishness. It had for a time carried an odious foulness. This foulness was in her house now, with an instinct parallel to the instinct of hunger, with similar acuteness; the crows felt the heat of it like the heart of a dying beast. Parallel, like a distorted reflection, monstrously wrong. It did not tempt their irascible hunger; the foulness made them sick, and they did not want to eat its rotted meat. Never, never, never.

She took this bag to interrogate the beasts of Mombasa but left the cursed rot at home.

White Breast and Gololi glanced at one another despite their reluctance to move so fluidly as one mind. They could not whisper their suspicions, for that would be repugnant, uncrow—nor could they yell lest all manner of animals discern the plot before they had a chance to execute it. Yet they could not move without the agreement of the rest of their kin, in the absence of their lordship. Locked in conspiracy and unhappy with the conditions, yet begrudgingly proud of their own slyness, even if it was confirmed by the lesser other.

Fifteen years ago, in an event the crows remembered as *Fujo Fujo Kubwa Kubwa*—or the Great Noisiness—they had made a mistake, gathering in Old Snake's neighbourhood. This very neighbourhood.

There had been a wedding, and the crows had gotten carried away over the booty, spinning black chakacha across the roofs. They had not seen their lord for some time and had been careless in revelry, thinking Old Snake had lost his fangs.

But if Almassi was ever asleep it was the crows who woke him up. Almassi had eaten one of his special guests not a week before, and they thought he would be like the python, gorged and slow as he lay in his home, digesting. It was a delicate time of Almassi's cycle, and the crows had made it a careless time. It was one thing to make noise when Almassi was awake, and quite another when his body was in the process of nourishment.

The Burned One, house speaker, remembered diving into the sea, a hundred black crows, like a thrown buibui, in order to quench their fiery talons. They had underestimated a danger many years ago, and would not underestimate the girl who had killed the monster. Gololi and White Breast, despite their protests, had been charged with investigating her.

"We cannot approach Old Snake directly," the Burned One had said. "We must find proof, must wait for the other animals to ask him to act."

What greater proof than what was within the house? That poisonous foulness . . .

If the crows started a war then Almassi would kill them. Other creatures could be convinced to make an application to him and complain. Old Snake was not their lord but he was crownless warden of this island. The crows would not act recklessly again.

Outside the wedded dead wedding singer's home White Breast spoiled their camaraderie by proposing they break in. Gololi swooped down from his post atop the TV satellite to knock him with his talons.

Surely Gololi had only been looking for an opportunity to berate him, toppling him unfairly from the clothesline! The crows clattered down, caught in the weird girl's bedding.

They wrestled to get free of it, madly kicking at one another. And emerged from it heaving for breath, picking at their feathers, as though hunting some infection. It would not do to smell like the weird girl—what if she took notice of them?

They stood panting on the little yard roof, too afraid to even squabble. Their eyes searched for enemies. They had used up their bravery for the day and felt it no blow to their pride to evacuate and return to this errand at a later date, after discussing the next point of action with their superiors.

Just as they were about to do so, a presence made them tense and freeze. As though they were glued to their shadows. Even then, White Breast, that enterprising idiot, still had something to prove. It was he who turned his head first, and then Gololi, whose dignity was more precious than life and who would not be outdone by such a low member, turned as well.

Hassan stood in the roof's entryway with a tray of eggs in his arms. Gangly, long-faced as a dog, and insufferably *un*threatening.

Gololi was enraged. "Is it not interminably rude to come into a house when the homeowners are gone?"

Hassan stuttered at this welcome—rebuke is, after all, understood in all languages—and guiltily he flushed, glancing at the bedding they had toppled. Ah, had he spent all week trying to gather the courage to come? Her father's return meant he had the excuse.

"Look at the stupid look on his face," White Breast said. "Surely you must understand, Gololi."

They bent their heads, pitying him to remind themselves of their own power.

"I seek refuge from God and the devil," Hassan said doubtfully, seeming more confused than afraid. A true idiot. He said it three more times.

Cannibalistic devil massacrists the crows were called, but they were only demons in spirit; their comings and goings were not governed by exorcisms. They did not disperse but viewed him with the same odd fearlessness of crows—that intentness, hiding neither its attention nor its intelligence.

"He has come courting," the two crows said to one another, watching him from their place on the ground with a certain disdain, like two old uncles tutting at the nearly irreversible foolishness of youth as the youths went about pouring them coffee, pretending nobly that they could not hear disapproval. "Unforgivable, unforgivable."

"It is truly shameless."

"Death cure him. Death cure him."

"Truly, I cannot bear the sight of him."

"If he had any honour he would kill himself. Has he no honour?"

"A stupid, right in front of us. Look how he sighs."

The crows had been so frightened before that to make up for it they spoke civilly to one another, as though they were in no hurry to leave, talking now like two professors whose prejudices had been set aside to murmur at oddities that confounded them both.

Hassan must have known he was being discussed, but his human mind could not negotiate with this notion—rejecting it to place the tray of eggs (a prop!) behind the door as though to safeguard it from them.

Hopping aside, the crows saw him pick across the cement floor, through its broken glass and sharp rubble, and kneel down to pick up the bedding. Their disdain deepened as he shook it out, and they were supremely disgusted when he scolded them as softly as he would a pet that had gotten into his work things. A scolding! Fondly delivered! This they could not abide! But he was shaking out the bedding loudly, drowning their dismay, their cries of affront with the nonchalance of a true idiot, typical of his breed.

It was a faded white sheet, with a little bit of a flower border. Drab, even by the crows' understanding. But he was smiling at it as though he saw something familiar in it, that comforted his heart. Hassan sighed, sickening them, and Gololi was so upset that she aborted her plans to smash all the eggs behind the door, grown too despondent to act even on mischief.

Mischief itself is as crow as the crow's own blood, so naturally crow that it did not even need to answer any action as retaliation. Mischief enacted itself without prompt, inviting itself upon everything, as easy as breath. Mischief made the crow as much as its blood, as much as its beautifully black feathers. To see mischief drained from a crow? And not even have malice to replace it? No!

Alarmed, White Breast could bear it no longer. "Have you no shame?!"

Gololi settled into the earth, mindless as any hen. She had now seen all of living, it seemed, to understand she could no longer bear it and remain in her body. Exasperated to the point of defeat, at the indignity of others.

"At least have mercy and chase us!" White Breast demanded. Never one to accept running from weaklings without being given the proper send-off. "Chase us! Disgusting!"

"This is even worse than Old Snake," Gololi whispered, the eerie pitch frightening her fellow agent to tears. If Gololi, the loudest upstart in the flock, could *whisper*, things were truly dire. "He thinks that he is in love."

"How can one be in love with a monster girl weirdo?"

"What understanding have I of these ridiculous customs?" snapped Gololi, suddenly defensive. "Look at his stupid face. Oh, I can't look at it and stand him to live. I must die if I do not kill him."

"He wants to make a wife of her," White Breast realized, as the boy tenderly folded the unstylish bedding back onto the line and stood there smiling gently like an idiot. "How does one make a wife of a monster girl weirdo?"

"Perhaps they are eaten in the attempt," Gololi *drawled*, reticent and tired until White Breast pecked her savagely, surprising Hassan, who swiped worriedly at them to break up the fight.

"Fly!" White Breast wailed, bloodying his brother's side. "Fly!"

Gololi turned murderous, even as the boy stomped around foolishly, trying to save them from each other by crushing them clumsily.

A fight would have erupted for true, incompetent peacekeeper be damned, except Gololi now heard what White Breast had heard—the slither along the floor—and all the blood fled from their brains, into their wings. A torturous hiss they heard, like a breeze rasping between many branches, rattling gently the tinder-dry leaves.

The crows hurled themselves into the air with such madness their feathers shook free of them—as though their hastiness had mauled them from their bodies.

Hassan watched them disappear, standing in this odd slow rain. "Subhanallah," he exclaimed, untroubled, finally, done with the matter and moving from it without feeling any lingering curiosity to investigate it further or keep it at all in mind.

He grew embarrassed, worried that someone had seen him (and someone likely had, for Mombasa had a hundred eyes for every mouth) and worried that father and daughter would find him here, doing suspicious things with their washing. Which was how the girl's father came upon the boy, folding the laundry.

~

The new bride was weeping, and around her, family and wedding guests upturned the outdoor carpet. They lifted their skirts and tiptoed, shuffled, searching the grass—they whispered wildly to each other, investigating all the while. Children were caught by their shoulders, shaken, turned upside down, and questioned, poached into the search.

Gololi landed next to White Breast, beak too full to mock him—the sun searing off her prize in great glinting sparks. White Breast was astonished by the ferocity of his dislike and his affection.

Gololi's beak went to talon. Now in her grimy fist was the heavy gold earring. "Daktari Kunguru," she said, "suits you better, brother."

"I hate wailing brides. What care you for gold? If they look up here they'll see, then they'll start killing crows again."

"It's this caution and weak-heartedness that keeps you from greatness." Toying with the bauble, she broke off a piece of red ruby. "I love wailing brides most of all."

"Gololi . . ."

"Should I drop it on the ground then? A servant will scoop it up and not return it."

"Ah, the courage to take it I see," White Breast mused to himself, "but not the brazenness to return it."

"You think you are very sly?" she huffed, but flew down nonetheless.

With awe did White Breast see her perch on the knee of the bride, who was too shocked to scream. When Gololi dropped the earring in her red, velvet-wrapped lap, returning it, then she really did scream. Gololi beat a hasty retreat then, White Breast sweeping after her. They glided through the air, landing on a minaret in the next neighbourhood.

She still held the ruby in her fist, probably worthless costume jewelry. "I wanted to see the wild dancing," White Breast said.

"What kind of bird are you, always so fascinated with human affairs? Crows dance best of all."

White Breast still burned from the wild escape from the rooftop of Aisha's apartments. The mischief at the wedding was meant to refresh them; certainly it helped Gololi regain her bearings. She was in a better mood now that she was certain of her abilities to cause trouble, and White Breast, despite his irritation, felt better too. After wild fear came a comforting anger, and sitting by her now in the glow of the setting sun, he grew less and less angry.

"Daktari Kunguru is a human affair, it's what the children call my ilk."

Gololi huffed. The ruby sat at the very edge of the ledge, glowing between them. It was a fiery eye, sharding up with red light. "You are my ilk, you idiot."

"With this disgraceful white patch?"

"And your weak heart too, and your lack of cleverness, and your lack of spontaneity, Brother."

He did not want to talk about Almassi, nor did he want to argue. To his surprise, he found himself no longer angry, not at all, not even a little.

"Here," Gololi wiggled, swaying with her wings and cawing. "Let us dance."

And as she spun on her talons, screeching and wiggling, doing the black-hearted joyous chakacha across the orange ledge, White Breast watched her and thought with fondness he would never on pain of death dare speak aloud:

I like being called brother by you best of all.

~

Ali scrambled kima in the bottom of the pan. Hassan shuffled in the kitchen. Every time there was a sound, his head would jerk up in alarm. Or in hope?

"Aisha won't be here anytime soon," Ali said. "She's busy with her lessons."

"Oh, has she returned to school?"

What a tender, silly little boy. Ali, feeling sorry for him, made harmless small talk.

He was a sweet boy, Hassan. Good to his elders, respected by his peers, and gentle to all. He would make anyone a good husband. Full of faithfulness, good heart. Dutiful, true.

Was he a man who would cook for others as he expected a wife to? Perhaps. Yet he lived in a pedestrian, willing blindness. All his ambitions for his future *earthly*, human dreams. Money for a better house, a wife he'd treat with the honour and amenities she deserved, parents he would release from hardships. Children he'd provide for, to make them grow healthy and godly. He prayed, dutiful. He lived, dutiful. He meant with all his heart to do the simple good that God, he prayed, might give him power to do.

But Hassan did not worry over the attention of crows. People like Hassan had to go on with life instead of dawdling and occupying themselves with unexplainable things. God's mysteries would be unlocked in heaven. He was patient, without curiosity.

Ali served the meal to the boy who thought he loved Aisha. Wasn't it cruel to try to make a wife of a girl who sees? Who wants, more than anything, to know?

Ali had long known his wife was wiser than him, yet he could never hate her for it. He had been her protector since childhood and her protector till death. It was an insult to her. Loving him must have felt to her like accepting defeat, as it hurt her pride.

But she did love him, in her way. Shida's way of love was thorny, unsure of itself, suspicious—yes, she felt weak, yes, she felt thwarted. But it had nothing to do with any particular person. It was all of them, faceless they were made by it. It was this place, this heat, this insufferable cementing of sole to home.

She was born one hundred thousand years too early. She could not bear empty gestures or the space cordiality took where truth might have stood. She hated pity, and she hated pitying others. It was an insult to them to pity them, waiting for them to catch up to her where they had delayed. The sickness in her body inescapable. If she'd had strength enough she'd have been a pirate, a conqueror, a traveller.

Ali loved her and it was difficult for her to forgive him that.

They sat at a little table in the kitchen, staring at each other over flash-cooked mince and yesterday's chapati. Hassan's family must know of Aisha's oddness and oppose his desire to wed her. Hassan did not care a fig if Aisha was discussing tax reforms with the birds and planning coups with the goats, and because he could not know, he could not examine faulty flaws in his logic, or that things he could not accept existed.

Though an unselfish boy, Hassan was blind to the incompatibility of their differing dreams. Hassan's goodness lacked consideration. Hassan had no awful pride, but a good man's lack of consideration is never manifested in such horrid ways. His pride is even humble in its appearance, godly and kind. His punishing goodness is so sly and subtle, it is a secret unto himself.

Even a good man can be a prison. Hassan must have imagined a future where Aisha's strangeness was made forgivable through a natural domesticity coming forward, a marriage that was an opportunity to listen to these instincts. Aisha, a satisfied wife, humbly attending to their house! Aisha loving him, blending seamlessly into the iron that his own path struck out into, like a ribbon twining itself around a stick.

Hassan's dreams may not have been able to fully imagine the colour of her wedding dress, or even the style with which she would wear her wild, boyish hair. He only knew that the colour would be beautiful, and that her hair would be long and pretty and Aisha would settle easily in that prettiness in a way she had never done before, settle into it as though she had been born to it, born for their life together.

Straight, stiff Aisha, whose eyes went only a little half-lidded and yet communicated her rude and underwhelmed exasperation. Sphinx-faced Aisha, with the wild royalty of an animal that belongs only to itself—did Hassan think that Aisha would evaporate? Some imposter-Aisha replacing her? A soft Aisha, leaning on him, relying on him, smiling at him? Ha! Aisha was too suspicious to smile at someone like Hassan.

Hassan saw Aisha as a future wife, made the best of women. He intended, with pure and faultless heart, to love her forever.

But Aisha didn't see Hassan at all. The more Ali spoke with this poor prison of a boy, the more he saw what Aisha saw.

Aisha saw Aisha sailing the sea—skin dark from the sun and grinning with all her teeth, zigzagging through the air, plunging and disappearing as perilously as a lightning bolt.

Too alive to be the kind of good woman who would be sufficient for a good man.

Aisha saw Aisha hunting—Aisha saw Aisha striking out like a general, a master of her future.

Aisha saw Aisha and the House of Rust.

~

Aisha went between the fruit stalls, mabungo on the brain. Parched from running around, she wanted the sweet-sour iciness of the fibrous juice to refresh her. Were they in season? She reached for one to test the toughness of its shell when it was snatched from before her eyes.

Aisha raised her brows, but Ibrahim grinned, his gold teeth glinting like copper in excuse. "The boss here is very adamant," he offered, weighing the fruit with another bunch and packing it away.

Just when she was about to ask who this boss was and where he was, Ibrahim put the purchase in the basket of a young boy. In the basket were rows upon rows of halwa tightly rolled in brown paper and labania za kopa from *Lamu*, of all places! "*Omar?*"

Her surprise did not have time to turn to suspicion, for Omar yelled, "It is none of your concern, freak!" and with a battle-cry, fled so that he was lost to her eyes, swallowed up by the other market-goers.

How undeserved that was! She forgot about the fruit, losing appetite, gaining irritation. What a brat!

She expressed her dismay to Ibrahim. Amina would never send her little tyrant out so trustingly—Aisha felt careless herself for neglecting to offer to help with the market duties. She had been so occupied with her desire to find the cat that she'd forgotten all about her neighbours.

"He's becoming responsible," Ibrahim said. "He runs errands."

Refraining from saying anything unkind, Aisha thanked him and left. Amina and Rukiya, who were so careful with their money, would never have sent the child to stock up on so many sweet things. Of course he would run away from her. He was embezzling funds to fill his selfish little belly!

Aisha marched back home, sure to pay Amina a visit to get to the bottom of it all. At the tenement, a figure swathed in black came down the stairs, greeted her. Aisha frowned at the shadows, ready to berate all the demons that sought to greet her. But it was no demon; the girl pulled down her veil. Aisha tilted her head in hazy recognition, unsure but not impolite, *yet*.

The girl smiled nervously, trying not to be disheartened. "I came the other day to see you, with Khale Hadia."

Ah, the milk-coloured girl. Aisha stepped forward and endured her face being kissed in greeting with much less suffering than she usually felt. She was surprised at that too. "Oh, how are you?"

The girl smiled tightly when Aisha searched behind her with dread. "She couldn't come, she's busy preparing. The house is full of guests as well, so I had to come see the sugaring lady at her house. She wouldn't have let me go alone otherwise . . ."

"Khale Rukiya is so strong, sometimes the girls cry with how hard she scrubs them."

"Yes, she warned me against being a brat, so I didn't complain. But I'm grateful she let me come to her house, and if she scrubs my skin hard, I suppose it's what she has to do." The girl paused. "I'm glad to see you, though. Would you mind—I mean if it isn't any trouble—you see I tried to memorize the way here, I was very attentive to it, when I came last time, I didn't have too much trouble coming here—but you see, it's the coming out of it that's really worrying me."

"Makadara isn't a pit full of degenerates, you know."

"I'm not very good at walking around. I've always gone wherever Khale Hadia has gone, I'm really sorry to be troubling you—I suppose I'll just—"

"It's all right," Aisha said. "I'll take you."

Aisha did not offer her arm, but felt that she should have. Something about this girl inspired you to be gentle with her. She was soft and sweet-smelling, a girl in all the ways Aisha wasn't. Aisha expected to hate her but did not. Aisha began to lead her out of the maze of buildings, after asking which stop she wanted to go to.

"You said . . . *Khale* Rukiya. Are you related?"

"No," Aisha said, which made the girl look even more embarrassed. No doubt the unsavoury situation of Shida's birth had everyone assuming whatever they wanted. "It feels odd just to call her Rukiya, as I've known her since I was a child."

The girl reddened. Aisha could never get red. Her skin sometimes turned a blotchy, energetic dark when she got heated—but it always looked like a rash. Never so pretty or delicate. The girl saw Aisha looking at her over her shoulder, and remembered her face was uncovered. She quickly tugged the veil back over her features. All her prettiness was meant to be hidden so she could shine even brighter on her wedding day.

There was a reason why the girl had an abundance of khales and Aisha had to make her own. *That's what I call most of the women Hababa knows.* Aisha thought it pained the girl. "I thought Hababa Hadia was your grandmother."

"Oh no! She's my mother's sister."

"Couldn't your mother bring you then?"

"Ah, no, uh, my mother died. But it was a long time ago."

Aisha's mother was dead, too. "Is she like a mother to you?"

"Mother and father both," she said. "They died in a car accident."

"Poleni," Aisha said quietly, and told her to take her arm, readying to cross the road.

"Tushapoa."

"I was glad to know your father came back." She sounded like she meant it, too. "I'm sorry about Khale Hadia, I know sometimes she's . . ." She rolled backward and forward on the balls of her feet, vibrating in place. "But we prayed together for your father."

Oh, Hababa Hadia's prayers! Curses, more like. Aisha did not want to hurt the girl's feelings. She should have felt bitter, but she found that she meant it when she thanked her for her prayers.

They crossed the road together, the girl's hold on Aisha as tight as the knot in a rope, as though she were afraid of being run over or dragged away by a sudden tide of cars or people. Bravely, she kept it from her face, thanking Aisha with the seriousness of a man.

Aisha decided to be brave, too. "I don't know your name."

She was relieved to have reached this stage. Her laugh a beautiful, girlish sound—neither shrill nor cunning, just a true and startled peal of brightness. Aisha saw the noor in the girl's face as though it was shining even through the veil, and knew, with surprising tenderness of her own, that she was not being laughed at.

"You know!" She wiped at her eyes with gloved fingers. "I really admire that about you. When we visited last time, you didn't look away from Khale Hadia's eyes once—you held her gaze!"

"I didn't do so in challenge."

"It was just like you weren't afraid of anyone. Like she could not hurt you."

"That's not true, she did make me angry."

"But not in a way that mattered. There is a directness to your stare and a frank openness—as though you hide nothing, it is only that we cannot find it out!"

"You embarrass me when you say it so admiringly."

"She hated that you looked at her like a peer. I'm sorry that she was like that."

"I'm sorry I didn't congratulate you." Aisha cleared her throat. "I forgot about your wedding between all the scorn she was giving us. Mabrook."

"Mabrook, *Aisha*."

"Mabrook for what? What have *I* done?"

She laughed again. "I mean, mabrook, Aisha. Because that's *me*. I'm called Aisha too!"

That evening, when Aisha readied for bed and organized her things, a bright ball rolled from the bag and disappeared beneath her bed. Aisha went to her knees, hunting for it.

When she found it, she put it on her lap. It was a little dusty, but it was an orange. She had rested her satchel on the stall, she remembered, ready to fish out money for her purchases before Omar had distracted her.

Ibrahim must have put it there.

A month ago, she would have recoiled, her insides would have resisted this kindness and shame would have embarrassed her. She brushed the orange with her sleeve on her way to wash it in the sink. When she wiped it again it shone as bright as a sunset; she inhaled its sharp bright smell and closed her eyes.

It was sweet. She did not hate this thoughtless kindness. She did not flinch.

It was very sweet. She tore the skin and, smiling, ate it alone.

CHAPTER TWENTY

The more Aisha tried to hold on to the air, the more she used. At first the creature was as small as a house on a hill, and then it was a hill, and then it was a mountain, and then it was the size of the moon, crashing into the earth. Fragrant flowers exploded in her lungs. Jaws sprang open, dragged apart like a rusty trap, and the water seemed to bulge, forced into its great maw. A great force pushed at her but she was fixed in place, as though held by wrist, heel, throat. She tried to keep her eyes open as the salty lash whipped at her.

Her eyesight blurred, her heart failed.

And she woke.

Every night since Aisha had returned, she had these dreams. The same dream. At first they were terrifying with their intensity and their frequency. But she wanted to see what was at the end of it: what happened when the beast reached her?

She spent her days training her breath, filled her lungs with air and held it, held it, held.

She felt Jicho's gaze through the pillowcase, through the cupboard, through walls and doors. When she slept, when she prayed, when she was just sitting there with her thoughts. What was he planning for her? She would stomp on him with a cleaver, she thought darkly, at the first sign of treachery.

He understood his captivity and wanted to be free.

*Do you miss your Sunken King so much? He struck off his own limbs
to throw you to the sharks, so he might flee.*

What will you do once you are in the sea again, Jicho?

What flesh will you latch yourself on to, and what monstrous thing
will you be?

~

White Breast had had a tough time of it, disowned, alienated, and, all
in all, made a bird most non grata. It was one thing to be cawed out of
a family of crows, but to be cawed out of all of crowdom? His disgrace
cut deeper in his heart than the sharpest of swords.

He was to be murdered on sight, or at least murdered if he was a
nuisance.

How had his intentions been so misunderstood? It was, if one
were crafty enough to think it, almost deliberate.

Had he dared approach the other crows, they would tear him for
his feathers.

So he hung around Aisha, the weirdo who had caused all the
trouble in the first place. For so long as others feared her, White
Breast was safe. To escape the teeth of the roaming wolves, he hid instead in the snake's abode.

He watched, with no one to report to. It felt that something must
be left to him, if he had nothing else. *I was given a mission, I will not
abandon it.*

Hurled out of crowdom, he was also denied conversation with
them, and thus the network of information that had seemed so vast
and intimate all at once, stretching back centuries, thousands of years,
to the beginning of all crows, was shut to him. He was but a faulty
edition, past knowledge, rather than the organic, ever-growing uni-
verse. To be as lonely as a book forgotten on a shelf as history went on
being made! To be forgotten, abandoned to time, never to age well, so
all information he used to have would be but far too *dated* a shadow.

Had he known how to weep, he would do so bitterly. But he must keep his courage! Or die. Surely his honour might be returned to him in time? And yet he could not shake the feeling that someone had conspired against him.

White Breast watched Aisha through glassy rain and through humid afternoons that writhed with steam from yesterday's rain. Dawn to dawn, he shivered at his post, scrounged pathetically from her garbage, the loneliest bird that had ever flown. He, alone in Almassi's abode.

Already Gololi and he had barely escaped with their lives from the roof of the apartment building. Almassi rarely bothered with humans these days, but a crow's memory is as long as first crow existence. It would not do to forget that Almassi had once been easier to anger, happier to act on violence.

First it was the selfish cats of Old Town, then goats under Kamau the Peaceful, and then it was those Luddites, the chickens. She asked the dirt, the trees, the lizards (indoor and outdoor), the shark hunters, the mangy dogs that roved the sandy fringes like mercenaries ready to set upon pilgrims.

And then she asked White Breast. Hand over brow, shielding her gaze from the mid-afternoon sun, she hollered, "Hello!"

Had he been compromised? He nearly fled. How the beaks of his brothers would rend his flesh! He stayed, staring ahead at nothing with great fortitude.

"Do you know of the House of Rust?"

What kind of stupid question was that?

Endure, you noble bird, White Breast told himself. None of the other creatures had answered her. She'd had food for all of them, though. Where was his? Yes, indeed. That wouldn't be fair at all.

He glanced down, tried moving his eyes without adjusting his skull. Just quick enough a flick of his attention as to see that she held . . . corn in her hands.

As if!

"Corn is for bothering you," Aisha said. "And this," White Breast felt her shift beneath his perch as her palm opened, and he got the unmistakable scent of something delectable, "is for giving me answers!"

Ha! She had tried pulling *that* with the other animals—she always ended up giving them what was in the other hand as well.

He had already lost so much, he couldn't make the words true. They had called him uncrow! What burdens White Breast had on his tiny shoulders. No, he could not take the corn. Even if it would mean . . . oh, it was absolutely *divine*, stewed lamb bones.

"Do you speak the language of Adam?"

The language of bullheaded tyrants? Why should one bother?

"Do you know of a cat called Hamza?"

Oh, was that what he'd chosen!

Crows and cats had precious little to say to one another. In his day, White Breast used to go to wealthy neighbourhoods and tease the cats that roamed the gardens with mocking crowlike "meows," chasing away whatever the pampered house pets were hunting, with malicious relish. How he longed for that petty mischief. He missed his brothers ever so.

"Do you know of a cat who had no shadow?"

Everyone had a shadow. Cat or crow. This talk of cats bored him to death.

"Where is the House of Rust?"

None of your business!

Under one cliff face, before a rattling wall of salt-slimed crabs, White Breast watched her ask these same questions. Cockroaches of the sea—brinier, with sweeter meat, cockroaches all the same. They see-sawed on their legs, sprang their bodies rightward, leftward. They may not have spoken Adam's language, but that was probably for the best: the code they tapped out with their clubs and claws said things best heard from a mob. She brought those ones little dried freshwater fish from the lake up yonder. They hated her all the more, and feared.

Like White Breast, they had not touched the food that was proffered.

What an obnoxious girl.

The camels had none of the gentleness of goats and sheep when Aisha disturbed them. "You have no gold dinars, silver kilwa, or even copper mafiya for me—no coin with the name of a king or god or holy saint—no shilling with the style of poetry? Why should I listen to thee?" Mfalme wa Ngamia bent his head toward her, sniffing her feet in the beachy sand, puffing at her stance. Gritty eyelashes wild and long, thick as the teeth of a carpet brush. Scars went down his back, long dried, healing into pale, rubbery strips. Mfalme wa Ngamia outlived everyone who had ever laid a hand on its kin. "Doth thou bringest us honey? Or fruit? Or long, inky eel?"

But of course, she did not understand. None of them spoke the language of Adam, that poor and feeble tongue. Better she learn how to speak crow, goat, camel, crab, and all.

Skinny was White Breast becoming. He could not roost with his brothers, so poorly did he sleep, perched on the electric pole in the dreadful drizzle. His loneliness was abject.

A bird landed beneath him. Why, he would recognize that dark coat anywhere! The beady roundness of her black eyes . . .

Gololi jumped and careened against the night winds, then on them, rose. Night-time was for sleeping, for guarding nests. White Breast watched her go with ugly exhaustion, and huddled more securely, to return to sleep.

She returned after five minutes to clip him in the head.

White Breast, fuming, woke to follow. To the sea, the sea—black-bodied, sleeping, white lips worrying the cliffsides like a child teething on a chair leg. Gololi flew, swift and dark, kiting downward along the face of the plummeting cliffs of Lighthouse.

The air had the buttery sweetness of roasted sweet potatoes, the snappy, spiced bark of the muhogo. The cloudy nectar of madafu with its sweet, melty meat. Oh, when had White Breast last bullied a child into abandoning his food? He dropped into the abyss, abandoning his wings to become a stone, rushing, rushing. And then he opened and glided, finding Gololi on the slippery rocks.

The lights of a crossing ship glimmered. Ferries lay asleep until to-morrow. The rock they perched on had been uncovered by the tide, and ahead was a great and boundless horizon so dark, the sky had lost the seam that separated it from the deep in the day. Beneath that sleeping, darling water were the movements of sharks who followed ships and the ferries, lying in wait for the garbage, scavenging the un-lucky. The busy world had gone to rest. Now was a time for liars and for thieves.

For the whisperers. *What have you brought me here for?* White Breast wondered, morose. Killing was always done with an audience, and crows were allowed no secrets from one another.

The cold pulled and tousled at their feathers. Gololi's coat was inkier than ever. White Breast thought with envy and hurt of his own wasted appearance, compounding his feelings of disgrace.

"For whose benefit do you come here now?" White Breast spoke. "Guilt is as uncrowlike as remorse, you do not come here to assuage your own feelings!"

"To think that you, the disgraced, would be so ungrateful . . ."

"And how did I become the disgraced?!" White Breast shrieked.

Gololi leapt on his back with her talons, hopping in distress. "Be quiet!"

White Breast, despite his incredible anger, fell sullen and quiet.

"Do you think I am here because I am sorry?" Gololi chastened. "I came to hear your apology."

"Do you *hear*—apologize for *what*?"

"Quiet, you idiot!" Gololi pounded at his skull. "I can't be seen with you—the others will think we are political dissenters. Or worse: in *love*."

White Breast shook her off, disgusted and *outraged*. "Who sought who out?"

"It was you who disturbed the order of things! What did you *expect* would happen? You can't call for votes over nothing. Ours is a de-mocracy, yes, but when one makes a motion, it needs to have some sort of reasoning."

"The Burned One controlled all of the crows' feelings. I wanted someone fair."

"Then you did not even propose yourself. How weak!"

"It would have been a play for power, which I don't want."

"You thought that would have been selfish? At least ambition can be a virtue, selfish or not. What little character you have to be afraid of power, be critical of those who have it, and yet, not want it for yourself. You wouldn't know what to do with it! Either you are a power-hungry rival or an anarchist. If you are so useless you cannot decide which, then of course you'd be voted out."

"I believed that you could do it, Gololi, I voted for you and you betrayed me!"

"Betrayal?! Ridiculous!"

"I voted for you!"

"I was tricked into volunteering myself—I made myself a political rival, of course I would have voted to chase you out, everyone was already voting for the outcome. If I'd been against it they'd still have thrown you out, and I'd have been in danger indeed."

"The Burned One manipulated the process."

"That is a hefty accusation!"

"Isn't it clear to you? Takataka the Magnificent has garbage on her mind, not democratic process. Red Eye is more concerned with farming a ready supply of ticks for him to munch on. Both are part of the Burned One's gang, both eat from the same seamstress *shradh*. Both have admirers of different subgroups, the vain young ones, and the grizzly older uncouth ones. Only you, Gololi, could not have been accounted for. They were put there not to win the election but to divide the vote. It was all a trick!"

"That would have required planning," Gololi said, not wanting to believe. "They could not have known beforehand that you would call for a change in speaker, you impulsive, naive idiot."

"If you were in power for decades, you'd have systems in place to keep it as a precaution. Just because the Burned One didn't know this would occur doesn't mean he wasn't always prepared."

"This is stupid!" Gololi declared. "And certainly irrelevant!"

"How can a conspiracy like this be irrelevant? Our lordship would not stand for this. How can we not fight it? Has the work we have done together meant absolutely nothing to you? Why have you come then?"

"For your apology—"

"*I absolutely, absolutely reject it!*"

"—*and* to tell you that following the weirdo will not get you back into crowdom. The matter is taken care of. You have stuck to her as closely as tongue to tooth, true," Gololi said. "But we have watched from a distance as well. I have seen the ants ring the hotel in Old Town; they have sought an audience."

"Almassi has awoken?"

"Not quite," Gololi hesitated, "but his attendants have opened the books and are taking complaints. If the ants have proceeded, the other animals will not further delay. All will press this concern until . . ."

"*Until it is heard.*" White Breast did not know what to feel. Matters were moving so quickly that his aid—his spying—was unnecessary. Old Snake would wake up. He would do away with the girl. And White Breast's small, moving circle of safety in a world hostile to him would vanish. The girl may be dangerous, but the terror that followed kept away those who would do a disowned crow harm . . .

"For your own safety," Gololi murmured, "you must go to Mecca."

White Breast's thoughts evaporated.

"It is the only place where you can be safe from humans, and tolerated by the rest."

Even birds were wary of shedding blood in the holiest of holy places.

"I cannot," White Breast said. "I must regain my honour!"

"You are so earnestly stupid!" Gololi hissed. "You have no hope of that! It is gone, it is *finished*. Enough, do what you like! If you will not go to Mecca, you will die in Mombasa. They have marked you for killing. They will eat your heart and peck out your eyes and stab you till you have more holes than feathers and leave your corpse out on the road for the cars to run over until you are crow-and-maggot mush. And then they will bring all the young to see what happens to traitors!"

"I will take this name traitor—you force me to eat it!—for I cannot abandon what I was ordered to do. Nor to pretend ignorance when I see ill being done. When I see in his lordship's absence lowly governance, I am no obedient, voiceless voter. I will take this name traitor, though I know with all my crow heart I number among the betrayed. I am no pious pigeon, flying over pilgrims. I am the shadow of a monster girl weirdo, and I will see this through to its end!"

"Then, Brother, be ended!"

White Breast huffed—"Sleep peacefully, Brother!"—and flung himself into the great, cold air laughing with terrible misery. "I have a monster girl weirdo to shadow!"

CHAPTER TWENTY-ONE

The cursed hotel in Old Town received all manner of creatures in the days following the girl's return: those who met the monster killer, and those who saw her and feared for their lives.

First the ants went, and when the ground did not shake and the palm trees were not sucked into the earth as if yanked by the roots, then the rats went. And when the sky did not rain fiery stone, and the underground wells went unpoisoned, then the dogs went. And when the thunderous din did not come with more than its usual disagreeable intensity, the proud camel went.

When the great goat went, it was regardless of the weather, without looking for changes or fearing them. Kamau the Peaceful took no human guise, unless it was to teach a lesson. He went alone, for a masterless goat is as purposeful and direct as the angels.

The illusion was in full force to accommodate the guests. Though to think of Almassi as welcoming and generous outside was unwise. He was the host of all hosts, the last one for the cruel and unlucky he chose. Kamau saw, with all three of his sights, the layering of lies, and let a winding shadow lead him into a groomed garden with deep pools of shade. A gazebo was bursting with bougainvillea, inflamed by the gold of bright midday, the woodwork ornate and in symmetry of design godly and divine. Guided toward it, Kamau caught sight of a swinging, hand-woven hammock between green flushed palm trees. The chicken was not far away.

Around the gazebo were littered beautiful garden pieces, furniture imported from countries that had once been under the heel of empire, from a different time entirely.

That was Almassi's vicious irony shining through.

Kamau knew that he was in a limestone hovel with half its roof missing, that it was raining when he came upon the old hotel. Such beauty might capture a human heart and trap it in luxurious sceneries, as impossible as they were darling. Kamau had not come as a guest, for a night in the hotel stretched on and on and on, purgatory in the jaws of a snake. You ran in circles to escape the labyrinth once you knew it was a falsehood designed by that architect of balance, Almassi.

Guests looked for doors, clawing at their eyes. They witnessed a production perfectly tailored for their absolute immersion, and prayed for escape while trapped in a dream, not knowing they were dissolving in a snake's belly, where there was no escape or forgiveness. Only punishment. Almassi's attendants were frantic, busy ferrying the visitors here and there with such worry one would think their lord was interested in these affairs. Shadows were shaped like black snakes, streaking fast through the air.

Under one of the smaller gazebos, a young Swahili boy stood on a spill of green-dyed kashata, a stockpile of labania za kopa, and halwa. Omar was arguing with the attendants in a mess that looked like something he had burglared. "Be quiet! Of course the paper's wet! I am not yet trained to *see* under all these lies you've layered! I am carrying him on my head all the time! All that demon does is eat people and take naps!" He collapsed in the mess and rubbed his eyes, sniffling.

"My buttocks are wet," he wailed, "because you're so cheap, Almassi!" He curled up on his side and began to cry in earnest. The attendants rushed about him, crooning and distressed. He swatted at them, missing each one. "Get wooden floors, Almassi—get a ceiling, Almassi! I refuse to watch the crows watch that freak. Why are peppers in another person's farm burning your mouth, Almassi? I hate you bitterly. I am going to start school and become a pilot. Almassi, do you hear me? I am going to fly a plane and you can stay here impersonating tourists you can never be. You freakish prisoner. If you eat me, I'll kick you very hard. I dare you to eat me, you stupid snake!"

The snake-attendants pitied him. Almassi would not wake up. The boy was wise enough to have a tantrum now.

"Shikamoo, Peaceful Kamau!" the snake-attendants greeted him.

At the centre of the gazebo, a small, antique box held a sheaf of papers that shuffled themselves. A whittled stick, capped in bronze turtle-shell, dipped itself in ink and danced across the report it readied.

Behind Kamau, the chicken floated in the hammock. Innocent of the world, he swung delicately back and forth. The chicken roamed Almassi's house, unmolested and unaware of danger, the only one immune to the trap. The only one other than Almassi and his attendants who needed no guide. An ignorant creature, no more than what he was, and because he lacked knowledge of all worldly dangers, they ceased to exist. A vulnerable creature, yet the most protected of all.

"Great Brother is at rest, please let us know how we may help you."

"There is nothing great about your brother," Omar whimpered, sorry for himself. "He's a big bully. I carry his big, fat life on my head!"

Old Snake's naps could last days, months, even years. Rarely did he like to be woken. Yet his illusions were as polished and glistening as a prized jewel. Sleep or no, one could not pretend he had left such trickery to his servants.

Almassi's greatest acts of terror often came when his sleep was interrupted and yet . . . not a whisper from him. Not a head punished, not a crow scorched. He was a barely reformed monster, and his anger reminded you best of all how he was the worst of all creatures to cross.

Kamau blew out his lips in bored disdain.

"Not a complaint?" The shadow wiggled, one of hundreds of Almassi's attendants, yet as nervous as a new helper. "Then what have you come to bring to our Great Brother?"

Kamau said what he had come to say.

"Peaceful Kamau, I certainly cannot say that to the Great Brother. No, I cannot say that at all!"

Despite the shadow's distress, the beautiful pen worked away, recording their words, charmed into an unflinching and unforgiving obedience to form and function.

"Oh, I wish you had not said that, Peaceful Kamau. Now it is on the record and I must bring it to Great Brother."

Kamau had said his piece. Another shadowy snake sailed through the air to herd him back to the exit, through the garden and the old, colonial-style lobby that did not exist. The other attendants were twisting, writhing, like cloth being wrung—bemoaning how Kamau had made it infinitely more dangerous to please Great Brother with their services.

How could they tell Great Brother, well, *that?*

Kamau saw the chicken again. His feathers gleamed from the rain, though the eye might be tricked into thinking it the pleasing glimmer of garden dew. As nonchalant as though nothing in the world had ever meant it harm.

"It is not two crows," Omar muttered. "But one now. A white-chested crow. Write that down, it's important. Write that I hate him, too."

He had left the hammock and migrated under one of the many Bombay chairs that littered the garden.

"I don't want her to come here," he said, finding tears again, though more quietly. "This place is not for her. It's *mine*. I stole the chicken, it was me."

There did he fluff out his wet feathers and there did he settle to doze in a nonexistent summer afternoon.

~

Something was dreadfully wrong when Aisha returned. On the steps of their home she saw, in abundance, like the molting skins of snakes, men's shoes.

Her father had a few friends and played cards sometimes. Compared to the person he had been before he'd disappeared, he seemed to be more social. Still a little shy, but smiling more genuinely, and not keeping to himself so much.

Still, men gathering usually meant trouble for women. She bent to organize the chaos of sandals, but Hababa hauled Aisha in so fast she hardly had time to protest, and quickly enough that she couldn't glimpse the majlas as she was herded into the kitchen as though she were a secret to be hidden. Hababa, who *never* trusted her to make the kahawa for men, foisted this task upon Aisha before rushing back to the kitchen to chew on her fingers by the door, *eavesdropping* on the visitors.

Aisha, summoning patience, set up a tray, trying to tally up the number of shoes she'd seen, sort them into pairs, in order to count out how many cups she would have to set. Six? Or eight?

Hababa was no help. Aisha buried a sigh and, greasing her knife, proceeded to slice through the sticky halwa, warm because Hababa had forgotten it by the window where the little sunlight would blaze through. That was unlike Hababa, too.

Zubeir stepped into the kitchen grumbling for the tray and was shushed. Aisha's annoyance grew. She felt that everyone knew something she was too slow to follow—she was slow when Hababa snapped for her to pick up the tray, slower still when Hababa shoved her through the door. Aisha was so slow she might as well have been moving in reverse. And she stood there a little in shock, gears ground to a halt. Not understanding.

Her father was there, and other long faces, their features . . .

These were Hassan's kin.

Aisha was so outraged she nearly shouted. The audacity! She had to bow her head to hide her expression of anger, murmuring her salam. Not a day after getting talked to death about conducting herself properly in front of men, about not making herself a nuisance—and now Hababa had thrown her to them so she could serve them afternoon coffee!

To sit among them and be a meek thing! Aisha settled down on the floor with the tray, going about filling the little cups as though she were shy. She had never had the presence of mind to pretend that men made her shy. She usually ignored them instead of doing a great deal of acrobatics to acknowledge them. Cold indifference was present in her now and she paid attention to none of them, doing her duty plainly. That was even worse than being shy, because it could not be a virtue.

Fear could be a virtue. A lack of fear was arrogance of the highest order. She was not afraid of men. At best she found them obstacles to tolerate, at worst things to deflect. She'd never done a thing to please a man.

She felt a keen anger that their performance sought a performance of her own. That she was here to perform some girlishness, some meekness, some properness. Ha! She was a flat-faced creature who would not deny her nature. What was this stupidity? Had she not been clear before?

Done pouring the kahawa, she stood with the tray and paraded around the room. Hababa scolded her when she served things on her knees so she dropped to one knee to pour everything, then rose again to serve it. She went right to left, looking at none of them, keeping her gaze impassively on her tray. Brown hands taking what she proffered, murmurs of thanks.

One of them was Hassan. He nearly knocked the cup off the tray for how nervously his hand shook, thanking her quietly and quickly, as though she were stepping on his throat.

She hoped he burned his tongue.

The next hand was her father's, not as sunburned as it had been before. Now quiet and deliberate, he said, "Thank you, Aisha."

Aisha let him see her cold and empty eyes—but instead of quavering beneath her rebuke, he frowned with a gentle one of his own. It warned her to be sensible, instead of communicating his sorriness.

The tray empty, she looked at everyone in the room. "I need to bring more cups," she said quietly, as two other men, and Zubeir—who had slunk in shadow-like, to sit again—had remained unserved.

Ali nodded once.

Aisha tucked the tray under her arm, opened the front door, and stepped through it.

There was a glimpse of grey, rainy street before it (along with Aisha) disappeared.

Ali's face took on a tinge of weariness, rather than the polite disbelief that his neighbours were struggling with.

"Are the cups . . . outside?" someone failed to whisper.

Hassan went pale and were it not for his father's discreet hold on his shoulder, he might have done something stupid, like stand and run after a girl.

And likely get walloped by this same girl.

"No," Ali said, "they are not."

They waited for an apology that never came.

And waited, and waited.

Hassan's father, a barrel-chested man, decided then to laugh—it was sudden and deep as thunder.

Aisha had run out without her shoes—they would have delayed her if someone had the idea to stop her. She ran out into the street, the tray over her head. She was aware that she looked like a crazy person, and she did not care. But to save her family further embarrassment, and to stop herself being found by them too early, she went on quicker and farther.

Her anger did not keep her warm for long—it sat in her like a jagged ember, but the rain had come down again, pouring cold on her. To think that Mombasa had been a boiling stove not so long ago!

Hababa would have her head for this, Aisha thought. But she was so angry at her family members that she was not sorry. Hababa had left halwa out because Hababa had known guests were coming, Hababa was at Ali's house because she had known the whole time! Zubeir must have known, too.

And Ali . . . that hurt her most of all. He knew that she had no interest in these matters, how could he do this to her? How could he not warn her? How could he even *entertain* that stupid Hassan's wishes?

So blinded by anger, betrayal, and rain, Aisha didn't see the goat until she had tripped over him. She crashed into a wall and, falling into a puddle, lay still, stunned and drowning in two inches of nasty water.

Aisha rolled over and sat up, her clothes sodden with dirty street water.

"What are you doing here?" she murmured once to herself, and then again more loudly—standing up so she would be more dignified.

But the Big Billy of the masterless goats of Mombasa paid her no mind, moving past her insignificant self.

Aisha, hurt and suspicious, followed it down the road. Where were the other goats? Usually they went wherever they wanted, but the streets of Old Town were narrow and winding—not a lot to graze on here. Further, he was alone. Where he was going was one thing, but where he had come from was quite another!

What did an old goat have to do in Old Town, coming alone like that?

Aisha was sure she couldn't be mad, was sure her hunch was correct. She couldn't afford to doubt herself.

Rain pelted the tray when she raised it over her head, seeking to follow the goat—but the noisiness of the rain couldn't muffle the sound of birds, crowing at one another.

Aisha tipped her head upward. Two crows sat on the edge of a roof, heatedly squabbling, but fell quiet when she looked at them.

Aisha looked down again, scowling—and they started up again.

"Am I being discussed?" she shouted at them.

They were not sure how to respond. Daktari Kunguru crowed at her and was pecked at furiously by his neighbour. Aisha frowned, losing anger to confusion. She *was* being discussed.

"Aisha!" Hababa's cry warbled through the sheets of rain, rippling like it came from underwater. Never had Hababa called her and Aisha refused to answer, or run to see why she was being summoned. But Aisha's heart closed like a fist, stubborn so she wouldn't have to be hurt.

She shot a look at the birds. "How timely!" she spat, not finding this at all to her liking. She ground her jaw and ran through the rain, away from the birds and away from Hababa.

Though Aisha and Zubeir had done their best to repair the leaks in the roof of the shack, she found that they had missed some.

She sat on the table, shivering under an old sheet, staring sulkily at nothing.

Her feet were torn up and stinging from a sanitizing dip in the salt-toothed ocean. Her eyes burned from the pain and she blinked, looking upward—loath to let tears gather. The wind rattled at the door, protesting the lock she'd fixed, which latched it closed.

The protests of the wind turned into the pounding of fists. Aisha did not rise or answer—knowing that despite her silence, the rattle of the latch said enough about her presence within. She slapped at her thigh in irritation and trudged to open the door.

Baba stepped in, his shirt drenched, making his skinniness real again, making what he had suffered in the belly of the beast real again.

She had not expected him—but he was a fisherman, and he must have known of Zubeir's shack. He shrugged his shoulders, shaking off what shivers he could and looked up at the roof. "We used to say demons lived in this house, but it looked like a wretched hovel before . . ."

This was an opening for her to forgive him, or begin the process. But she wasn't surprised enough to forget the ill that had been done, or so she'd thought, but even that anger faltered when he brought out from under his shirt a pair of her shoes, kept mostly dry.

He set the shoes on the table they'd dissected him on. She felt the memory become a rock in her throat.

Ali meandered around with curiosity, his gait more loping than it had been. She worried that he'd hurt himself in the rain coming to find her. He examined his surroundings, smiling at the leak and doing what she hadn't. Opening a box and rummaging within, he found what he'd been looking for: a tin he set under the leak, for water to gather.

He hefted himself onto the table and fished around for a packet of mostly dry cigarettes. He lit and smoked one long and thoughtfully, as though sucking marrow from a stewed bone. "So this is where you go," he said, his smile faltering. "I'm no good right now, I feel light-headed."

Aisha went to sit next to him, her feet dangling off the side of the table. "From the kahawa, the sugar, and the smoke?"

"The sugar and the smoke," he murmured, smiling to himself before he sobered quickly enough. "Does he deserve to be hated for liking you?"

"Why am I paying for it? I don't want him."

"So just tell him that."

"But *why* do I have to? Why can't he just understand it and leave me alone?"

"You and your mother aren't that different," Ali said in wonderment. "You always expect people to understand things in the same exact way you do, and when they don't, you get impatient and give up on them."

She had nothing to say to that; she was surprised he spoke of Mama at all.

"Not everyone can be as quick as you." He smiled in irony at her expression. "Your Hababa says I indulge you."

"It is my life!"

"That's why you cannot recklessly dismiss each option," he said gently.

The smoke made her eyes sting. "Are you accusing me of being coy?"

"No, but marriage isn't an indignity. Don't look down on married women." His sharp look quieted her. "I want to be sure you're refusing for an honest reason. Your future is important to us, Aisha."

"If I say that I'll think on it then it will be a lie."

"Then don't lie, and think on it seriously."

"If I say I'll think on it then it will give you hope, and you will grow angry when I say no. You'll say I was lying anyway."

"I won't."

"I don't have any faith in that!"

This admission startled both of them; she saw his silence and his shocked hurt. Ali looked down, smoke weaving between his fingers. "Aisha," he said, "I know I haven't given you any reason to trust me. I certainly haven't been very reliable. But I want that to be different. I want to be your true father, not some shadow. So when I say to you, think on it—I'll trust you to do so properly, if you promise me you will. And I promise that I will listen to your answer, and abide by it."

"But you will be angry with me!"

"How can I be angry with an honest daughter?"

Aisha's mouth wobbled.

"You've already told me you have dreams of the House of Rust," he said, "and I honour that, as best I can. But time has passed, and some dreams change—yes, yours hasn't—but it's all right if it has, as well. Changing your mind doesn't mean you're wrong. You're just . . . different from the person who you were yesterday. Maybe the person of today wants different things."

"She doesn't."

"Promise me you'll think on it."

"So that they don't feel insulted? Why delay a refusal?"

"Did you think I came running after you because I care about insulting someone?" Ali said with a little more sharpness. "I didn't invite them, it was the women of both families, making their plans. I was as surprised as you that they came. No matter her scheming, Hababa wants what's best for you. As do I. Though sometimes what's best for you is decided by yourself."

"Hababa will punish me."

"Mama will just have to live with that," Ali said, "but think on it seriously."

At her expression of disbelief, he raised a finger. "All right, if you won't listen to what I'm saying. Listen to this." And he knocked on his stomach.

She heard the thunk of each tap of his knuckle.

"Oh, so you're intrigued!" He fished the object out from underneath his shirt and placed it on her lap. It was a book.

Her father could barely read.

"This is a book on sailing."

"I know, that's why I bought it." But her expression only grew more confused. "It's for solo sailing across the deep sea. That's what the store clerk said, though he wondered why I would want it. Just like you do."

Aisha brushed the title, its letters standing out in relief. It was old, second-hand. "Can you blame us? I don't have a sailboat."

"Don't you?" he wondered. "I managed to get one. You can have it if you like. And I could afford it too, though I hear it's the unluckiest sailboat in Mombasa. It's killed every rich heir who ever boarded it."

She could not understand a single word. Though that didn't keep her father from going on speaking. "Zubeir is calming her so she doesn't whip your backside. And I . . ." Ali sucked in a breath, put out his cigarette on his knee to her cry of protest and outraged worry. He regarded her properly. "I have come to a decision."

"You are not a rich heir and there is no such thing as luck, good or bad. Whether or not you will have the boy, I have decided to treat you newly. I tried not to interfere too much with you," Ali said. "I wanted you to rely on me, but never to feel I ruled you. If I was not God from the beginning, you would not hate me in the end. But I realize now the worst way I could fail you is not by not being God, but by being a hypocrite."

Aisha waited for her father to finish unravelling his thoughts, intrigued and a little confused by these unexpected words—she wanted to see how he would end them.

He stood.

She rose slowly, mirroring him.

"I will treat you now like my heir," he said finally. "I will trust you with my knowledge and my teachings. If you will accept them."

She couldn't help her surprise. "Baba—what do you mean?"

"You said that you will go on a journey one day. If I try to trap you here you will go, with or without my permission. Because you are wilful, and I must admire that now. I'm proud of you. You will go to sea, but not unarmed. You will learn how to sail, how to fish, how to gather drinkable water. I will learn how to let you go."

"Baba . . ."

"I'm saying I will not stand in your way. But let them say I was a man who had a child, let them say I was a father, not a bystander. It's selfish, but I want to be proud of you. One day, you can look back and know that your strength came not out of spite, but because there were people who loved you, who wanted you to be strong. Who were proud to see you on your way. Wherever you go, whatever beasts you face, I don't want you to look back and think I wasn't proud of you, or that I thought of you with regret. Think of me and let it add to the strength in your heart."

He needed to teach her just as much as she needed to learn, and she could never dream of refusing him. The words she'd been waiting to hear for eternity were finally being spoken. Would he have said this before? Long, long ago, he might have taught her these things, had not the long, inky one intervened—or would he have simply suggested that she set the sea aside like children's playthings?

She loved the sea that had betrayed him. It was not easy for him to go back to it. He used to swing her on his shoulders, all the way to the sea. She remembered the joy he'd taken in her company, and the ugly things too—his hand wriggling through the gills of a fish—and what he had been trying to teach her.

What she was now readier than ever to learn.

CHAPTER TWENTY-TWO

Hababa was willing to forgive her. She said Hassan's kin had decided her exit was an attack of incredible shyness. This would stand in for all the virtues she lacked, and so her rudeness was misinterpreted and became a credit to her character.

Hassan's father's laughter had boomed and rumbled like thunder. He had no right to take amusement from the situation, as though it could somehow belong to him despite not going according to plan, for pleasantly surprising him. "Make my refusal clear to them," Aisha said in a hard, angry demand, dripping all over Hababa's kitchen floor.

"Yes, yes," Hababa laughed. "Of course, it doesn't do to be too eager."

"No, Hababa, I mean it. I'm not being coy. I don't want to get married."

Hababa did not laugh anymore, but stood there struck and a little slow, then her anger crept up slowly on her, like a thief. "What do you mean? He's a good match for you. He's respectful, not bad looking, kind, and he has a head for business. Ambitious without stepping on other people. And he wants *you* for some reason, despite . . ."

Hababa seemed to regret that last bit, but Aisha roused angrily. "Despite what?"

"You know what!"

"Because I'm strange and alarming? Or because my mother didn't know her father?"

Hababa's inhale of air seemed to cut her as it went in. She grew meek and grumbly, caught out. "We don't speak of that. Your mother paid enough for my sister's wildness. But she grew up to be a good and godly girl."

"And you married her to Baba because no one else would have her!"

"Even if they wanted to, she would never have had any of them!"

"I don't dispute it! I won't feel responsible for what your sister did, I won't be guided by an old fear, Hababa. If no one wants to look past the fact that Mama's—"

"*Don't!*" Hababa hissed.

"—a bastard, then I'm meant to accept either their pity or their ridicule quietly? And just . . . take whatever is offered? Say yes before he changes his mind? Because it's more than I deserve, right?"

"You deserve so much more than the world will give you, Aisha! But people are—"

"I am not people. I *won't* be!"

"Oh, is it that you are so beautiful that you can refuse whoever, whatever? Because you're the Queen Bilquis?"

"Stop saying things and acting like I'm the one who spoke these words!"

"Ever since your father came back you've been wild and unreasonable. What has gotten into you!"

"I'm the one who brought Baba back!"

She opened her eyes to see that surprise had swept all the anger and poison from Hababa. Aisha was breathing hard. She swallowed, trying to wet her throat. But it felt like dry and itchy paper.

"When Baba went missing, on the third day, after you slept— I went out to sea."

"What kind of crazy story . . ."

"I went to sea with a cat called Hamza, and I faced monsters and I found Baba in the belly of a great beast, who stank of death."

Hababa laughed, mesmerized by Aisha's anger, and allowing herself to be irritated so she would not get swept away by impossible things.

"Why is your hair wet, you asked me, remember? It was wet because I was half-drowned when I came back. He didn't accidentally wash up on shore like they said. You knew Baba's dealings with the sea were never normal. It's why you were so harsh when he disappeared! Mze Zubeir cut his heart and bled the sea from him. That's why Baba isn't fishing, why he's a carpenter now. You said Baba was sick, and I don't know how much of that is right—but if he was sick then he isn't anymore."

"Your father survived an incredible ordeal. He changed his mind about a lot of things."

"No, he didn't. I *made* him. I told Mze Zubeir to cut out the sea from him. It wasn't right, but that was the decision I made."

"I don't believe it."

"I've been trying to find out where Hamza went. He invited me to go with him to the House of Rust, but I couldn't abandon you without saying goodbye."

"Your mother always had a mean streak in her. Sometimes I told myself I deserved it. But you . . . this is a really cowardly way of being cruel."

"I don't need you to believe in the story, Hababa," Aisha said through tears. "I just need you to believe in *me*."

Hababa's mouth twisted, and Aisha felt the tears spill over, and her chest hurt.

"You're so stubborn. Your mother always looked down on married women. Do you think it's wrong for women to marry? Do you think you're better than the rest of us?"

"You married Jedh."

"Because he asked me."

"You said you were lucky that he was dead. And went on miserable for *years!*"

"It was not all misery. He was a good man, sometimes we were happy. He was a withdrawn and reserved man, but I did not hate him."

"But you relished your independence after he died."

Aisha's cheek stung. It took her a while to understand that she had been struck. The sound of it seemed to travel slowly after, reaching her mind belatedly. The sharp clap of it, lost in a faulty transmission from some distant country. She saw Hababa's raised, trembling palm. She saw the painful crease of her eyes. How hard her grandmother was breathing, as though she had run in circles.

For a moment she hated her grandmother, but she was ashamed—for being so surprised by a blow, for being so angry that Hababa had hit her, and for hurting Hababa at all. And she dropped her eyes, so Hababa would not see in them what Aisha could barely understand enough to control.

"The loneliest years of my life were long and hard. I had no male guardian, and your father was barely of age. I had to protect myself in ways you will never understand. I worked day and night to provide for this family, I was *alone*. I had no confidant. My son was a wanderer. My niece hated me for trying to teach her how to survive, she hated me for knowing what her mother had done. When she was sick and your father was gone for days at a time, and you were so young, who do you think scrounged for medication and tried to take care of you all?

"Do not make light of me just because I have been familiar with you, Aisha—because I have been fond of you. I've done my best all this time. I know you talk of me as though I am a gossiper, as though I am idle, when you see me at the pot, cooking what I can sell to pay for whatever it is I can provide for you. I do not do it for your thanks, nor do I do it to make you forever mine, but you will not treat me as though my life has all been a string of trifling events and dramatic misfortunes. I loved your grandfather, I needed him. He was the only one who asked. Had I said no, I would have been very stupid indeed. With him I learned responsibility. I had support, and my parents had someone to lean on. Because I decided to live in the real world and be a real person, I had my own house, my own life, my own future."

Aisha's jaw felt numb. "When it came to the man you love, Zubeir did not ask Baba, he asked *you*. When you agreed, you spoke as *yourself*. As a person who belonged *to* herself."

"But before that I was a possession? A mindless donkey with no will of her own? Don't look down on me!"

"I won't dismiss your destiny in order to trust in mine! Why can't you see that choosing what I choose for myself is not an insult to you? Why must you take offence that I seek to determine myself? And why am I forbidden to protest when you bar me for the sake of your own pride? You would rule me and say you love me!"

"Get out."

"I hate him, I hate him—because you have chosen him over me!"

"You think I even care about that boy? Even once that this had anything to do with some boy?"

"You would throw me at him as if I were old cast-offs!"

"You are so determined to see what you want, and then you say I put words in your mouth. We will ever misunderstand one another just because I won't go along with your silliness. I'm disappointed in you."

"I always did what I was told," Aisha cried. "I did *everything*, I was careful to be good and polite, even when it was hard, even when I felt empty and false. And now when I say what you do not like, you act as though I've *always* been wicked, that I've always been my mother.

"I never wanted to be rewarded for being good. I just wanted you to be proud of me, to know that I loved you and accept quietly what was good for me. But that was before, Hababa—when I didn't know what I wanted. Now I've found what I want, I'm not a ghost anymore just inhabiting some lie, who let you call me my mother's name like it was a stain on me. I don't want what you want for me. I need to go to the House of Rust."

"So just because you've found what you want, I'm meant to accept whatever it is? You're truly foolish. Get out, Aisha. You are no longer my granddaughter."

Aisha's lungs were on fire.

"Do not come back until you've come to your senses."

"Until I've changed my mind to something you approve of, you mean."

"You have gone astray."

"Then you will never see me again, Hababa!"

Aisha fled.

Gololi came again to White Breast in the night or in the rain and railed against him, told him to go to Mecca because Almassi was coming, he was coming.

But days passed, and the girl went on. Only now she was with her father, struggling after him like a son instead of a daughter. The two of them oddities, her father watching her pull a boat up to the sand using her own strength—her father teaching her how to tie rope in different knots. A task at which she lacked coordination. Line after line, loosening ineffectually in her lap. Was this the girl who had slain those monsters? Truly?

Almassi is coming, Gololi warned with superiority. *All the animals have complained. Any day, he will smite her and you will be lucky if you're in the way—if you survive, it'll only be to get killed by the other birds.*

Aisha grew leaner, stronger. They were repairing a boat. Each day it was coming alive. Gololi watched this monstrosity with him, as though the two humans were putting together a leviathan, growing a horrible beast to wield against the world.

Gololi's passionate resentfulness began to flag, being replaced with a grim fear. The boat was coming together. Aisha was being taught the fishing spear, the sail, the radio. No one was coming to stop her.

No one was coming to kill the enemy that grew stronger and stronger each day, to retake the sea. White Breast saw that first frightened panic turn into a grave, stony terror in Gololi's chest.

White Breast was not so afraid, and that was frightening. He had been watching her so long, she had become too familiar to properly fear.

"Why does he idle?" Gololi wondered, cold and dead. "Isn't he afraid people will say he is frightened of her?"

"Old Snake is resting."

"He is afraid, or he is indifferent."

"Perhaps she is of no danger, then," White Breast suggested. "Perhaps we ought to leave her alone."

"Don't pray for that, Brother. If the crows cease to be afraid of her, this monstrous shield will disappear, and you will die," Gololi warned. "It is one of your great talents to exploit loopholes in order to aimlessly waste time, so you must waste time for a little longer."

"Ah, you flatter me, Brother—to hear such from someone who specializes in appearing where they are least wanted is high compliment indeed."

"He is not afraid, but he is indifferent. Do you not remember the cursed object she carried with her, have you not seen it? Would a peaceful person have such a thing in their possession?"

White Breast had never seen it. It sat somewhere inside her room, behind all those walls. Yet it stared like the point of a spear hovering between his wings.

"Perhaps she does not know what it is."

"She knows enough to keep it a secret. Whatever it is, even being ignorant of it is dangerous. *She* is dangerous."

"If Old Snake will not move, what makes you think you should take matters into your own hands?"

"I shall not touch her," Gololi said, grave as iron, "but Old Snake *will* move. For all of our sakes."

White Breast did not see how a bird like Gololi might achieve such a thing. Crows were shrewd creatures, but they were also simply crows. They had spread word, they had gossiped in the midst of other animals, hoping to be overheard, they had spread the tale and sowed worry into the minds of their neighbours—they had prompted the animals to seek out Old Snake, without having to go themselves. A crow's strengths lay in more subtle matters. Not a single crow had gone to see Almassi.

The mercenary dogs had gone, the old camel and the old goat—those who had been here since long, long ago, some who had even known Almassi from the worst stories, from the Great Before. Yet none had moved him. None could have made him come.

What could little Gololi hope to do?

CHAPTER TWENTY-THREE

Each night the silky white silhouette came closer and closer—Aisha would fall into her bed and snap into sleep like a strained cord released. Ali had been driving her hard, preparing her for the dangers ahead, both the mysterious and the man-made.

What was her vessel to do when she was caught in a following sea? Avoiding pirates. What to do in a storm. How to repair a leak. She felt a little sorry for having thought him somewhat incompetent, and she learned how wrong she was, for sailing was hard and unforgiving work. It whittled down whatever little fat she'd had on her bones, and she saw her face grow narrower, sharper, harder. They pored over navigation: using maps, using stars. And she held her breath as she read, held the book, and traced the words, keeping time by pages.

Then one night the jaws opened, the water bulged, forced away and into its great maw. At first the creature was as small as a hat, then a house on a hill, and then it was a hill, and then it was a mountain, and then it was the size of the moon, crashing into the earth— she was a grain of sand before a racing fist, the fingers opened, ending in bone-white teeth, calcified as stalactites, rising, rising. Her eyesight blurred, but her heart did not fail. Her lungs screamed, but did not yet burst.

Plum petals glistened like a fistful of thrown jewels, hurtling past her cheeks. She stared into a blanketing night at the end of its teeth, the hollow that opened without sound, the teeth that raced past her, and the jaws came down, closing off all light, swallowing her whole.

Bougainvillea.

~

White Breast followed Aisha everywhere. It was familiar now—routine. She raced around like a boy. She sat now on the sand, fixing tears in a net, waiting to show her father when he would come from his new workplace.

White Breast's eyes slipped shut, listening to the pick in her hand nibble and tuck at wire. The sway of the leaves in the trees, the quiet in the wake of the usual evacuations that took place wherever they went. Niggling at his skull was a sense of foreboding. But he knew no unusual storm would be rising from the ocean today, no great wave or change in the earth as to make him feel so on guard.

Then he heard the screaming.

His brethren—he knew those voices. He rose to attention, legs aching with the panicked impulse. The girl looked to the air in curiosity but did not do much else. If he left her, he'd be in danger—to leave Aisha was to be among those who would hurt him.

But his brethren were screaming, and he felt ill. He cursed himself and swept into the air, wings beating hard. Past spires and pulpits, through the branches and following the roads, White Breast raced.

The noise was in Aisha's yard. White Breast saw that the window was open. Gololi was dancing in a shatter of smashed glass. She moved as though she were on fire, with a terrifying rhythm. Three others were with her, leaping frantically from side to side.

White Breast flew to the window and saw Aisha's room, burgled and in disarray, the cupboard open, the bedding torn. A wet brick encased in the shattered half of a pickle jar.

"What have you done!" White Breast raised his wings.

Gololi's companions were too frightened to hate White Breast. Gololi was laughing, Gololi was screaming. "What you should have done yourself!"

On Gololi's beautiful coat crawled a great tick, as white as corpse flesh. White Breast felt its foulness like the stench of death. It was the cursed item. The ugly thing. Why had she come to take it?

"Get it off our brother!" White Breast roared but none of them dared. "Cowards, all of you!"

White Breast leapt up, but Gololi swept out of the way, tossing into the air with a horrendous laugh. She could barely fly. Her body was at war with the thing that had gotten into her; half of her tried to peck at it, the other half tried to escape.

White Breast roared, launching himself against her body, and she kicked at him and tore at his flesh. He cried out in pain as she tore at him, as the tick writhed and crawled, evading his beak. He stabbed at it as Gololi stabbed at him. They tore at one another, her cries bloody and frightening, full of murder for him.

"It is not you!" White Breast wailed. "She is not herself! It is this evil, foul thing! Help me!"

The crows danced around them, edging in and leaping away, too frightened.

He was to die here. And he became so angry that even as he felt his eye rupture beneath her beak, and his sight fill with blood, he did not let himself be blinded. He found the cursed, wriggling thing. Suddenly diving with his beak and snapping it between his teeth, he tore its hooks from Gololi's flesh. He broke it in his beak, and it burst in his mouth. Gololi heaved on the floor, crumpled and crying, bloody.

White Breast felt acid burn in his throat, felt hooks grow all around it. He had not destroyed it. He had given it a new home. His brothers viewed him with horror. Blood pooled around Gololi. White Breast stumbled backward. Vines grew down his throat and into his belly, twisting around his guts and heart.

The eye shredded at him. *They will tear you for your feathers.* Pain filled him, as complete as the air, fire writhed in his marrow, and all his bird bones were engulfed in a ravenous poison, his heart pounded, his half-sight blurred—Gololi did not rise, Gololi did not breathe. The thing was teething at his bones and slicing at his neck. He collapsed.

Shadow engulfed White Breast's twitching body, but the pain in his bones halted—seized up in his veins. He thought perhaps it was death. But he had seen the finely woven sandal, and above him was the wide-brimmed hat thrown to shade him, landing around him, redistributing puffs of dust.

Feet stirred the earth where the crows had landed.

All the crows had fallen silent, all the better to hear this new stranger speak.

"I have heard my name with a frequency, spread among the populace maddened as a fever," came the voice, light and dangerous. "I came to hear who it is that chews my name like dead and rotted corpse flesh."

A hand rested on the top of the hat, compressing it at once.

White Breast heard the voice no more, disappearing where he was sent.

Almassi disappeared the next crow before brushing off his hat and placing it on his head, its brim wide around the untamable hair that crowned him as the mane does the lion. But Almassi was no lion. The chicken perched on his shoulder with gentle ease.

"You have chewed me awake," Old Snake growled, smoke winding out from the end of the old ornate medwakh with elegant laziness. "Now, who shall pay the cost?"

CHAPTER TWENTY-FOUR

The bougainvillea was wilting in the rain, but for the creeper that fringed Almassi's House of Smoke. Iridescent, the creeper bloomed eternally, so long as he fed the illusions he had so exactingly created.

It took a wicked heart to know what pleased another wicked heart; an evil one can catch an evil one. To the good and the peaceful, this was but a simple, smoke-stained limestone square in need of renovation. But to those horrible ones, this house was an inviting hotel, glittering with worldly beauty, jewelled in ever-blooming bougainvillea. To the evil ones, his was the House of Shadows, the House of Smoke.

The rains had come with the girl.

The rains would have come, with her or without her.

A girl cannot change the weather.

But she can change the taste of the rain.

His tongue flicked out at the coppery tang of magic, not unlike the zing of blood. His painted collar vibrated against his skin, like a hum starting in his throat.

It had been a long time since he'd had to reckon with such an enterprising human. He had always had a fondness for bastards, and for the children of bastards. Tenacious, like the shark hunters. He knew the smell of them as a cat knows the smell of another cat, entering the room it has vacated. A tingling sense, not unwelcome, not invited, yet seeping in. Felt along his entire jaw, pulling.

The sea churned away, ruminating its own self.

Almassi leaned against the window frame beneath the balcony of riotous bougainvillea. The rain darted at an angle, lightly soaking the grass. The old chicken keeping dry beneath the sill, dozing on the old carpet.

Almassi thought of his mother. The great snake that had ringed the island, turning the molten rivers to mush. She had carried the egg in the steel cavern of her mouth for twelve days. Almassi had hatched in the shape of a human child. He was half his human father.

His infamous bloodlust thoroughly convinced his peers and kin not to take him lightly. Travelling as he pleased, Almassi had done what he liked, taken what he wanted. He killed wicked men, holy men, ate their children. Then in Mombasa he was trapped by the spell of a painted collar.

In Mombasa, he settled his heart and learned his lessons. He even become a revert, accepting God. He repented his wicked past in his own way. The wild Almassi who cared nought but for his own desires, quick to act on his own wishes, to punish . . . had become a patient man with a calm heart.

They said that Almassi had forgotten his teeth. He had chafed at his bonds for the first two centuries, and then he had bent into good with natural easiness.

The trap was not Mombasa, but his old life. Once he'd been full of fury, righteous with his own pride—cold as ice. He had been a war god, a death god. No one wise to what he had been could easily forget.

Old Snake, they still called him, admitting his seniority, not his weakness.

"Great Brother!" Tumbling shadows came flying on the air like paper streamers—racing through the labyrinth. Mortal men had been eaten in these endless corridors. "Great Brother!"

Almassi drew the medwakh away from his lips, exhaling smoke as they related to him all that had happened, and he listened patiently, lazily, as though hearing it anew. "There have been a great many complaints, Great Brother! There has been another monster killer, and the wild beasts of Mombasa are worried indeed, Great Brother!"

The snake-attendants were but strips he had cut of his own

shadow—and he heard what they had learned as he had slept. He had heard the heart cutter Zuzu's pacing outside his home; his worried feet had threatened to erode the earth.

The heart cutters had not bothered him in decades.

Almassi heard of a girl who kept with her a great sea eye, held ransom a trapped dream; he heard of the blood that slicked her when she came tumbling out of the sea with her father, and he heard she was looking, they said, for a cat with no shadow.

A cat from the House of Rust.

~

When Aisha returned home, she was so tired she collapsed into bed immediately. Baba had brought muhogo for dinner and she had hiccups all through the night no matter how much water she drank. But she did not have the dream.

In the morning, she listened and with a slow-gaining alarm heard only the sounds of the birds outside, the people rolling their wares down the road. She pressed her ear to her pillow, her heartbeat at the side of her skull like a closed drum, but nothing else.

Under the bed, she prised open the halwath khania tin with an old coin and stared, unseeingly, into the dark contents.

There was nothing in there. When she put her hand in, no water. She scrubbed around, and only oily, sandy clumps of sesame sugar clung to her fingers.

In the cupboard, Jicho's jar was full of bright orange lemons in green chilli and carrot brine so strong it perfumed her clothes. She sat, speechless, trying and failing to grasp the happenings around her. Was she dreaming?

In the washroom, she dunked her head, scrubbing her eyes. She had woken up for morning prayers a few hours ago and performed them, blind with exhaustion, before tripping back into bed. But now, awake for the second time, she felt alight with awareness.

She went back and saw that she was not asleep, there really was a great achari jar in her cupboard and the remnants of halwath khania

221

in the box. For her prisoners to escape was one thing. To have these things take up where they had been . . . was quite another.

This was not the work of her family, and it was not the work of Jicho or Ndoto, else they would have done this long, long ago. Some other hand was at work, some other mouth was laughing at her, scolding her, warning her. Who had taken them? A foul thief. How would he use them? What about the dream?

She worried a great deal for the things she did not know and how they might complicate matters. Had she lost Jicho and Ndoto earlier, she would have been far more out of sorts. She had needed them as reminders that her journey had been real. Now with her journey coming closer, her convictions whole and fortified, she did not need to lean on reminders of the fantastic. She was sure of them now and wouldn't be frightened or scolded, no matter what mouth was laughing at her.

This was magic. She wiped her hands on her hips and in a short time had put the pickle jar outside of the house, near the front of the garbage, and in a second trip took the empty sesame sweet tin box, which she put on as its hat. Both she put in an old crate.

She went back in and resolutely performed ablutions, sat on the floor, and spent the morning reading the Quran to cleanse her room. She was a slow reader, though not out of practice, and was finished with her juzu by noon. Her stomach rumbled, empty, for she had not eaten. After afternoon prayers she ate some leftover chapati from yesterday's breakfast. If she was absolutely starving she could have gone to Hababa's, but that would have required one of them bending their necks again, and Aisha was discovering new avenues of stubbornness, and refused to do so. She was also afraid that should she go to Hababa's, she might realize that her convictions to stand her ground would reveal their weaknesses. Asking for forgiveness would destroy her, and she had to preserve herself, whether or not she was wrong. It didn't matter who was right and who was wrong, she could not afford to back-track.

Zubeir came upon her starting a fire on the beach; she meant to arson away wet pickles and oily sweets. His face, on which age lay so artfully as to make the handsomeness of his youth more pronounced, was now a grey-tinged pallor. Underneath his eyes, his sleeplessness dragged. He asked her what she was doing with a sigh that said his mind was on other matters.

She told him what had happened, and when she returned to destroying what was probably witchcraft, found that Zubeir had picked up the pickle jar. "As the halwath khania is empty," as if that *explained* anything.

"Mze Zubeir," Aisha began, preparing to chastise a troublesome child, "surely you cannot think to eat things like that."

"I have a wife to appease," he said, "for someone has angered her."

She clicked her mouth shut, stoking the dried kindling, coaxing it to catch.

In truth, she was surprised that Zubeir was not more harmed than he was, or angrier. He obviously saw no danger in the items, which meant he knew their origins, or possessed some idea. He would not bring undue harm to his wife. Besides, she did not want to talk about Hababa, and she couldn't say sorry for telling Hababa the truth. She asked if he knew how such things had come into her room.

He did not, he confessed. But he turned the jar to show her the pickles as though she were meant to recognize them. "These are Mwembe Kuku oold, high quality, from Mama Arjun," he said, rejoicing in his good fortune. "Come to your grandmother's and we shall have them with fluffy pilau."

"I hate pilau."

"Lying really should be left to those with skill." Zubeir tittered at her as though she had embarrassed herself, and danced away with a joyous step, without looking back once.

What a greedy old man. He was unbothered by what she'd relayed, as though there was nothing frightening about these events. That he had sidestepped her question so easily told her outright that he knew *exactly* where they had come from. If she wanted to know more she'd have to bully him, but that meant going to see Hababa.

That wily old man! She shovelled kindling into the halwath khania tin, the smoldering, burning sesame sugar as strongly perfumed as the pickle jar. Its nutty sweetness sickening when she stood near it too long. She had other things to do.

The weather was clearer today, grey and smoggy clouds stretching far back in the horizon where a storm was fighting itself out. But the shore-line was brightening, sunny. Aisha decided she would go into the shallows and practise fishing, so she'd have something to show Baba when he came back from his work.

She had readied her line and flung her bag of bait down before realizing she was being watched. Glancing at the shore, she sighted a figure. That gaze like the sun on her brow. The figure wore a tall hat. Aisha scowled and busied herself with the work of her hands.

The unlucky sailboat would not have a name. When she and Ali had first entered, its insides were furred in moss, its outsides frosted in lichen. Its last coat of paint was as flaky as an old snake-skin. Aisha had hung over the sides of the boat and painstakingly scraped away each dead scale. Otherwise, it was a good ship. *I expected rats and cockroaches*, Ali said, surprised but untroubled.

Father and daughter fixed the sails over the next few weeks and attended to the repairs. It wasn't in so bad a way. Only it remained in the centre of the creek, and no one wanted them to bring it to the shore with the other boats. Its reputation made it an unwelcome spectre.

Aisha patted the sides of the beastly omen as if it were a beloved ox, hardy and strong. "Men make wickedness. Let us look after one another."

Aisha glanced up as the tall hat raised its arm. It waved.

She ignored it a second time, though it irked her. She flung her line into the water, thinking of the small fish that grazed in the creek. On her journey she would have to travel along the continent rather than away from it, and there would be waters as murky and muddy as these, or as clear as the word *aquamarine*.

The sails weren't up, yet the mast creaked a little as the boat buoyed up and down in the harmless creek. She glanced up again and there was no one on the shore.

Aisha wound the wire around her index finger, making the bait dance thoughtfully in the depths. Slowly, as though nothing was amiss, she unwound the wire from her finger and hooked it around a nail she'd hammered into the boat. She rose, yawned, and made her nonchalant way to the hatch—and then she leapt out, spear in hand. Ferociously, she pointed it at the intruder.

For someone had come to stand on the deck. The wide brim of his peaked date-palm hat was ringed in purple and red, blushing bougainvillea. Beneath that hat was a great deal of black hair, wreathing his beauty.

The spear blade was honed on her own whetstone. She'd seen to its dangerous sharpness. "How did you get here?"

All human beings feel beauty instinctively, as the attraction is natural and instantaneous—and yet, Aisha's instinct was matched by a stronger reaction, something learned: a determination in her, a refusal to grant beauty power.

"Did I swim?" he said. His garments were dry. "Did I walk?" His sandals were traditional and finely made, not a speck of sand or water. "Did I fly?"

Aisha moved around the boat's edge, cautiously, glancing around to see if there was a dinghy he'd come on, hiding more hooligans, not quite taking her eyes off of him. "What is your name?"

"What will you pay to earn it?"

"Courtesy is not earned, but it is lost."

"How clever." He admired her words, dark eyes narrowing in amusement. "Almassi."

She had not expected to have the name so promptly and so simply. Precious stone. *Diamonds.* It was a man's name—its syllables were perfect and beautiful. A strong name. Neither inherited nor borrowed. It was full of belonging, soul. Said in any corner of the world, and heard, no matter the distance.

His features were far too smooth for time to cling to. Each hand grasped the hairless forearm of the other. His jacket hung on his slender shoulders, each empty sleeve lightly billowing. His kikoi was well made, the folded roll beneath his folded arms. At a glance one might think he was a young man, but she felt his wardrobe looked less like the flashy, *bobbish* attempts of the younger generation of boys—and more like the old country chic of the old Muslim men who played cards in town. She half expected to see the cud of miraa round one cheek.

But the hat was strange. She had never seen anything like it.

The more she watched him, the more he was amused, content to be taken stock of, and pleased by her slowly growing suspicion, as though it were a compliment. "You are that person who killed the beast."

His mouth was as generous as a woman's. She saw two clawlike curves flash, bending around the lift of lips—wry, like a gill.

Her culottes were tied around her knees, naked shins sticky with the salt and grit. She did not drop her spear. She saw his feet, no shadow around him.

He lifted his head in interest. His dark brown eyes shone copper and then gold in the direct sunlight. All shadow was gone from beneath his hat, except for one, its fine collar thin around his fine neck. "Do you look for my hoofs, fishling?"

"That is *not* my name."

"Hm. The beasts of this town have come severally to complain to me of you. They tell me your name. They are used to the attentions of the mad on occasion, but to be pursued by a questing girl like you, knowing what you have done, troubles them."

"I'm sorry I disturbed them, but I've killed no one."

"Sorry? You did what you thought you must, didn't you? Now, you were asking about, what was it called . . . the House of Rust?"

At her rapt expression, even his laugh was beautiful, a short rumble, soft and charmed. Hababa would have commended it as sophisticated had Aisha any grace to mimic it. Effortless and natural, without the pretence that usually came with sophistication.

"Yes, you go around asking and asking: Do you know of the House of Rust? Do you know of a cat who gave me a name so I could miss it? Do you know? Do you know?" Almassi sighed, taking pause in his delight. "Did it ever occur to you, Aisha, that you are standing upon it right now? The House of Rust is just a riddle."

His laughter had such a pleasing lightness and tenor. Aisha shook her head, clearing it of these chimes. "Once I'd have doubt enough in me to believe you. Now I wonder what a strange man who is not a man—what stake does he have in my belief or disbelief?"

"You're not so stupid as to forget to be frightened of anything," he said, and his tone was as comforting as the meaning was alarming. "But I am not here to prove myself the most dangerous person in the room. I never have needed to. Let me say this: This town is dearer to me than gold, than the dead is dear to the grave. You have created an uproar, and the citizens are bloodying their excitable imaginations over your dangerousness."

So the beasts had understood her? She'd thought at worst she was an annoyance—she'd always tried to be careful, sensitive in her approach. Now, she felt guilty and she wavered.

"You are safest when terrifying things are afraid of you."

How did they learn of the night journey? She had only ever told three people, and supposed the shark hunters knew of it vaguely since theirs was sea business. "What do they *think* they know?"

"A rumour spread by the crows."

"But how did the crows know?" For they could not have seen her deeds, they could not have known.

"Because I whispered it to them as they slept. I whispered of dead monsters and wild, frightening girls."

"I did not kill anyone!"

"Be quiet and don't undo my work," Almassi drawled, his gaze cold and lightly hooded. "Notoriety comes with strings attached. You are a weakling with no powers of your own. Did you think you could escape the sea unremarked upon? Do you think you could come here and not be seen as a challenge to the authority of other kings? Better they be frightened of you, even if by rumour of non-existent strength, than to take an interest in you."

Aisha watched him. "It was you," she realized. "You were in my room, you thief!"

"I have been trying to sleep for the past three weeks, and have been inundated with rabble complaining of *you*. A theatre of disarmament was required. Do you know what you caught? That was one of the great sea eyes. A poisonous parasite that plays interpreter to monstrous kings; had I not intervened it might have caused chaos. What you have done is careless. I have protected you. Some gratitude is polite."

"What gratitude?" Aisha demanded. "You just came here to be shady and mysterious and talk down to me."

"Have I been very rude?"

"You come to talk to me too, without a chaperone."

"My bride-stealing days are long behind me and I take no interest in children. But you have questions, and I can answer some of them. If it's wonders you seek, there are wonders still here. You need not go so far."

"I seek Hamza from the House of Rust, and I'm going to find him. He helped me, without asking anything in return. If you can tell me where he—"

"He helped you and then he left you. Everyone knows your name, Aisha. Understand it best from me: to become notorious is dangerous. Leave the House of Rust to the scholar's cat."

"I will go, whether you like it or not."

"I forbid it."

"And where were you when my father went missing? Did you protect him?"

"I do not go to sea."

She glowered at him in abundant irony, considering their current location, but he did not explain himself further. "Then you will not follow me."

"Ha!" Almassi took off his hat and turned his head slightly enough to give her boat a brief and condescending scan, and with an elegance as coy as it was cruel, he touched the hat over his mouth so she might know how poorly he hid his laugh. "The vessel that sinks," he said coolly, "has no navigation."

But Aisha would not let him have the last laugh, slamming the spear into the boards. "Mombasa cannot *stand* the pompous!"

The hat slowed, its fluttering as slow as a courtesan's fan, and when Almassi turned fully to her it was with a colder expression in his gaze. "I can see," he said, the hat that hid his mouth no longer an elegant tool of beauty but a helm's shadowy guard for his dark eyes contemplating her, "that the thanks of a donkey are still in its kicks."

"A friend in the eye," Aisha stubbornly jerked her chin, her fear schooled from her words, "but a hypocrite in the heart."

Almassi's voice lowered in warning. "Do not play with the lion and then put your hand in its mouth."

"The mouth is the house of all words," Aisha said, more quietly but no less meant, and knew that she had him. "To speak the truth before a tyrant takes no little courage."

His laughter now was princely and terrible, like lemon juice sharp on all her wounds. The hat lay over his chest now, in some mockery of sweetness, and when he straightened himself he became taller somehow, his swaying spine rippling into his shoulders, his head adjusting to the gaze of a predator catching sight of prey in the undergrowth.

Almassi's lip lifted. "*Kitendawili.*"

Like magic, the word stirred down her back in a sudden wash and Aisha's blood went cold. She was staggered by the old spell, by its alarming familiarity. Yet she could not fall short and now lack in daring. Her boldness evaporated. She had reached for a rotten branch in her arrogant climb, and it could not bear her stupid weight.

She was never very good at vitendawili. Had Almassi somehow known? Perhaps he did, but he did not care enough. She felt herself slow in panic, but she could not let him make the childhood game his. Aisha growled. "*Tega.*"

They faced each other as though with drawn swords. It was an old game, older than she was, perhaps as old as he.

Almassi spoke the riddle: *He who declares to the crowd to own me ceases at once to have me in his possession.*

Almassi leaned against the mast. Aisha scowled, walked back to the edge of the boat, and tested the wire. Sitting down, spear over her lap, she rubbed her knees as though that would begin the process in her brain.

It was not the knowledge of the thing that nullified it, but the declaring of it that destroyed it.

Or set it free.

Truth?

No. She had been afraid of speaking the truth, as though speaking it would falsify it. The truth was always the truth, no matter who tried to bend its shape, or bury it.

To falsify by speaking, therefore to be contrary . . . some sort of hypocrisy.

What was true, and then becomes a lie, once spoken. What escapes, once announced.

Something . . . that should never be spoken?

Deed? He who declares the deed has no more power over it?

But deeds would always have power, they were the only thing that had to have power. You could not escape your deeds even if you changed your . . .

Name?

My name is Aisha. She used to think that to say her name was to give it away forever. Names were dangerous things. They were your strength and yet they could be injured by wicked tongues, and be spoiled by the speakers.

No. What becomes nullified once declared? What loses value, or runs away once announced?

Wealth? If declaring your wealth and blessings automatically destroyed them, there wouldn't be a single pompous person on earth. Certainly to be smug over one's fortune could threaten it, for all our lives follow a kind of narrative sense and irony delightful, threatens . . . there must be some poetics, if not, they will be invented.

No, not a thing, but an *idea*. A thing could be killed but never uncreated or unmade. So it must be . . . an idea. Some smugness that undid.

But she had no idea as to what that idea was.

Aisha rose up decisively and faced Almassi. "I don't know the answer to the riddle. The only thing I could come up with was 'a secret.'"

"As expected."

"I don't think you're very good at riddles."

He narrowed his eyes, irked, but he was too bored to be angry with her. He covered his yawn with the back of his palm in a gesture he somehow made look gallant. She didn't reprimand him for his rudeness, lest it earn another lecture about how terrifying she was supposed to find him. "The answer is *haya*, humility."

Aisha felt cheated, and did nothing to hide this feeling.

"The man who declares himself to be humble is performing to a crowd. He is not humble; he wants to be congratulated for virtues he does not possess."

Aisha was even more openly annoyed. "I'm very sure some prophet or other must have called themselves humble, do you say they were liars?"

"Do you accuse me of blasphemy, little girl?"

"I only think you're awful at riddles. And it's even worse, because it seemed you were boasting of your talent."

"You're just too dense to think of the answers."

"Your riddle was too vaguely worded. The answer wasn't satisfying at all, and how poorly constructed! The wordplay is non-existent. What musicality? Putting together both arrogant people and holy men. You really go out of your way to look down on people."

"Oh, and you could do better?"

"Of course not," Aisha said. "I don't have the time to sit around thinking of ridiculous puzzles all day, am I an old man? You really amaze."

His mouth tucked, his impatience turned to sour dislike, but she did not care. Odd games have always been a weakness of such creatures. Almassi was no different from the beasts in the sea, who could not resist an offering, no matter how bogus it was. Such creatures have a weakness for being right, even if they know they are being tricked.

The flowers were beginning to wilt, fluttering from his hat. The band on his neck had thinned even further, and now it gleamed ichorous: blood in a cut. As though his throat had been freshly slit. Sweat struck along his temples, with the loathing restraint with which he tried to resist, and the hateful, irritated way with which he succumbed. He had strained himself. He was growing weak before her eyes, perhaps it was true. He could not go far to sea.

He saw her see, and it rankled him. "Come here." He ground the words with the back of his teeth as he kept his temples clear and unwrinkled, haughty and proud. "I am tired from walking."

"Ah," she said sagely. "You are one of those people with weak constitutions."

"I simply prefer to be closer to my house."

She accepted the explanation too agreeably for him not to be insulted by it.

"Come, let me have my prize."

"There was a prize?"

"I did not say that I would tell you where to find the House of Rust if you answered correctly, yet it was implied. I would have told you." He raised his brows at her expression. "Do not accuse me of lying. I would have. We were operating under those assumptions."

"If that's how things worked, we wouldn't have a system of government."

"Hm," he said. "Step forward a little."

Aisha raised a brow, dubious—but found nothing outright evil about this request, and could not reasonably deny it. Her spear was light in her hand. She had no qualms about stabbing him. Almassi observed her bare feet critically. He cupped his chin. Asked her to take three more steps back, and she obeyed. Humming, Almassi directed her to make minor adjustments in her stance, and it felt comforting to obey, because it was all rather simple. Now that she had refused him outright, she would not have to give up anything. His sudden, reasonable air and direction after their disagreement felt like a much-needed guide toward a better place at which she thought they might resume negotiations. Could she move to the right a little, he asked.

"Yes, right there," he said, stepping forward once. "It is done," he said.

Aisha jumped back. And saw that as she did so, she lost something to Almassi. Not simply ground. Her feet had lost worse than their toes. Everything was there. Except her shadow stretched long where she had stepped *out* of it. Almassi had anchored it with his feet, keeping it with him.

Aisha yelped like a bride whose dress has been ripped by someone else's treading. It was not an elegant noise, not at all like her. There was nothing beneath her. The sun at her back had flung her shadow forward. Now it lay on the floor like a discarded garment. Shadow or not, she was being stepped on. What illusion was this!

He shook his head at the hope in her despair. "None. You have been separated."

She stepped on her shadow, but it would not stick to her feet, no matter how she adjusted herself. "No, this is impossible. Give it back!"

Almassi slipped back. Aisha's shadow lay flat on the ground like a murdered body. They looked at it, he with a grave stare and she in mounting panic. She crouched, fingers trembling along the outline of her shoulders. She touched the hot floor and the shadow shivered.

It was *breathing*.

CHAPTER TWENTY-FIVE

Not shadow, not darkness or night—but the complete absence of all light, and a silence permeating all, as White Breast woke, choking on blood. His body felt soft and shattered, porous in the absolute, unmoored from time in a depthless nowhere.

He felt his battered bird heart with its sleepy pounding, sluggish as though in a dream of its own, beyond his controlling or command. The wrongness in his body still remained. It prickled his flesh, like scabby, salted lashes—that wanted to hiss and smoke, like hot stones dashed with cold water.

Every crow knew that life carried death. Death grows along life, going through the labyrinth of every creature's body, making the body grow older or toward life's final severing. Death, whose heels had been fire, racing through White Breast's veins, now froze mid-lunge. This felt more awful than the dark, for death held him, aloft—no floor beneath him and no air above him. He was not restrained but he had nowhere to go. As apart as a dying star. He was not the saved, or the living—he was the halted, the postponed, the preserved.

"Brother?" he called out, voice cracking on hope. "Gololi?"

His cry went forward and nowhere. He listened closely, but nothing answered him, as he had known. A crow does not grieve, it is not for a crow to weep, but to witness. It is not for a crow to hope, but to know.

Gololi was gone, he knew.

Blinded, White Breast felt tremors begin in his shoulders as air squeezed and wheezed through the clotted nostrils of his beak.

Unseen, White Breast slowly began to cry.

~

Sharp, dry weeds crackled beneath Almassi's sandal, and he stopped there, in the undergrowth. Head bowed, Almassi felt the sun heat the back of his neck, and sweat licked down it like slobber. Laughter puffed out from him at the oddness of human discomfort. A friend that time and distance had altered and made a little new. It had been a long time, after all, since he'd walked this far toward the prison limits.

The wild shrubbery that fringed the coast was hard and coral-like, dry and calcified. Itchy bugs sprang everywhere like mites, prickling on the skin, tickling the nose. The air was suffused with the burning, nutty smell of sugar and sesame.

Almassi tucked his thumbs into the fold of his kikoi and laughed again. "Zuzu!"

And there did Zuzu sit, ganglier than he'd been when he was a child—as long of limb as a spider, and as dark, as handsome.

Almassi raised his arm, and the wild undergrowth parted, snapped, and prised apart.

Nearly hidden by the fallen, dry brush—a monarch cross-legged on a long-dead log. He was as light on his feet as he'd ever been, disturbing nothing to find his perch. A panga sat across Zuzu's knee, a fitting weapon, never meant for a sheath. Always open steel. If one was not careful, there would be no welcome ever again from such a man. How forbidding. Zubeir forbade Almassi as the old chiefs of Pwani had forbidden him long ago.

Almassi's gaze went behind the old heart cutter's son to the jar of pickled lemons.

"One day perhaps I will die," Almassi said. "But I will not be killed. Anyway, you have spoiled the effect."

"If I wanted to kill you, I'd properly prepare myself."

"So for now we must comfort ourselves with a show of strength."

"Better that than miserliness," Zubeir said, unsmiling. "You can fill a jar full of pickles, but not a tin with khalwath khania." He kissed his teeth, tittering at the shame of it. "Thought there was nothing you could not conjure."

Almassi folded his arms and corrected his brief pout. "You can taste the pickles, they are real from the market. But sesame sugar paste from Hadramout of that quantity . . . alas, I can no longer control the movements of the ships on such short notice."

"It is embarrassing. Is that little boy my replacement?" Zubeir hummed. "You've gone far today, has the ink not stoppered your heart?"

"It's been a long time since I walked the shore . . ." Almassi's wistfulness was not a lie. Mottled light fell on his upraised face, and he shifted beneath his skin.

"Oh, Zuzu," Almassi sighed. But the man was grown, and no longer flinched at the insult. A long, long time had passed. "You do not even visit me anymore, not even with tobacco or sweet things."

"I had gone on a journey," Zubeir said, eyes averted. "Your attendants can get you all you desire."

"That is a cruel thing to say to the marooned."

"You are not marooned or imprisoned."

"Careful," Almassi said. "Foul magics hold me."

Zubeir flung the machete into the earth, where it vibrated. "You must not hurt her."

"You know that I will not."

"You must not demean her then. There are other injuries one can inflict."

"You do not want me to test or discourage her."

"Don't underestimate her."

"Oh ho, is it me who underestimates her?"

Zubeir rubbed his knuckles, caught out. Not all that different after all.

"I say that I will test the will of that child," Almassi said, "and challenge it."

Then he softened his features, absorbing the sight of the man before him. "Oh, Zuzu," His laugh was warm, his eyes bright as though with tears. "How old you have become, how handsome and how tall. You used to be so serious! Come and tell me all that has happened, and how it came to be that your heart has settled its restless turnings."

~

Life went on with unnerving simplicity and a little loneliness—though Aisha was loath to admit it. The shadow was everything Aisha wasn't—like a carnival mirror, it became whatever people wanted beheld. It said all the right things, with no voice, and yet was heard. It apologized so sweetly to her grandmother, and was proof of a girl growing into an excellent woman.

Aisha, without a shadow, did not frequently leave her base of operations. She concentrated on working, on her lessons, on readying her boat for the journey ahead. She thought she'd be too distracted to know what her shadow was doing, but she was her shadow, and Aisha would be listening to her father speaking about how to know when the ocean was turning ugly and still feel her shadow rolling and kneading the dough in Hababa's kitchen. It was like having a separate consciousness running beneath, constant, not overly focused, not worryingly distracted. It was like stirring a pot with one hand as you fanned another with the lid.

Her shadow was perfect in every way, just like the Aisha made of milk whom Aisha had thought she could never hate. Racing around the house as quiet as Aisha had been as a young girl, doing all the work that needed doing and even the work that didn't. The houses underwent thorough cleaning: curtains were washed, ceilings swept, floors polished. And the best thing about Aisha's shadow was that it never, ever talked back when it was being lectured. It sat there, absorbing the criticisms with the sweet piousness of a student savouring the teachings of her guru.

Was this all it took to fool those people? Aisha's contempt reared its head. Her father knew enough to disapprove, and Zubeir enough not to interfere.

Was that all it took to buy Hababa's love, an eternity of obedience? The shadow was whatever you wanted it to be. Aisha felt ugly. She thought she was mocking her grandmother, but she was only mocking herself.

The days trickled by with maddening slowness. The success of her understudy project was frustratingly efficient. The ease with which she'd let herself be overthrown by the self she had trained . . . a coup, so perfect, and yet . . . without satisfaction.

She wasn't allowed to feel spiteful. This excellent strategy she'd thought to use to escape was a long-term betrayal of her truest self. It was meant to be perfect. So why did she feel so irritated?

She had thrown herself out of her own life, she had chosen this. She was meant to feel happy and free. What cut her was that she'd had to choose at all. That to pursue her future, her present was to be incompatible, and her past forever estranged. She could not be Hababa's Aisha and be her own self at the same time.

She had done this to herself; it was meant to hurt less. She threw herself into preparations with unfailing vigour. Her shadow spent the day appeasing and loving everyone, the way each wanted to be loved. Then at night it would swim through the air and come back to Aisha, where Aisha experimented with this new limb.

The farther away the shadow was, the less aware of its movements she was. She sent it far, far inland and could not feel it for an entire night. For a while she thought she had lost it as surely as one loses a paddle tossed into the sea. But it came back to her, and she knew it had gone as far as Malindi, where Aisha had never been. That it had done as it was told, scouting ahead and crawling on the roofs of Italian restaurants and giving to her mind the shape of the reefs shimmering with moonlight.

She wrapped the shadow around her wrist like a bangle and stretched it between her fingers like a band, testing it. It was elastic where she wanted, and tight, without give, where she wanted. But it was still weak, this new part of her, and sometimes it tore, or crumpled.

The shadow was a prancing goat and a soaring bird. Then it trotted around her like an actor, swept its high, peaked hat off of its head and bowed low and long, as though to soak in the adulation of the masses. Her shadow was everything that was Aisha and more. It was a sword in her hand, and when she brought it down on a pile of branches, the whole lot snapped and spat slivers of bark, cut by it.

She had her boat, she had her weapon, and she would have her navigation sooner than she expected. One morning she went to the beach just as the dawn had come. The sun was clear off the waves, and the gold and blues, an astonishing shimmer of pastels and slashing metallic colours, darted over and under one another. She saw the familiar silhouette of that snake sovereign, Almassi.

Her shadow had crept back into Aisha's bed, and made the shape of sleep.

Almassi turned his head and smirked, letting her greet him. He looked soft in these lights, less like a drawn sword and more like one dozing pleasantly in the sheath. He did not look as tired and sick as she had seen him last. His bougainvillea were a plum purple, stirring in his hat like they too were sleeping, sweet and gentle.

She couldn't gather enough of her day sense to be afraid of him this early. The night had slipped away, but its sense remained. She was soft from it, too.

"When I was a youngling, I had little kindness in me," Almassi said. "But even at my most wicked, there was always a truth in me, a tenderness. Sentimental and yet I could not deny it. I ached and yearned to see always the colour of the sea, I could not long be away from it. I would kill and kill, but I would grow sullen and heartsore if I hadn't seen the sea in too long. It felt like I was dying."

Aisha had read about mountains and deserts and yet . . . "I think I can't be long from it either."

"Some people have lived all their lives without setting their eyes on the ocean."

There were many in Mombasa who couldn't even swim, which should have been impossible to imagine, and it made her sad.

"You should always remember that you are a luckier girl than most," Almassi said. "Some things, once given to you, can never be stolen away. So you have to hold on to them with more thoughtfulness, you understand?"

The few blues had evaporated, and the searing gold and silvers lifted like a vapour, their shimmer going as the dawn sense and night sense dried up and the sun shone higher in the sky, with less sentimentality or other such notions of romance. It was a work sun. Not a reminiscing sun.

Almassi swept off his odd hat, extending it to her for her inspection.

Aisha turned it in her hands. It was made of date-palm material, tightly woven in a way she did not recognize. She peered into an empty hat. He seemed to want her to confirm this, and despite having received a few unwelcome surprises in the past by doing what seemed reasonable when he offered reasonableness of his own kind, Aisha put her hand in, feeling the inside of the hat and then the outside.

Almassi received the hat once she had proved it was empty. He shook away his sleeve. His elbow disappeared into it, then his shoulder. The hat was tall but was far deeper than seemed possible. He fished around as though for a sock at the bottom of a soapy bucket. After a little rummaging, he began to pull his shoulder out, and then, as his elbow resurfaced, the brim of the hat shook. Almassi's hand reappeared not closed around the ears of a rabbit—but in feather-flutter, black talons closed around his fingers.

A pale-grey bird, covered in stony sores, did not resist him. Sores like cuts, grey and sealed. Cuts that twitched, clenched shut. He was no grey bird, but a crow. Bleached of his colour, as though he had been sucked dry of his liveliness.

She thought of the blinking sea-serpent's eye and the air was cool, the little heat of her body sucked out of her.

"It's odd that you are quiet." Clearing aside his arm, he resettled his hat. "Usually you'd be accusing me of some barbaric thing."

"Did you do this?"

"No," he said, then squeezing the air between two of the fingers of his other hand, to show her the measurement, he amended. "Perhaps most of it. Some of it is you, as well. The crows broke into your room. They thought if they brought me the sea eye, they could prove you were wicked and that I had to kill you."

He was a sorry-looking animal, an imitation rendered in the shape of a crow but without all that *is* crow. None of the noisiness, none of the springy rebelliousness, the shrewdness that made you suspicious. He sat in Almassi's grip like a tamed hawk, but his head was not buttressed by leather helm. Body tucked inward, head bowed, beak against chest. His eyes were closed, as though his body could not bear the cold.

Had such an animal wanted her dead? How terrified he must have been—to want her dead. She felt sorry for him, and guilt scalded inside her like bile.

"I wanted you afraid." Almassi raised the bird, addressing him. "I thought it would keep you safe. I was not so wise as I thought, crow, to use the old strategies of war."

Was that his apology? It sounded as sorry as one, but the words did not match the sound. Aisha felt her eyes sting with tears.

"My brother is dead," the crow said, cold and wretched. "My brother is dead," the crow said, his voice shaking. "My brother is dead."

From his body, a grey wetness dripped through the clenched cuts. It began as a trickle, perspiration-like. Then it raced, streaming through wet grey feathers, mercury-like. It dripped over Almassi's fingers, a run of moonlight, ivory-silver.

"My brother is dead."

Silver dropped on the sand, sizzling oil.

Almassi's flesh melted away—and she saw the line of bone, peeking faintly through the ruin.

"My brother is dead," the crow wept, with his eyes clenched against daylight, against life. He did not fight, he did not rankle or attempt escape. Almassi did not tighten his grip, did not hiss in pain—his face was free from hurt or hatred, anger or scorn. He let the crow weep and let the acid eat his fingers away. "My brother is dead." He held on, gentle. His smooth, inscrutable patience, without harshness or hastiness. "My brother is dead." Each word she felt like the sharp twist of a knife. "My brother is dead."

Aisha's hand reached out, not to touch Almassi's shoulder, but to hover over it—so he might feel her plea. She wanted it to stop, but had no right to demand an end to grief, especially when none of it was hers. When it was her fault.

Almassi glanced at her, giving her his attention.

Stop, she mouthed. She wanted to tell him to comfort it, to soothe it. To do something other than stand there, keeping it aloft, revealing the bones of his hands beneath black talons.

"Now, what is your name, crow?" Almassi spoke gently, quietly.

That was not what Aisha thought was correct to ask. But the crow stopped his weeping. His eyes were still shut. "White Breast."

"A good name," Aisha said fiercely. "A very good name."

The crow did not speak. "Yes," Almassi murmured. "She can hear you, she can understand you."

Did the crow hate her?

"What do you mean to do with your life now, White Breast?" Almassi said. "Is there vengeance in your heart, for me, for the girl, for the rest of crowdom? Who is worthy of your anger?"

"You are a devil, Almassi."

"You've finally the courage to say it to my face instead of eating my flesh with the rest."

"Brazenness is the luxury of the strong," the crow said. "What could we, little crows, have done but hiss among ourselves? It was my brother who sought to move you."

"Your brother did not want you to redeem yourself. She thought you would do the same and earn your place back into crowdom. Who would leave such heroics to someone else?"

"I tell you that you are a demon, Almassi, to say such things."

"The brother you mourn envied you."

"Perhaps it is true. But I loved my brother, as I love all my brothers," the crow said. "Either way and forever, and I hate you, Almassi."

The tears had ebbed; the last of the silver clung to the fine, naked bones of Almassi's fingers. In the pool beneath his hand, the silver was speckled with black drops of blood.

"But I cannot blame only you," the crow said. "Vengeance is poison, I wouldn't know where to start. We crows have been too long without our lord, and wretchedly we have had to make do. None of this would have happened had we been united under our lordship's guiding hand."

"He has been gone a long time."

"He is not dead, you told me so."

"I have not heard word of his death."

"And no other word of him."

"I am not best placed," Almassi said guardedly. She realized this was embarrassment; admitting this limitation did not come easy to him. "To hear anything beyond what my short net catches."

"And he has left us here with you, an odious snake."

"There must be some reason for it, White Breast."

"Yes," the crow agreed, "and I shall hear it from our lordship. Perhaps he has abandoned us, or perhaps something keeps him. I must go to him, I must find him—and learn, not by word of mouth or crow hearsay, the truth. I must see him myself and hear him speak, and then I will know for myself."

"You have a better disposition than most souls," Almassi said, "and more wisdom."

"I don't want to hear praise from you, Almassi."

"Then I will not voice it again. In a few days' time, you will go with this girl. She is looking for the House of Rust."

"I have never been."

"But the great sea eye has improved your vision, enhancing your already crow-perfect sense of direction. And you have inherited its tongue, too, and its ear. You can speak all the languages of all creatures and man."

"I am ugly and wretched, I am no fit companion."

"You can find the House of Rust. I have stopped the devouring eye where I can, it is fixed in place, but death is in you yet, White Breast. The House of Rust may give you access to healers far more enlightened than I."

"I have never been."

"But you have a sense, don't you? And you will learn."

"I will die," White Breast said, mistrustful, his loathing turned inward. "So I must go with her, or die here."

"I will not kill you, White Breast. It was not my intention to harm but I must take responsibility. Go find your lordship," Almassi said. "Go with the girl, and look together for the things you want."

"What of my brothers?"

"I shall take care of them."

"Say you shall care for them, and protect them. Not trick them with dreams and campaigns of rumours and lies. Not plant fears of genocide of the likes we faced when Nunda, eater of men, was hunted and we along with them."

Almassi did not quite apologize, and did not quite accept the chastisement fully. He bowed his head. "You are free to stay, or to go—but if you want to leave with the girl, take to the air now and finalize your affairs."

"No," White Breast said. "Put me back in the darkness. Today the sun is eating me like it eats the dawn. Put me back in the hat and take me out when I go with the girl."

Almassi nodded and dropped his hat over his hand. When he wore it again, the crow was gone. Only the smoke rising over his unfurled skeleton, and the pool of acid evaporating in the sun, said that anything had happened.

Almassi's arm fell back by his side, his sleeve slipping back over his fingers.

"That crow is hurt because of me," Aisha said.

"How self-important." But he was gazing not at her, but at the sea. "When do you leave?"

Fishing boats and their little fishermen, silhouetted, looked like wooden carvings against the diamond-like light of the sea.

"At dawn, the day after tomorrow."

CHAPTER TWENTY-SIX

She hardly rested the night before she was set to leave. The events that had brought her to this point replayed themselves. She thought of what she was leaving behind, she thought of Zubeir and Ali, and of Hababa, who did not know the truth.

She had tricked her own blood and given to her an impostor, so Aisha could leave quietly. Hababa wouldn't pray for her journey or her safety because she would be showering her affection and blessings over Aisha's shadow. Deceiving her grandmother was cowardice and she could not bear it. She had not seen Hababa since they'd argued, but Aisha's shadow—biddable and sweet, taking on all the shapes Aisha never could, with enviable ease—had made things all right again.

The dawn of the day she was set to leave, Aisha sprang from bed and went running from the beach. She had gathered in Zubeir's shack, for easy packing, all the little she had.

She ran as if possessed. She could not leave things as they were. Let Hababa strike her, let Hababa say she was no granddaughter of hers—but Aisha could not lie to her as though Hababa were just like all those people Aisha had lied and pretended to. Like the wedding singers and the monsters and the sea.

But Hababa was not at home. Aisha asked the neighbours but they did not know where she was. She checked Ali's house and she was not there either. Aisha had to find her today. Eyes clouding with regret, she jogged back to the hut and heard Hababa before she saw her. Attacking and heaving at the ground, Hababa was crying and wheezing in rage, pounding at cloth on the earth with a great big beam of wood.

Hababa whacked at the earth aside the cloth, and Aisha launched forward, fearful that Hababa was dealing with some manner of snake. But it was only Aisha's shadow, dodging the attacks as they came, swinging left to right as Hababa tired herself out.

When Hababa saw her she burst into tears. Flinging the wooden beam from her and instead stomping at the sand with the heel of her feet like a bride, Hababa cried, "I knew it wasn't you because it put on the subha dress with no complaint!"

Aisha rushed forward and embraced her weeping grandmother, who clutched at her as though she would tear her in half for her silliness, if she were not falling apart herself. Hababa cried and cried, and Aisha herded her into Zubeir's shack, rubbing her back gently. She was so glad Hababa had been able to tell them apart.

The cloth behind them rose as Aisha's shadow quietly slipped back into the sand-studded dress.

Aisha gave Hababa an old chair and knelt before her until her grandmother had calmed down a little, sniffling and observing her surroundings with weepy red eyes.

"I always knew," Hababa said, voice rough. "To some extent I always knew."

There was the surgeon's table, there the old stove that must have eaten a hundred dreams in its lifetime. Before her a wild little girl with her mother's eyes.

"But I was afraid."

Aisha touched Hababa's knee, trying not to hope. "And now?"

"I'm still afraid."

Aisha looked down at their feet, Hababa's swollen at the ankles, the straps of her sandals biting into her flesh. She wanted to soothe the pain away, but did not dare.

"Was that a demon?"

Aisha shook her head. "Just my shadow."

"Have you entered into a magical pact?"

"No." Aisha said. "I have not."

"I have to make a choice now, Aisha. That I let you go with regret or that I let you go with love." Hababa drew herself up, ironing out the trembling of her voice. "I can't stop you."

Aisha didn't voice her agreement. She was waiting hopelessly for Hababa's decision.

"I can't stop you but I can choose how you go. You foolish girl, I love you. If I cannot forget you I mustn't forgive you—but you are mine and I love you either way, and you can't love and not trust, not believe. So leave with my love, my trust, my belief."

Aisha blinked to clear her eyes. Her heart was shaking, and when Hababa took her by her shoulders they rose together. She could hardly believe what she had heard. She wanted to cry. "I'm so sorry I tricked you, Hababa!" she burst out. The grief and joy were a tide that tumbled her, and she cried. "I didn't want to trick you, I didn't want to go without you knowing it was me. But I didn't want to leave you alone."

Hababa hushed her, rubbing her back, surprised by Aisha's outburst. It was not like her granddaughter to cry, and so openly. She wiped Aisha's face with the edge of her leso, patting it dry only for it to go wet again.

"No more, no more," Hababa soothed her, walking them back outside. "You can really cry a lot, can't you?"

Aisha hiccuped. The shadow was waiting for them, resplendent in slightly wet, sandy subha robes. When it saw Aisha it toppled forward, tackling her with arms wide.

Aisha accepted the thudding embrace with a wet laugh, and felt the wedding dress melt onto her body. She touched her hair and felt the tight rows of braids, and in them the woven flowers. She felt, wondrously, the black ash that split her lip, and had never dreamed she would be in such finery.

When she looked back she saw her shadow was drawn behind her, attached once more to her body.

Hababa looked at her with bright, proud eyes and patted the sand from her dress gruffly to stave off tears. "You best look the part."

"I don't go to be a bride."

"Subha isn't about going meekly into marriage," Hababa sighed. "It's about going to war, and the people you love gathering to give their blessings. Just as proud, just as warlike. The family that's taking you as their bride makes you debut as a married woman, one no longer a girl. The subha is so that you never forget you have family and womenfolk of your own who do not let you go gently as if into slaughter, but with hard grace into your destiny. I wish I'd seen you dance your hair even once."

"If ever that time comes, I won't do it without you there."

"Don't make those kinds of promises. I might die before then."

"I might die first."

"Anything could happen." Tears welled up in Hababa's eyes again. "But no promises. Let me know when you're safe, and when you're not."

"I'll try."

Outside, Hababa touched her cheek. "I leave you in the care of God," Aisha said, "as nothing is lost that is in His care."

"I leave your religion in the care of God," Hababa said, "as well as your safety, and the last of your deeds. May God give you piety as your provision, forgive your sins, and make goodness easy for you wherever you are."

Hababa wrapped her in her arms. She smelled of chickpea flour and wilting wedding yasmini. Aisha breathed into her chest so she would not cry. Hababa rubbed her back and swayed them both, as though she were a child again, small enough to be picked up and hugged, as though she were precious to her, and always would be.

At high noon, the girl kissed her father and hugged her grandmother's husband—and pushed, with her own strength, her boat into the water.

In Uhuru Gardens, the shadows flowered on the ground, unfurled beneath the branches. Rows upon rows of crows waited, as a man not-man stepped through the boundary, striding from darkness and into full view.

"It has been a long time since we convened," Almassi said. "It has been a long time since I came to you as a beast. You see, I did not want to remember what it was like to be the Almassi of old. So I stayed out of your affairs and did not interfere unless I was interfered with. I am not your lordship. I have never been anyone's lordship."

Kamau the Peaceful and his brood absorbed him with their cool glass eyes. And the Burned One was silent, on the highest branch. It was a stadium.

"I thought to myself, I will be asleep. I will continue my sentence quietly."

What was heard here would be carried forward to the camels and the dogs. To the other birds. A crow is a great traveller.

"I played the prisoner, I did not want another war." Almassi said. "But I was wrong."

Astonished silence greeted him. Almassi made a philosophical hum. A girl was saying goodbye to the trees, to the sky. The girl rolled up the sleeves of her robes and tied them, edges soggy from the sea. She wrapped her veil around her head in a turban, tight.

"This be the island of war, the place of hiding," Almassi said. "Will you let them say that we did not know our own? That we did not send to them the very shining example of our coast? When they fight, let her say, I am that island, I am of that war. Let others fear the girl, and let us embrace her."

You must be able to bear the elements and the punishments of a body going without; you must be hardened to hunger, patient of thirst, and mightier than the cold.

"Did they not take us too lightly? Is she not the shining example, of our most triumphant, our most terrible? We are no longer asleep. Enemies will come for her, what will we say?"

She had passed the test. The bird kited ahead of her. Had she not the courage to say goodbye, regardless of how that farewell would be received, he never would have let her go.

Don't go to sea with a leaky heart. They will smell the injury and come running to slip into it. Nothing calls the devil as well as doubt. Your own convictions will be turned on you, as poison on a spear.

"Fight. And when they come to Mombasa, what will we say? Will we be afraid?"

Not with the dawn, or the night, fleeing like a thief. But with the sun on all of them. With no hiding and no escapes.

"Let them remember why this place has such a name."

In daring what you have dared, in attempting to endear yourself and court answers with such persistence, you have acquired an evil name.

"If you look for me, you will find me."

A good name illuminates itself. It glows even in the dark.

"And if they look for us, they will find us."

Mercenaries or missionaries: all are variations of the same garbage. Now, a person who can go, without conquest in his heart—that is extraordinary. Had there been conquest in your heart, I would have killed you.

"Go forward, go swiftly, Aisha!"

The winds were good and the sea drove her forward. Her destiny stretched before her.

And eager, and afraid, and whole of heart, she went to meet it.

This story is one told by Khadija Abdalla Bajaber. If there is any good in it, then that good belongs to all. If there is any ill in it, that ill belongs only to she who told it.

ACKNOWLEDGMENTS

This book began as an amusing, self-indulgent experiment—a way to write what I know and to know how little I know it. A project led with love and tenderness, with curiousity and imagination unfettered by questions of what anyone would think. I was writing it for myself, to prove something to myself. I had to believe in me, and little by little, I began to realize just who else did that too. When I was writing the book it was a private, closely guarded practice—no one read it, they heard about it before they saw it, long after I was done. So, I cannot say they were directly involved in the process as it happened, but these people are a part of me, the marrow that goes through the bones, as much a part of me as gills are part of a fish. The more I wrote, secretly, quietly, the more my heart grew, you were all living in it without even knowing. A few pages closing a novel aren't going to be enough, it is difficult to talk about. It is too wide, if I don't name you in the written word, I've named you in prayer, in the heart of my heart.

Almighty God, who has brought me to where I am, you've taught me hard lessons and sweet ones too, thank you.

My mother, who every time pieced together my torn-up work, because she saw its value even when I couldn't and didn't want to. Baba, with his strange slyness, pushing me, making me want to be better even when I thought I couldn't and didn't want to. My parents, the two of you are so locked in this conspiracy against me, that I know the only way to truly be in love is to be in cahoots.

My brothers, the best of men, who tell the most useless of jokes; Taib, I knew I could always lean on you as an annoying younger sister, you don't know it but your goodness has always guided me. I am happy only when you are happy, you're the best, big bro. My little brother, Omar, who was one of my first and insightful readers, how stubborn and clear-sighted you are, how much you wanted this to go well for me. Thank you both for taking me seriously when I least wanted to be.

For my sisters, who are heroically surviving unreasonable climates, we have been in the trenches, haven't we? Little sister Gamar, who is far kinder than I am, who has been so excited, so ferocious, I love you more than the grave loves the dead. Sihaam and Rawya, who I have liked so fiercely from the moment I met them, you two and Gamar, are my sisters in heart and in war.

For he who arrived unexpectedly; Ali, you weren't here when I first started writing. A wonderful surprise and all too cunning for your age. Bright boy, my prince, stay crafty.

Najah, you gave me my fond name, you're the first one who ever did. Thank you.

My neighbours, your generosity and friendship with my family, has brought me to tears. I will remember it forever.

Violet, in that gloomy, cold place, I'd have drowned without you. I miss those years! Thank you.

My kin and clansmen, there's enough of us to make an army quail, aren't we? Aunts and uncles, cousins, nieces and nephews, my elders, my peers, and the youth who come after. All those who are living and all those who are dead. Those who have not been my kin in blood (or not only in blood) but have been my kin in heart. My heart is so full of you, my people.

Hannah, glorious girl, you saved my life. Thank you.

Thank you to Graywolf, Caroline Nitz, Fiona McCrae, Yana Makuwa, and all members of staff and team. You have made everything so smooth that everything still falls over me like a dream. Your hard work and good care have meant that things go easy. Thank you.

Katie Dublinski, the copy-editing process is something I previously understood as notoriously unpleasant, but it has been such a joy to work with you that I feel incredibly spoiled. Thank you so much for your attention to detail, your patience, and your encouragement.

Steve Woodward, my editor. Who knew that first draft could turn into this? I have learned so much from you, you connected me to my own work in a way perhaps I'd have otherwise tried escaping. Draft after draft after draft, from A to Z, you've supported and guided me. You are an alchemist, this book wouldn't be half of what it ended up being, if it weren't for you. Thank you.

Kimberly Glyder, who made the book just that much more real, it has been an exhilarating experience. Never did I imagine that one day I could talk so much in detail about the clothes of coastal men, thank you for working so hard and portraying the signs of my people so beautifully.

Igoni Barrett, how wild it was, to find someone speak so kindly and earnestly about my work. For so long I wrote in a bubble, and you and Graywolf helped shove me out into an extraordinary light. You and all involved in the judging process, I don't know what happened, but I'm glad that it did. Thank you for seeing the promise in my work, your words have meant so much to me.

Mombasa, will you forgive me my trespasses? So many try to escape you. If in trying to honour you I have instead dishonoured you, forgive me. You are a city of wedding singers, wily merchants, mkokoteni pushers, grand matriarchs, dandy old men, cunning fishermen, and quarrelsome crows—but above all, you are a city of story-tellers. You are so much more than my words alone could ever hope to embody. I am only one story-teller in a city of raconteurs, and I can speak for no one. To the sea-kin, my countrymen, my neighours, the folk of this place, for your kigelegele and your kelele equally, thank you. I am endeavoring always to one day be worthy of you.

And you reader, who have this in your hands. What a funny thing. I am learning my way around these worlds of words, I am a traveller like you, if I can dazzle or bore, or excite even a little—the place where I live is a wonderful and wild court, thank you for coming, for you come as a guest and there are blessings in those.

In closing, I would like to thank the several Unseen for leaving me so far unharmed. May we continue to walk aside one another.

God bless you on your way, and guide me on mine.

Khadija Abdalla Bajaber is a Mombasarian writer of Hadrami descent and the 2018 winner of the inaugural Graywolf Press African Fiction Prize. Her work has appeared in *Enkare Review, Lolwe,* and *Down River Road,* among other places. She lives in Mombasa, Kenya.

ABOUT THE GRAYWOLF PRESS AFRICAN FICTION PRIZE

The Graywolf Press African Fiction Prize is awarded for a first novel manuscript by an author primarily residing in Africa. Founded in 2017 to facilitate direct access to publishing in the United States for a new generation of African writers, the prize is awarded every other year. Winners receive publication by Graywolf Press and an advance.

Submissions must be full-length, previously unpublished novel manuscripts, either originally written in English or a complete English translation. If the submission is a translation, the translator need not live in Africa and the original-language book may be previously published. Agents are welcome to submit manuscripts for consideration. For more details, visit www.graywolfpress.org/submissions.

The House of Rust by Khadija Abdalla Bajaber is the inaugural winner of the prize. The next winner, *If an Egyptian Cannot Speak English* by Noor Naga, will be published by Graywolf Press in April 2022.

A. Igoni Barrett, the prize judge for the 2017–2021 prize cycles, is the author of the acclaimed novel *Blackass* and the story collection *Love Is Power, or Something Like That*. He is the recipient of fellowships from the Chinua Achebe Center and the Norman Mailer Center, as well as a Rockefeller Foundation Bellagio Center Residency. He lives in Nigeria.

The text of *The House of Rust* is set in Adobe Jenson Pro.
Book design by Rachel Holscher.
Composition by Bookmobile Design & Digital
Publisher Services, Minneapolis, Minnesota.
Manufactured by McNaughton & Gunn on acid-free,
100 percent postconsumer wastepaper.